Spaceships Passing in the Night
K. P. Kilbride

K. P. Kilbride

Copyright © 2025 by K. P. Kilbride.

All rights reserved. No part of this book may be reproduced or distributed in any form without prior written permission from the author, with the exception of non-commercial uses permitted by copyright law.

Paperback ISBN: 9781068599002

Ebook ISBN: 9781068599019

Cover painting by K. P. Kilbride.

Book Cover Design by GetCovers.

This is a work of fiction. All the names, characters, businesses, places, events and incidents in this book are either the product of the author's imagination or used in a fictitious manner. Any resemblance to actual persons, living or dead, or actual events is purely coincidental.

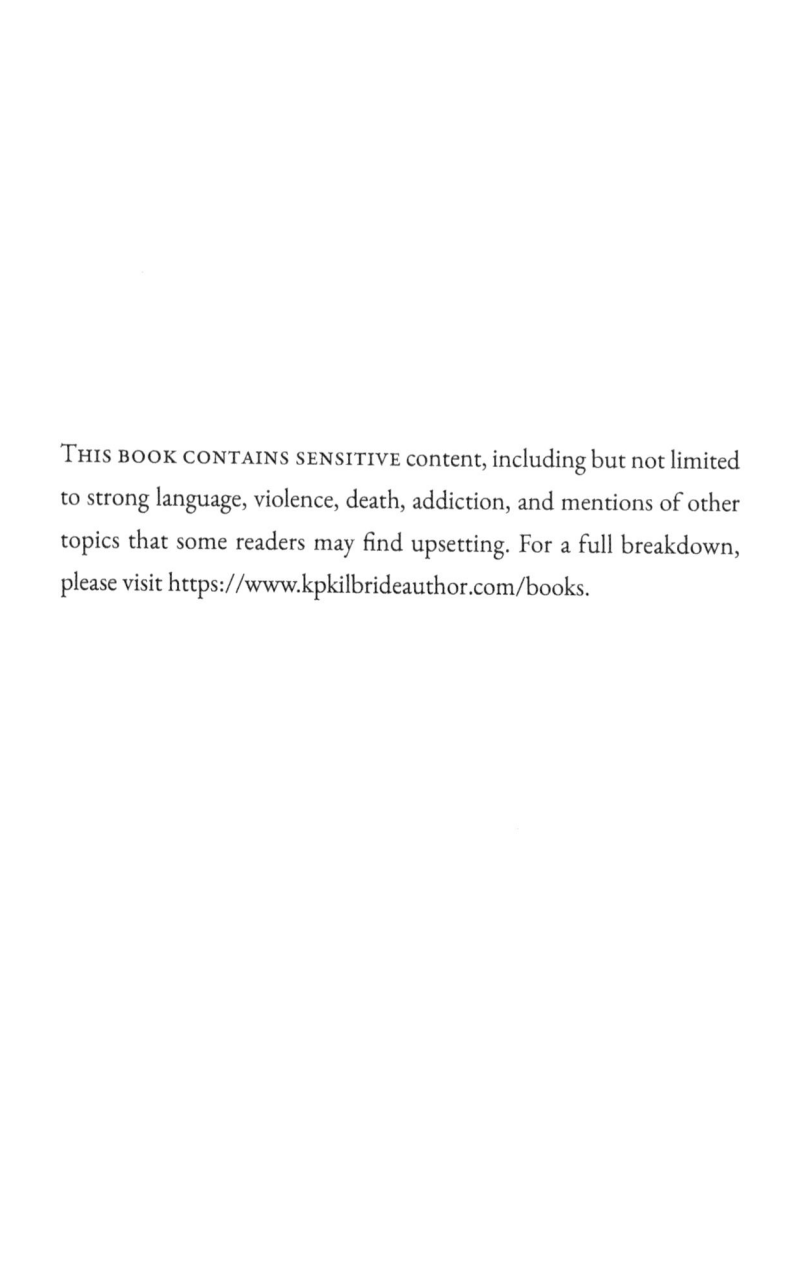

This book contains sensitive content, including but not limited to strong language, violence, death, addiction, and mentions of other topics that some readers may find upsetting. For a full breakdown, please visit https://www.kpkilbrideauthor.com/books.

For my grandparents, who have always encouraged my creative projects.

Prologue

It was a generally accepted fact that the universe didn't care about anything. It was the cosmic elephant in the room that species liked to avoid. There was no meaning behind it all, no logic, just miles and miles of empty space speckled with stars burning themselves to death and sentient civilisations doing much the same. When each year brought more reconnaissance reports mapping more of their galaxy, the "civilised" universe seemed to shrink and the fear of the unknown crept in. A lack of focus crept in. People became fixated on what might be out there, and slowly but surely, an undercurrent of unease eroded the stability and unity the Interstellar Alliance of Homeworlds had built. In the face of it all, what had the galaxy's best and brightest come up with to tackle the vast existentialism? Relentless bureaucracy. It was so relentless, in fact, that even a day before the human holiday "Christmas" and the Hyfb celebration "Feast of the Fifth Sky", politicians were meeting in a space station to discuss trade routes that had worked perfectly well for fifty standard years and would work for another fifty with or without their input.

Any excuse to get the good whisky out, the human minister thought, rolling the golden liquid around a spherical crystal glass. *Any excuse for a change of scenery.*

Avery couldn't say he disliked the meeting or the people. None of them could. It was as much a tradition as the festivals they were eager to get home for.

He chatted with his alien colleagues with ease as they moved from a long, sleek meeting table to a collection of low couches. At this point, they were old friends on a social visit they'd assured everyone was essential. The couches were grouped together in small L shapes, looking out over the space station. Avery admired the view, one of the best in the city. As the artificial sunlight dimmed, the dark buildings lit up with signs of life, and the glow of the news boards and adverts that hung from them began to show. From their vantage point, they could see most of the station, including where it ended: the gratified bulkhead on the other side of the city, illuminated in the city's glow of light pollution.

"Best be leaving soon," the Hyfb ambassador said, clapping what could loosely be described as a hand on his back. Avery looked at them over his shoulder. The Hyfb were a bulbous, light species filled with enough gas to allow them to hover just above the ground. They were also, disconcertingly, translucent. Avery had learned not to stare. "If you want to get home in time for Chris..." His brow furrowed as he tried to remember the pronunciation. "MAhss? Are you assured it will be a 'white' kind?"

A smile tugged at Avery's lips.

"Only in some places, my friend." He turned back to the window. "Unfortunately, I won't make it to Earth this year, but the weather-people of my home space station can guarantee us snow, of a kind."

He looked past the cityscape outside the window, seeing instead his home on a not-so-different space station. The weather, as a subset of environmental control, could be managed down to the smallest details with precision engineering.

Yes, there would be "snowfall", though not as someone on Earth might know it. A white substance would fall. It would be cold and melt on the skin. It would be pretty on the ground, but there would never be so much as to disrupt daily life. Weather for aesthetics' sake. With modern engineering, almost all life's little inconveniences had disappeared. The space stations truly were the best place to experience humanity. He sipped his drink, smiling to himself.

Behind them, the bottles of whisky and collection of glasses on the meeting table began to rattle. The room turned to look at them, frowning. He exchanged a glance with the Hyfb official.

"Meteor shower?" they suggested.

"Or somebody in engineering is going to get fired," he agreed, turning back to the window. Signs attached to buildings wobbled, as did the people visible inside. Together, they watched the memo screens, waiting for some kind of announcement. None came. The shaking only worsened. Avery grit his teeth.

"What's that?" someone asked, pointing out the window.

A brilliant pink light was piercing the bulkhead. Avery's eyes stung and watered, and he threw his arm up to shield them.

"What the hell is happening?" he mumbled, downing the rest of his drink.

He squinted at the city around it, trying to see what was occurring. The light burned his eyes, leaving a haze of extreme light and extreme dark that consumed every shape. As he tried to grasp onto the image of something, anything, the light exploded outwards. Cold sweat trickled down his back as he realised that the whole scene was silent, his ears filled with the sound of his own pounding heart and harsh breaths.

Anything not bolted down was sucked away by the pull of what could only be the vacuum of space, and everything else bent and groaned under the strain. The world outside became a blur of things rushing to meet the void. Avery's breath caught in his throat.

As the metallic scent of ozone and the bitter scent of the space station's fire suppressant foam reached him, he found the courage to speak.

"We need to leave," he stressed, eyes wide. But it was too late. There were already cracks in the window and the strain was beginning to show on the floor. Although he turned his back to run, the building snapped and gave way, knocking them all off their feet and through the window, where they were sucked into the vast, uncaring void.

1

Strictly Speaking

Roz's fingers danced across the control board, doing a million small tweaks at once. It was only half skill, the other half made up of tiny assistive implants in her fingers. She didn't just work for the radio station; she *was* the radio station, adjusting music, mixing, presenting, and playing adverts from one cosy room filled to the brim with tech. It was her dream job. At least, that was what she told herself. The presence of both her supervisor and a detective on the other side of a piece of soundproof glass told a different story.

She looked back at her hands. For now, there was a job to do. She tuned out one song and began speaking.

"Good evening, weary travellers, and welcome to Radio Broadstrokes." There were three holographic screens in front of her: one for technical checks to ensure everything was working, one to allow her to find and play songs, and one, to her misfortune, that showed live social media feeds with questions and requests from listeners. At least, that was what it was meant to be used for. Her jaw set. As soon as her voice began, it lit up with a torrent of hate messages once more. "I'm Roz, and I'll be here all night long for all your music needs."

She stared fixedly away from the third screen, but the flood of messages equivalent to a digital boo from millions of people was hard to ignore.

"In the news tonight." She took a drink of water as her voice grew hoarse. "There has been another attack on a space station. 12-Nesc-A becomes the fourth in a strange chain of attacks, the cause of which is still unknown. Our thoughts are with all those affected by these tragedies. The authorities are doing everything they can to get to the bottom of this. We'll bring you updates live as we get them." Her breath hitched as she forced the next words out. "In other news—" Violent banging on the window interrupted her. Her supervisor signalled frantically for her to stop. Nodding, she said instead, "Here's a word from our sponsors," and cut to an ad break.

Her supervisor yanked at the collar of his shirt, looking ready to collapse. Beside him, the detective looked calm and confident. A shiny black beard and moustache covered warm russet skin, lined with age and experience. Golden brown eyes watched her keenly. *What do they see?* she wondered with a shudder.

She could not ignore it any longer. She turned to look at the third screen. "Spy", "traitor", and most of all "angel of death" flooded the display. She'd always known that fame would be a blessing and a curse, but today's flavour of curse was paralysing and plain insane. It was the court of public opinion, and it had decided she, a small DJ from the middle of nowhere, was guilty of massive acts of terror. Four different space stations had been destroyed now, in four different systems, at four different times, with no other links than being unfortunate enough to be mentioned in Roz's broadcast the day before.

She dismissed the screen and tossed her work glasses aside, rubbing her face. Without them, it was just her and the beautiful console of buttons, dials, and aesthetic blue and gold lights. Her and the music. Her and her thoughts.

Panic had been a constant companion over the last few days, nestled in her chest. She worked hard to keep it in check. But in moments like this, moments where she was alone, it rose inside her and broke free. Horror came hand in hand with it. Millions were dead and a large group of people had determined that she was responsible. Maybe it was more accurate to say they *needed* it to be her fault. In many ways, she couldn't blame them. Everyone was on edge. Revalin, for all its efforts to hide it from the inside, *was* a space station, and the attacks had been so sudden, so random, and the lack of a motive, the lack of a sensible person to blame, was so far beyond terrifying. Her brain shut off when she tried to think about it. She blinked away tears. All she'd ever wanted was to do this job. Now it might be snatched away by some cruel coincidence. She eyed the officer behind the glass. What was he going to do?

As the chain of adverts played in her ears, she sank, putting her head on her arms. *A few minutes of peace,* she thought. A few minutes to recover. A few minutes' break from... whatever was happening out there.

"You're a small fish in a big pond," she told herself. "Why did you have to leave? None of this would have happened if you'd kept your old job." But she'd had to take it, hadn't she? Her dream job served up on a platter. She sighed.

"Did I make a mistake, Ambo?" she asked. At once, her AI assistant, a small hologram in the shape of a bird, popped up in front of her. "Coming here?"

The bird blinked in a way that always unsettled Roz, then replied.

"Probabilistically speaking," it began in its synthetic female voice, "it is very likely."

She nodded to herself.

"Glad I asked," she muttered.

"Would it make you feel better to know that many humans in your position also often regret their decisions?" it asked.

Roz closed her eyes.

"No, Ambo," she replied. "It would not."

Reluctantly, she pulled up her screens again. Twenty million listeners across multiple galaxies and only a wee few minutes before she was back on the air. Her personal communicator was not much better. Whenever she touched it, there seemed to be a hundred more messages: concern from old friends and colleagues, inquiries from reporters who had somehow found her contact information, and pinned above them all by settings she needed to update, a message from her ex. She didn't know how to deal with any of them, least of all that. If she never opened the message, she would never need to acknowledge that their relationship was well and truly over.

Are you listening, Eva? She dared not say it out loud for fear that Ambo would tell her that, in all likelihood, the ex-girlfriend she'd left behind was not listening to the show. In fact, she was only one person in billions and billions of people in the galaxies in which it was broadcast. After a few months, she probably wasn't even *thinking* about Roz.

"I'm a long way from home," she said instead.

"Approximately 1678 billion standard units," Ambo agreed.

"*Fuck,*" was all she could manage.

Taking a deep breath, Roz straightened up. She couldn't stay like this her whole shift. Pulling her glasses on, she watched the horrendous comments continue to flood in. There was not enough time to steel herself. How could there ever be enough time to grasp this? What even was *this*? She couldn't focus on that right now, not if she wanted to keep her job. With half an eye on the detective watching through the glass,

Roz forced herself to breathe and began queuing up songs for the rest of the night.

2

A Little Broken but Still Good

"How can you be so fucking calm?" Olise muttered. "Your family was murdered."

Drake and Olise stood in a sea of mourners. They could not see the front of the funeral, but it hardly mattered. Olise turned to her friend and found him staring calmly ahead. Where usually there was a grin amongst his pink stubble, there was a thin line. His fair, peach skin was flushed red. His normally messy blonde hair with pink tips was slicked back.

"Being angry won't bring them back, Lis. Plus," he added and looked down at her, grey eyes cold, "We *will* find out who did it, for them and all the other dead people. The Thaler family won't let this go unpunished."

Olise nodded. Of course, the Thaler Family was a family with a capital F, and that made all the difference. A mafia, an ever-watching, long-reaching crime family who could do amazing things with their resources. She'd witnessed it before. But four destroyed space stations with very few leads... Well, it felt out of reach even for them.

She pulled a Twist, a chewing stick laced with a small dose of a relaxing drug, out of the depths of her pocket. Drake swatted it out from between her fingers and onto the muddy ground of the graveyard.

"Everyone knows funerals don't count," she said.

"Olise, you've been clean for months," he replied. "Don't start on account of a few dead people."

She huffed but did not pull out another. She closed her eyes, focusing on the sound of the rain and the distant sounds of the ceremony. There was a certain comfort to being here, with these people.

As a general rule, planets weren't in the habit of moving. At least not outside of their well-documented orbits. But the way the bounty hunter pair Drake and Olise went about their so-called journey to Porba would almost make anyone believe they did. They'd been heading there for three years now, and they would continue on their way for several years yet. Porba was little more than a week away from them at any given point, but there was always another job to do before they could go, always another little diversion to an interesting place. Olise glanced over her shoulder at a plume of steam in the distance that marked the location of their grubby, graffiti-covered ship. Always another breakdown requiring money and time to repair. She sighed. Perhaps it was less about the destination and more about the journey anyway, though she rolled her eyes at the cliche.

At least they'd made it to their destination on time before the old girl had given up the ghost. If there was any day to avoid missing out on, it was a funeral, though with the number of people here, Olise had a hard time believing they would be missed. But it was important to Drake, important to his family, and they were the only people who mattered to her. So here they were, suited and booted, crowded under an umbrella as sheets of water poured down around them, at the funeral of some extended family they hadn't seen in years.

Was it wrong to say it brought her comfort? Not closure or peace. She was perhaps the least affected out of the many people here, but because the Thaler family never forgot anyone. If you were a part of their family – and they'd taken her in long ago – then you mattered. With them, with Drake, she had meaning. She had a home to come back to and people looking out for her.

The rain lessened, and a mist settled over everything. The crowd began to shuffle forward, allowing everyone a moment by the graves to pay their respects. Olise took a deep breath as they stepped up. She looked over the new, polished headstones before nodding sharply and dropping her eyes to the ground. After a moment, Drake put a hand on her arm, and they joined the groups of people slowly filtering to the back of the crowd.

Everyone fell silent as the celebrant began speaking again, starting off loud enough that they could hear him before quickly dropping down. A murmur rippled back through the crowd, a final goodbye, and the funeral came to an end. As the crowd began to disperse, the pair turned to look at each other, then at the plume of steam coming from their ship in the distance.

"We're going to have to hitch a ride to this wake," Drake said before setting off to wave down someone who was probably a distant contact that he knew through some obscure event. Crime family or no crime family, Olise could not deny the Thalers were a unique breed.

They hopped into the cargo area of a ship, bracing themselves against metal crates inside. Drake chatted away with his relatives. Olise made small talk where she could, but she'd long since given up remembering names unless they saw them often.

"Listen," the cousin said, shaking his head, "as much as I want to get to the bottom of who or what is behind all this, I do *not* want to see what's capable of ripping up space stations like that."

Drake hummed in agreement.

"No ships nearby, so it must have been an inside job," he said. "But what weapon has that kind of power?" He shook his head. "Any word on it yet?"

"No," the cousin replied. "Nobody has any clue, including us. The news is throwing the word terrorism around, but the Family don't think it's that." He turned to Olise. "You don't have any family on a station, do you?"

She shook her head. *No family, period,* she thought, but stopped herself saying it out loud.

"Good." The cousin nodded.

The wake was a grand affair in the mansion of the family head. The entryway was almost flooded with the rainwater they brought in with them. The floors were marble and glowed a deep gold in the light of a chandelier. In a large dining hall, a few waiters served drinks and food was laid out on a long candle-lit table. Olise stuck to Drake as he floated around the crowd, paying his respects.

"Drake!" The pair spun to see the Thaler patriarch himself, the short, stout Uncle Remo. He was the picture of an old-school Earth mobster – perfect suit, perfect hair, and a round stomach. He embraced Drake. "You're good, I hope?" He patted him on the back before turning to Olise and embracing her.

"Olise, darling, you're looking well. Is he keeping you out of trouble?"

"Only sometimes," Olise replied. He gave a quaking belly laugh.

"That's what I like to hear."

He put an arm around each of them, leading them out of the worst of the crowd. "How's bounty hunting treating you? Business good?"

"Yeah," Drake replied. "The work is steady. Haven't been double-crossed in months. That's a plus."

"Good, good. Are you free for a job right now?" They nodded. "I have a proposition for you. I know we've had a little friction, and I know you like to keep it mostly above board these days in bounty hunting, but..."

"You know I'll do it," Drake said.

"Investigate these space station attacks. We've got people on it, but we swim in different circles. You have different connections. See what you can find for us." He extended a hand to Drake, who took it.

"Of course."

"We'll get to the bottom of it," Olise agreed. As she said the words, she felt them in her gut. Drake and Olise's career as bounty hunters had its ups and downs. Olise suspected they'd had more than their fair share of mistakes and failures over the years, but they'd learned and adapted and only improved with age. With the Family's resources, they'd only get better.

She looked to Drake, who nodded and added, "They won't know what hit them."

"They weren't coming for Thaler people," Uncle Remo said. "But we're coming for them." His eyes were distant, cold, even calculating as he stared into his drink. He snapped back to a smile.

"I should get back in there. Take care, you two."

They bade him farewell and then turned to each other, exchanging a nod. Another repair, another job, another while before Porba yet.

3

I Knew She Was(n't) Trouble from the Moment She Walked In

Detective Harsha Sobol watched the DJ on the other side of the radio studio glass with a frown on his face. Immaculate, bright eye makeup that stood out against her rich umber skin and matching jewellery gave the impression of a woman who was holding it together. The dark rings under her eyes and her restless hands told a different story. Watching her, shoulder-to-shoulder with Harsha, was her supervisor, stiff as a board and sweating uncontrollably. When the supervisor motioned for the DJ to stop talking in a desperate attempt to minimise any more damage, she looked up at them like a deer in the headlights.

She did not look like a terrorist, but people rarely did. If thirty years on the force had taught him anything, it was that people would do all kinds of things with the right pressure applied. He watched her grow flustered, looking at the social media response. The mob had already decided her guilt. It was his job to find out if it was justified or not.

He spun his hat around in his hands. It was no wonder he was uncomfortable. He'd be fighting against a tide of press and people wanting answers. Waiting on results when there was nothing he could do to speed them up. He had been assigned to the case because he could handle the pressure, and he was prepared for a rough few weeks ahead. The radio station was not making him feel better. Even holding his long trench coat hanging over his shoulder, he was sweating. The room that looked onto the DJ's broadcasting studio was small, dimly lit, and had the kind of warmth that weighed down on you and made you feel you were suffocating.

"Any time you're ready," he said to the supervisor. The man waited for an opportune moment and then signalled for Roz to leave the room. She did so jerkily, swaying as though she might faint. When she closed the door to the studio and turned towards them, head down, Harsha offered her his hand. She shook it only for a second, wiping clammy hands on her dark trousers splashed with colour. Despite the heat, she pulled a teal bomber jacket tighter around herself. Up close, she seemed so small, barely coming up to his shoulder. The tight, black curls of her natural hair had iridescent glitter through them.

"Detective Harsha Sobol," he said. "I'm here to ask you some questions."

She paled and mumbled a response he could not pick up.

"My office is through there," her supervisor pointed them towards the back.

"Thank you." Harsha picked up a slim briefcase at his feet and led Roz into an office plastered with awards and recognition. He sat on one side of an immaculate desk and opened the briefcase to reveal a neat silver and blue device inside.

"These questions will be recorded," he told her, "and with your permission," he handed her a collection of small plastic bands. "I'd like to use our lie-detecting system."

She nodded again and followed his instruction to put the bands around her fingers, wrists, and arms.

"I'm not going to bite," he told her. "Just ask questions." Another nod. "Are you ready?" She pursed her lips but mumbled in agreement. As he started the recording, she stiffened.

"Can you state your name for the record?" he began, watching her expression.

"Rosalin Dayne."

"And your current place of employment?"

"Radio Broadstrokes, late-night DJ."

As the detector readings showed it was ready, Harsha settled into his chair and clasped his hands.

"What do you know about the recent attacks on the space stations?"

"N-not much," she said. "Only that they were destroyed by something powerful. Only what's on the news."

The detector flashed green.

"Have you ever been to any of those locations?"

"No." *Green.*

"Do you know anybody there? Family? Friends? Old acquaintances, maybe."

"No." *Green.*

"Any connections to them? Business interests, political interests, that sort of thing?"

"None." *Green.*

"Do you know anyone who does?"

"No."

"Is Radio Broadstrokes the only job you have?"

"Yes," she replied. "I lived on Nonke until recently. I was a DJ there too, Nonke Radio 1."

Another green. Harsha paused. He clasped his hands.

"Did anyone tell you to mention these places in your broadcasts, or was it your own decision?"

"It was my decision." She appeared to tense further. She was a tightly wound coil. Harsha couldn't help but wonder how much more she could take before she would snap.

"Can you explain to me why you chose them?"

"Rugh-Cuwe was in the news because of the political talks there at the very end of last year. Then Shangris was in the news for going into high alert as the only other station in the solar system. We were running a bit where people would phone in and tell us about somewhere they wanted to go. My example was the gardens on Tenza-3. As for 12-Nesc-A..." She looked into the distance. "I don't know. I just remembered an old story. I'm on the air for so long I just... ramble."

She looked at him, and he gave an encouraging nod.

"You're doing well," he reassured her. "I appreciate your co-operation. Do you have connections with any of the following organisations?" He read a list of mercenary companies, private militaries, known terrorists and other potential threats.

"No," she replied to each. Another green light revealed she was telling the truth. The more questions he asked, the further he seemed from answers. It *had* seemed like a leap in logic that a random radio DJ on a late-night show was somehow connected to what otherwise appeared to be terrorist attacks, but in his line of work, there were very few coincidences.

"Tell me," he said, leaning back in his chair. "Do *you* think you have anything to do with these attacks? Any strange gut feeling? Any voice in the back of your head?"

"No." Her bottom lip trembled. *Green.* "I don't know why this is happening to me."

Harsha closed the briefcase. He tried to keep a straight face, but the truth was that this feeling was familiar. *She* was familiar. His stomach knotted.

"Can you do something for me?" he asked. "When you go back on air, mention the space station Amyra in your broadcast."

"Why?" she stammered. "I can't." A few stray tears ran down her face. "What if it's attacked, too? No," she said, shaking her head. A shower of glitter fell out of her hair.

"It's abandoned," he assured her. "Scheduled for destruction soon. I just want to test a theory. Do that for me, please." She did not look convinced, but she nodded. "The way you mentioned the first two stations isn't specific to you. Tenza-3 is the next closest station to the original two, so your mention of it could just be a coincidence. 12-Nesc-A is really where the pattern with you begins. Let's see if it continues. Then go home and try to get some rest. This is just the beginning. I'll be back in touch later for more information."

She hesitated, then removed the bands and left him alone in the office. As the door shut behind her, Harsha sank into thought. Everything she'd told him was the truth. Was there something he'd missed? Some kind of loophole? He didn't think so. So what remained? Was someone manipulating her without her knowing? Or did she only *think* she was telling the truth? There were still more tests he could run, more avenues to explore. Humming to himself, his eyes drifted to where Roz had been. Time would tell. He was sure of only one thing. Rosalin Dayne needed help, and he'd be damned before he gave up on answers.

4

Mystery on the Inter-Planet Express

Humanity had always had an interest in trains, Drake considered as he stared out the window of the galaxy's biggest train service, the Inter-Planet Express. Whether it officially counted as a train was up to debate, a furious one in some circles, but it was a string of carriages weaving its way through the vacuum of space. In the past, his ancestors had travelled "Europe" on them, back on a planet he'd never known. They'd robbed them, run them, smuggled on them, and, like so many people, ridden them to enjoy the view.

Sometimes, the further he got from Earth in space and time, the less things seemed to change. Using a small control panel on the table in front of him, he configured his surroundings. Sounds of a train chugging on iron tracks mixed with calming sea waves began to play. He could have changed the window to display something to match up with it, too, if he wanted, but he had always enjoyed looking at the stars. There was so much out there to admire. Still, when he closed his eyes and listened to one of the catalogues of experiences available on board, something inside him stirred, some kind of primal recognition that, at one point, the seaside had been his family's home.

"Bougie," Olise said, interrupting his thoughts. She slid into their booth across from him, dumping an assortment of packaged snacks and two colourful drinks between them. "Travelling courtesy of your family always has perks." She wrenched open one of the packets, sending small pink puffed snacks over the table. She shrugged off her jacket, revealing her bare arms and the network of detailed tattoos across her olive skin.

He turned back to the articles he'd been reading on his communicator, a touch-sensitive square tile. He pulled a small coin-shaped device from his pocket and placed it amongst the snacks. When he doubled-tapped it with his finger and then again with his communicator, it began projecting a hologram of his screen for Olise to see.

"Look at this," he said, pointing at a news article. "There's been another attack. Amyra."

"Amyra?" Olise said. "Isn't that abandoned?"

Drake nodded. With a flick of his fingers across his communicator, the news article disappeared, showing his notes hidden underneath. That made five attacks with no apparent connection, and they, like everyone else, struggled to know where to begin.

The galaxy was filled with suspicious activity. Drake and Olise were often a part of it. So, finding a starting point for their investigation was like trying to find a needle in a haystack, except they didn't know what the needle *was*. They would be meeting their repaired ship in a mechanic's shop in Revalin. Drake didn't love the idea of travelling to any space station, but he was trying to make the most of it. In the meantime, they were making use of the time, putting their ears to the ground and doing research. Hearing about the attacks wasn't hard; everybody was talking about them, but no one had anything to say. Beyond theorising and a few wild conspiracies, everyone was drawing a blank.

"What do you think of the DJ, Roz?" he asked. "She *has* mentioned all the places before they were destroyed, but... she's a *radio DJ*."

Olise hummed, looking at a picture of the DJ on a screen of her own.

"We'll be on Revalin anyway," she said with a shrug. "Worth investigating. Worth following the people investigating her, too. How a DJ would coordinate something like this or why is a question for later. A lead is a lead."

"I dunno, Lis. I don't get what there is to gain by destroying these places. Or who could stand to gain." He dismissed the screen and pocketed the coin. "The only thing that makes sense is power. But then why has no one tried to claim the credit? Or use it in some way. It all seems pointless."

"We'll find something," she assured him. "We always do."

She cast a cautious gaze about the carriage.

"Anything more on your mystery passenger?" she asked. Drake shook his head. It was a bad habit he couldn't seem to switch off, having a little nosy at the passenger list to see if anything was amiss. One thing had flagged. A name. Sabine Coren had boarded a transport yesterday a few star systems away and was now on this train too, unique ID code and all. By all rights, the distance between that system and this train should have taken weeks, not hours. He doubted it was anything. Someone wanted to hide behind a fake identity and had done a bad job of choosing one. It was more common than people realised. He and Olise used them often. In fact, "Sabine" was one of Olise's common choices. Although they had the sense to check who else had the names they were using in advance. Appearing several star systems away in just 24 hours was bound to set off all kinds of alarms. But maybe he wasn't giving the perpetrator enough credit. Its appearance in two locations may have been a deliberate move to hide something else. Still, he made a mental note of it.

"Everyone is on edge, though," he said.

"Aren't you?" she replied. "Someone is destroying space stations at random and we're in a public place that's much more vulnerable?"

Drake gave a measured nod. Lush red carpet ran down the centre of the carriage. On either side, small groups of people, notably better dressed than them, sat in high-backed private booths encased in iridescent, soundproof bubbles. They chatted away, attended to by a stiff waiter who, Drake considered, was keeping an impressive, neutral face, though their eyes betrayed how exhausted they were.

"Do you want to split up and investigate the train?" she asked.

Drake hummed.

"Maybe, yeah." He sighed. "I think we'll struggle to get far without being questioned though."

"And here I thought you were a charming liar."

Drake smiled briefly.

"And what do you think all these rich people are?" he asked. "The waiters will see through us quick enough."

"Then we'll be quicker," Olise said with a firm nod.

***

Phin Sayer swayed with the train, hands clasped in front of him, fighting to stay awake. He was dead on his feet. Four hours left on his shift, in his stiff, pressed waiter's garb, and no energy drinks were permitted. Something about "ruining the ambience". He was so close to solving his university project. So close to having something groundbreaking to write about for his dissertation. But close was not good enough. Not now, with only a few weeks to go and shifts galore during the train's busy season.

Phin was feeling the pressure. Work wasn't exactly a walk in the park either. The guests watched him warily, and he watched them right back. The terrorist attacks had them all on edge.

"Look for terrorists," they'd been told, though no one had told them what a terrorist looked like. There was no reason to suspect the train would be targeted, but then again, there was no reason to suspect there wasn't. His head spun with tiredness, but he couldn't afford to shut his eyes. If he fell asleep on the job, he'd be punished worse than if a terrorist destroyed the whole train on his watch. He ducked in and out of the carriage's store cupboard, pulled out a hidden can of glowing energy drink, and chugged it. He would just need to risk the warning.

The carriage was quiet. Most groups had a soundproof bubble around them, and even then, they were sleeping. A pale, peach-skinned man with ridiculous pink facial hair and matching frosted tips slipped in the back door and into a seat. Phin's eyes narrowed. Seats were assigned, but this man seemed to be coming and going a lot on this trip. Phin watched as his eyes floated over everyone in the carriage before finally meeting his. There was a long moment in which neither of them moved.

After a few seconds, the pink-haired man left again. Phin's heart pounded. What was that all about? *No need to assume anything*, he told himself. *You've had weirder customers than this.*

Before he could dip back into the store cupboard, a ping went off, signalling a customer wanted attention. He looked up at the ceiling where a small blinking light directed him to a middle-aged woman swamped in a cream jumper. Badly bleached platinum blonde hair stood out against lined, umber skin. Large round glasses magnified grey eyes.

"How can I help you, ma'am?" he asked. She beckoned him inside the privacy bubble and closed it off. When she spoke, she lowered her voice anyway, not that anyone would hear her if she screamed right now.

"That man, with the pink hair," she said, looking over her shoulder at the door he had left through. "He's making me very uncomfortable. He looks at everything so intensely."

Phin nodded. In his gut, he felt the same, but he knew what the handbook wanted him to do. He forced a smile and clasped his hands to hide the fact they were shaking.

"He isn't assigned to this section," Phin said. "But he might be looking for someone. I'll keep an eye on him and ask my colleagues to do the same. In the meantime" – he glanced in the opposite direction – "if you'd like to move, there's seating available in the next carriage."

She nodded hastily, gathering her jacket and belongings in a quick and messy bundle.

She kept her head down, cheeks flushed. The other passengers barely spared them a glance. As they entered the next carriage, his co-worker June came to meet them. Sparing only a moment to mutter an explanation to her, Phin returned to his bright, customer service voice and said, "My colleague June will take good care of you. I hope you enjoy the rest of your trip."

As June led her to a free seat and offered her a complimentary drink, Phin steadied himself. Now that a passenger had complained, he would have to investigate. On the surface, nothing was wrong – just a man in the wrong place, a man who looked sober, well-presented, and calm. But there was something of a predator in the way he watched the other passengers, it was true. Phin shuddered and returned to his own section.

***

Drake slumped into his seat with a groan and opened another pack of sweets. He glanced at Olise, but she shook her head. Nothing. So why couldn't he relax? All logic said there would be nothing, and they'd found exactly that. He was letting everyone else's fear infect him. *Get a beer*, he told himself, sinking back into his chair. Instead, he hacked into the train's network and watched messages go by. Nothing suspicious. Nothing that stood out. It wasn't long until they'd hit their stop: Revalin. He was pulled from his thoughts by the gentle ringing of a bell and their bubble changing colour. A woman waited expectantly outside, having "knocked" for their attention. She was middle-aged, swamped in a large cream jumper and round glasses. Drake opened the door, frowning.

"You're bounty hunters, aren't you?" she asked. Glancing at Olise, Drake paused, then nodded.

"We are," he replied. She stepped into the bubble and shut the door behind her.

"And you saw him too, didn't you?" she said hurriedly, sliding into the seat next to him. Olise raised an eyebrow. Drake saw her hand go towards the pocket where her gun was hidden, but she knew better than to grab it yet.

"Who?" he asked, trying to keep his voice level.

"The waiter, in the next carriage. He keeps going into the cupboard. Acting weird."

"The small one? Red-y, auburn hair? Floppy curls?" Drake asked. The woman nodded. He tried to remember his encounter with him.

He *had* avoided Drake's gaze, and his pale pink skin had been flushed red and shiny with sweat, but Drake had written it off as anxiety rather than guilt. Then again, Drake had been wrong before.

"I've been watching him the whole journey. I don't think he's really a waiter. He keeps going into a store cupboard."

"He could be new," Drake offered.

"Or sneaking food," Olise offered.

"If you're concerned," Drake continued, eyes narrowed. "Why haven't you contacted train security?"

"Just watch him," the woman begged. She grabbed one of Drake's hands. She was cold and clammy. "Please. If something happens, security will be too late."

He shared another glance with Olise. He could tell what she was thinking. Something stank here. But could they afford not to take this seriously? He clucked his tongue.

"Okay," Drake said. "I'll watch him."

5

City Lights and Restless Nights

Roz slunk through the city streets, the hood of her jacket up, head down, and hands shoved in her pockets. She would have preferred to avoid the busy thoroughfares around her work, but her knowledge of Revalin outside her commute was severely lacking, and the last thing she needed right now was to get lost.

She had never felt comfortable in Revalin. She'd been excited when she'd first moved here. She'd done all the tourist activities and tried exploring her local area, but the reality of the situation had quickly come crashing down. She'd moved away from everything and everyone she'd known. She was alone. Finding ways to meet people while working the night shift was hard. None of her favourite places were here, and it was lonely to go out and explore. It was lonely to have no one to share this new experience with. *She* was lonely. She could admit that now. She could admit it even before the label "angel of death" had begun. But… she had to get on with it.

"Ambo," she said softly. The AI assistant sat in her jacket's breast pocket, awaiting her call. It perked up with a musical chime. "Do I have food at home?" she asked.

"Checking…" it replied. "You have no fresh ingredients in the fridge. In the pantry, you have dehydrated bread, instant noodles—"

She cut it off.

"Stop," she told it.

"You have one shopping list," Ambo concluded. "Would you like to see it?"

Roz responded in the affirmative and glanced over the list before snorting. It had been made by the Roz of two weeks ago. When she'd found herself alone at home after work each day, she'd decided she would learn how to cook nice meals to make up for her lack of socialisation. The idea seemed laughable now. Still, she had to eat something. She dismissed Ambo and ducked into the first grocery store she passed.

Its bright white lights hurt her tired eyes, and she grimaced as she entered. Over a loudspeaker, music played and echoed through the store. At a brisk pace, she skipped over the fresh produce and went instead to look at instant meals. She stared for too long at the colourful spread of options, too tired and overwhelmed to make a choice. There was a break in the music and a presenter began to speak. Roz's stomach dropped. They were playing the news. She glanced quickly around her and found herself alone in the aisle, a small comfort as she buried her face in her hands and winced at what was to come.

"This is AO Central News. In tonight's headlines: speculation flies as investigations into the destroyed space stations continue without result; public discontent grows as officials attempt to prevent a mass exodus from space stations; and is there any truth to the rumours about the radio DJ Roz Dayne, as she heralds the death of each space station? With me tonight is criminal psychologist Dravyn Cohlin. What do you think of these rumours?"

"I think the idea that she's behind the attacks or even involved is a little sensationalised. Whoever is destroying the stations, I'm not sure they'd appreciate the galaxy being given a heads-up from a radio broadcast. It's an interesting connection in a very difficult case, and I'm sure the investigators will be following up on it. I believe Radio Broadstrokes took her off the air mid-shift this evening. Whether they know something we don't or whether they're just protecting themselves remains to be seen."

"What I wouldn't give to be inside those walls just now," the presenter responded. "Is there anything you can tell—"

The conversation continued with the presenter happy to continue asking dramatic questions, clearly unfazed by the accusations of sensationalism. Roz tuned it out for her own sanity. She lifted her head out of her hands and couldn't stand the sight of the food in front of her, couldn't stand being in public any longer. She left the store, but from every vehicle waiting in traffic, from every restaurant with an open window, it seemed like the broadcast followed her. The last few days had felt like a lifetime. How much longer would this go on for?

When she finally crossed the threshold of her apartment and closed the door heavily behind her, she was shaking. A cold, dark, and empty space greeted her. The apartment was a large, open-plan penthouse near the top of one of Revalin's skyscrapers. When she'd viewed it for the first time, the space had appealed to her, but the truth was she hadn't invested enough time or money into the apartment to make it feel like a home, and huge swathes of the area were empty and uninviting. A few boxes sat unopened in a pile, their contents waiting for shelves and other furniture to call home, but the reality was Roz hadn't brought much with her. Much of what she'd owned was shared with Eva, and Roz had left most of it with her, unable to cope with the memories.

Overall, the apartment was sparsely furnished with little more than the bare minimum: two couches and a coffee table, still pristine from their lack of use; very little in the kitchen, save appliances and a bare kitchen island with a single stool; an old beaten-up bed that had followed her through three apartments now, separated from the rest of the open-plan space by a half wall and a translucent curtain. It turned out that going from a bedroom that was little more than a cupboard to a bed in a studio was quite disconcerting.

She kicked off her shoes, shrugged off her coat, and threw herself onto a couch, lying face down. She let one arm and one leg hang off the edge and touch the floor. None of it really mattered. She closed her eyes but did not sleep.

Against her better judgement, she pulled out Ambo and put it on her coffee table.

"Ambo, show me—" she began, then stopped herself. What could Ambo show her that would change anything? Was there anything that would make her feel better? Now free from her pocket, Ambo's bird avatar appeared on her table and dutifully brought up a hologram of her home screen. A group photo of her, her mother, and her Aunt Alison beamed back at her. It was the last time they'd all been together. Roz rubbed her eyes and sighed.

"Ambo, without showing me everything else that's in there, are there any messages in my inbox from Alison?"

"No," it replied.

Roz rubbed her eyes and sighed. It had been like this since her mother had died. Longer, really, but Roz felt it more keenly now that her mother was gone. Alison had always been in and out of contact, off in one distant star system or another, pursuing her scientific research. Then, at least, it had felt like Alison always made time for them, to call and tell them about the things she saw in her travels, or to visit and bring them a souvenir. Now... it had been months, close to a year, since she'd heard from her aunt. Alison had never forgiven herself for being in a star system out of conventional communication range when

Roz's mother had died. Part of Roz had never forgiven her either. She knew her mother had worsened suddenly; she knew that her prognosis had been good until her last weeks, but the fact she'd had to delay the funeral for months, while firstly waiting to hear from Alison and then waiting for her to arrive, had just compounded the grief of her mother's shocking passing. At the funeral, Alison looked gaunt and hollow. She'd barely spoken. She could barely even look at Roz.

"You look so much like her," she'd muttered. The words had stuck with Roz long after they'd parted ways.

Alison had gone away for work again but had stayed in contact range. They'd met up twice after the funeral and had messaged for a while before... total silence. Even so, Roz wished her aunt was here. She dismissed Ambo with a lazy wave and stared into nothing.

Eventually, her stomach protested at her earlier decision not to buy food, and she was forced to sit up. She gave the fridge a cursory look, though, of course, Ambo's earlier report had been correct. She leant against her kitchen counter and took deep breaths. She couldn't stomach the thought of any food, but she knew at least part of her constant nausea these days was due to a lack of general self-care.

"Ambo," she said, voice cracking. "Can you order me some takeout? Whatever my last order was."

"Your order has been accepted, Roz," it said cheerily. "Estimated arrival in 35 minutes."

Roz nodded and returned to the couch, watching out her long windows for the delivery drone. Outside, life went on, even in the middle of the night. Chunky, rectangular shuttles, small, slim speed bikes, and small drones whizzed past her window in a blur of red and white lights in the artificial night sky. It was something she loved about Revalin. It felt like the kind of cities on planets she'd seen in movies. Not so long ago, she'd been thrilled at the idea of moving to the big city to pursue her dreams. Sometimes, it helped to remind herself of that. Sometimes, it just spurred a pang of grief. The move had been the point where everything had started to go wrong.

Ambo perked up.

"Delivery arriving!" it chimed.

Roz stood stiffly and walked out onto her small balcony, looking around for the delivery. A drink swooped in from above, coming to a dead stop in front of her, a small box hanging from its belly. Small clamps released, and the box was dropped into her waiting arms. She turned to go inside when motion caught her eye. She turned back, only to be startled by a bright flash. Another drone had appeared by her balcony, then another, each of them flashing lights at her. No, she realised, taking pictures of her. Paparazzi. Taking the box in one hand, she covered her eyes with the other. Another flash came, and another. In moments, a whole swarm surrounded her. She dived inside, slamming the door shut behind her. Her windows were one-way, but she snapped at Ambo, "Close all the blinds," for good measure. As she locked the balcony door, they snapped shut, plunging the apartment into darkness. Her heart pounded, and her breath caught in her throat.

"How did they know where I live?"

She hadn't been speaking to Ambo specifically, but it responded.

"Your name and address were on the delivery order, Roz," it said.

She sank to the floor and squeezed her eyes shut, cursing quietly. Of course it was. Why hadn't she thought about that? It wasn't like Ambo would think to use a fake name. She stared long and hard at Ambo's cartridge on the coffee table, feeling a weight in her chest. Biting her lip, she crawled towards it, turned the device over, and found its override off switch.

"I'm sorry," she told it. "It's just... I can't..." *You know too much*, she finished in her head. She didn't wait for the AI to respond before flicking the switch. Opening a small drawer on the underside of the table, she dropped it inside and turned away. "Wait here for now," she said, aware she was now speaking to nothing. "I'll restart you when this is all over."

"This is crazy," she breathed. It was decided, then. No more takeout or deliveries for her. She really would have to learn to cook.

6

Ah, Fuck

When Phin returned to his own section, things were quiet for a while. He served drinks, cleaned messes, and stared into space. Maybe the man had found what he was looking for, though even that made Phin uncomfortable. Maybe it was nothing at all. But when the man returned once again, queasiness washed over Phin.

Mustering all his courage, he walked over to him. He shoved his fidgeting hands into the deep pocket of his apron, put on his uncanny voice again, and addressed him.

"Can I help you, sir? I don't believe you're registered to be here. If you're looking for something or someone, I'd be happy to assist."

The man eyed him up for a moment longer, then broke into a smile.

"Yes, actually," he said, his voice smooth and his eyes bright and sharp. Almost Phin's type. He pointed at the door behind him. "Can you come with me for a minute?"

Phin suppressed a frown, glancing at the door. Internally, he groaned. Was Geo slacking *again*? Trust him to expect Phin to pick up the slack.

"Of course, sir." He waved a hand. "Lead the way."

He followed the man as they walked through one carriage, then another, then another.

"Sir?" he began.

"Just a moment."

It all happened in a matter of seconds. As the man stepped from the passenger area and entered what should have been a staff-only space, Phin stopped in his tracks. Something definitely wasn't right. Before he could turn around and call for help, someone closed in behind him and shoved him forwards, grabbing his arms and binding them tightly together in one smooth motion. Before he could yell, a hand clamped over his mouth. Cold panic washed over him. The pink-haired man said something to the person holding him, but the words went in and out of his head without processing. He looked around frantically for anything to help but saw nothing. Bright lights shone in through a service exit of the train. They were pulling into a station. This had all been planned, Phin realised. These people were professionals.

"You're coming with us, kid," the man said. When their eyes met, there was none of the friendliness that had been there before. His grey eyes were bright and sharp.

"No," Phin tried to say. Was there *anything* he could do? Surely, they couldn't kidnap him in full view of the station. He tried to thrash around in his captor's grip, but they were unmoving, like steel. He blinked, trying to focus. He might only get one shot at getting someone's attention.

As they waited for the train door to open, time slowed, the space between his rapid heartbeats seeming to stretch into hours. He braced, ready, his palms sweating. He winced as he tasted bile in the back of his throat. He tried to swallow, but his mouth was bone dry. His captors began to move, and as they did, he felt his shoulders release. It all felt futile.

Phin was not an action star; he was a *physics student,* and he was no match for the strength and expertise of his captors. Before he knew it, he was out of the train station, out of sight, in what seemed to be some small storage room.

He was dumped on a crate in the corner. The person who had been holding him, a muscular, tattoo-covered woman with a short, black bob, strode to the door and secured it while the pink-haired man paced. Would he remember these descriptions when the police asked? *If* he was still alive to speak to the police by the end of this. He gulped. *Someone* would notice he had disappeared from work, surely?

The woman stood a few steps behind the man now, looming over Phin.

The pink-haired man was turning something over in his hands. Phin peered at it. It was compact; a small metal casing with a few lights and buttons.

"Where did you get this?" the pink-haired man asked him.

"I don't know what that is," Phin replied honestly.

"It was in your storage cupboard," the man replied evenly. "Passengers said you kept going in and out of it. What was the target?"

"Is it a bomb?" Phin asked, voice wavering. The man stared at him intensely. Phin shivered. "Whatever it is, i-it's not mine. I kept sneaking in to drink energy drinks."

"Then whose is it? Did someone else tell you to put it there?"

"N-no-one. And it wasn't in there the last time I went in," Phin said, then added uncertainly, "I don't *think* it was there."

The man did not respond. Phin took a few harsh breaths. Hot tears pierced his eyes.

"Listen, I don't know what's going on," he said, almost begging. "Please don't hurt me." The pair looked at him and then back at each other. "The only reason I was watching you was because a woman said you scared her," Phin continued, unprompted. "She thought—" He gulped before continuing, "*I* thought you were going to do something to the train."

"You think *we're* the terrorists?" the man asked with narrowed eyes.

"I don't know what to think anymore." The words came out almost as a sob. In an instant, the mood changed. The room froze.

"Who was the woman? Was she middle-aged? Blonde?" the man asked after a moment.

"Yeah. Round glasses and a big jumper."

The man groaned, pinching his nose.

"We've been played."

7

HEAD ABOVE WATER

"Roz."

The detective's voice brought Roz back to reality. He had arrived at her door less than half an hour after the report of the attack. She'd been staring at the sea of messages again, lost in the pool, drowning, even. Amyra had been destroyed, and the more time went on, the more it seemed like it could only be her fault. She'd had enough sense to sit before it could overwhelm her, but now her couch dragged her down.

"And it's only 9am," she muttered to herself, shaking her head.

She looked at Harsha, who was offering her a coffee. She took it and warmed her hands. Despite retreating to bed quickly after her meal, she hadn't slept a wink last night. How could she, with all that was happening? Instead, she'd lain in bed for several hours, staring at the ceiling with a gnawing sense of dread.

"Everything will be alright," he assured her. He offered her a kind smile that deepened the lines around his eyes.

"With all due respect, Detective," she replied. "People have been telling me that for days now, and things only seem to get worse."

"Someone believes you're leaving them a message in your broadcasts," he continued, sitting down opposite her. "Do you have any idea who? We're investigating other members of the radio team."

She shook her head. The defensive part of her wanted to snap back that she didn't associate with terrorists, but she bit her tongue. The detective had been nothing but fair so far.

"Tell me about the people you know," he said.

"There aren't many," she replied. "Just the people at work."

"Tell me about the people you used to know, then."

"I had a group of friends. But we were all artists of some kind." She opened and closed her mouth several times without speaking. "I can give you a list of their names, but I don't—" She choked on a sob. "They wouldn't do this."

"Sometimes people get in with the wrong crowd," he said. "In trouble they can't get out of." She nodded, scribbling down the names with shaking hands. "My old co-workers," she explained as she added more.

"Any family?" he asked gently. She only shook her head.

"My mum passed away a couple of years ago. My dad died in an accident when I was young. We moved around a lot after that. It was kind of for Mum's work, but I think she also couldn't really bear to settle down somewhere without him. We had a good life, just the two of us. I miss her every day. I only have my aunt left, and she's" – she waved a hand, looking out the window – "in the middle of nowhere, in the outer systems or something. I haven't heard from her in months." A sharp pang of anger cut through everything else. Even her ex-girlfriend had had the grace to reach out, but her own flesh and blood, the *only* family she had left? Radio silence. Aunt Alison may have been working in a distant system, but she was still in contact range. She'd *promised* Roz that she would always be there for her. Why, then, had her messages gone unanswered? Her face must have shown a little of her frustration because Harsha continued.

"I'm sorry." He paused. "Any romantic relationships? Past or present."

Roz's shoulders sagged. She understood why he was asking these questions – she did – but it all served to rub in how much she'd given up and how little it had got her.

"An ex-girlfriend," she replied, adding one last name to the list. "We broke up when I moved," she offered as an explanation. "There's a war between us, and it's a long, long way. Doesn't exactly make for easy visiting."

The war over resources in the Maeh asteroid belt had cut off safe and easy travel to and from Nonke's star system. It was the first war in the inner systems for centuries, and everyone was so afraid of pouring fuel on the fire and spreading the conflict to nearby settlements that the attempts at resolution thus far were weak and ineffective. Roz remembered with a pang the weeks she'd thought that would be the craziest thing that would happen in her lifetime.

She did not hear Harsha's response to her statement, clasping her hands and staring into the middle distance.

"Roz," the detective said, pulling her out of her daze once again. He was holding out a small business card. "I'm going back to the precinct, but if you remember anything else, if you *need* anything, if anything else strange happens..."

He stared her down, not in an authoritative way but with the same concern her mother had when she'd gone out for the night. "Tap twice and it'll call me to wherever you are. I'll be there as soon as I can or send someone else. Alright?"

She began to reach for it, then hesitated. Smart business cards that guided you to the location of the business or person in question were common, but one that led the person to you... Well, under her current circumstances, it made her nervous. She looked at Harsha's concerned face again, then nodded and slipped it into her pocket.

"Alright," she said.

With the door shut and locked behind him, Roz paced like a caged animal. This was it. Whatever *it* was. She was in the nicest apartment she'd ever seen. She'd lived in places that barely classed as homes, but she had multiple walls that were actually floor-to-ceiling windows from which she could see a large chunk of the space station. So why did it feel like a prison? The station was in its early morning cycle, artificial sunlight filtering between the tall buildings, coloured adverts, and the moving specks of light from small vehicles. It was her *dream*, yet even before the first mention of the angel of death, it hadn't felt it. Not without Eva.

She paused by one of the windows, pressed her head against the glass and closed her eyes.

"Some things just aren't meant to be," she told herself, and she almost believed it. What could they have done? Both offered their dream jobs, in different galaxies? "Something," she stated. "I should have found a way." Maybe she'd been too greedy. She'd been a small-time DJ back on Nonke. What made Radio Broadstrokes so much better? The money? All that had got her was a beautiful but empty home. The opportunities? Well, she *was* known across many systems now, but not for the reasons she wanted. The people? They had a lot in common with her, but none of them were Eva.

She ran her hands through her hair and closed her eyes. She needed to find a way to stop the torrent of thoughts in her head before she exploded. A bath, she decided. A bath would be good.

Her bathroom had tall windows too, and as much as the estate agent had assured her that they were one way and no one could see her, it had taken her a long time to get used to the idea. The bath was set into the floor, hidden most of the time under the floorboards. It was the kind of bathroom she and Eva had dreamed about having, the kind only seen in movies. It gave the strange illusion that she was floating amongst the city. In a control panel on the wall, she pushed a button to uncover the bath and then turned on Nonke Radio 1. Even if she was several galaxies away, there was comfort in it.

She slipped into the warm water and shut her eyes, pretending she was somewhere else.

The air in the apartment was cold, so the steam from the bath rose, touched her skin, the windows, and the walls, and condensed into a cold stream. Outside, through the windows that automatically defogged, artificial snow was falling. It had been snowing on Rugh-Cuwe before the end, too. She shivered.

Roz was, by all accounts, a nerd. Everyone she knew was. She'd been a loner all her life until radio had finally introduced her to like-minded people. Who would believe she had a tie in any of this? Who would want to frame her? She thought hard again about what Harsha had said in their first meeting: had someone told her what to say, even subconsciously? Some stations had been in the news, but the others... She wracked her brains. *Had* someone mentioned them to her? She didn't think so, but perhaps that was the beauty of suggestion. Nothing happened during the daytime shows. Nothing had happened on the nights she wasn't on. *Was* it her? Or was it a coincidence?

She tried to shake the worries from her head. Harsha would help her; he seemed set on it. For now, the best thing to do would be to focus on the cold and hot spots on her body, the sounds of the radio, the snowfall sparkling in neon lights, and try, for the first night in days, to sleep.

There was a knock at the door and her eyes snapped open. She lunged for the radio and turned it off. *No one is home*, she thought to herself over and over. *Go away. No one is home.* There was another knock, then another. It wouldn't be Harsha, not without any warning.

Roz sank deeper into the water, up to her eyes. Had one of the angry mob found out where she lived? Had whoever was behind the attacks? Who, on Revalin, was calling with no warning? No one.

After a moment of silence, she heard her front door open. She froze. What did she do from here? *It's probably not your door*, she told herself. *You're probably hearing echoes from upstairs again. You're being hysterical.* Slow, heavy footsteps drew closer. There was rustling in her living room.

A deep voice began to speak. A second later, she heard the slight audio wobble of her implanted translator starting up.

"There's nobody home," it translated.

"Check those rooms, I'll check these," a second voice said.

Panic washed over her, and she glanced around the bathroom. The shower was too obvious a place to hide, shrouded only by frosted glass. The cupboard wasn't big enough to fit her by any means. Her eyes fell on the bath controls. Grabbing her towel and pulling it into the water with her, she pushed the controls, covering the bath in the floor once more, ducking underneath the flooring and plunging herself into darkness. She had to strain her neck to keep her mouth and nose above the water. When whimpers escaped her mouth, she clamped her hands over it, though her body shook. Could she drain the water quietly? No, the whole thing was electronic, either on or off, with nothing in between.

The bathroom door opened. Roz held her breath and squeezed her eyes shut. There was one slow step, then another. The floor above her creaked ever-so-slightly as the intruder walked over. She heard the cupboard squeak open, then the shower door rattle. Then, the intruder turned and left again.

"Nothing," the translator wobbled. The other intruder replied in kind. Whatever else they said was too quiet and distant for the implant to pick up.

Roz shuddered in the still-warm water, hugging herself. What the *hell* was going on here?

She strained her ears, listening for something more. The footsteps continued around her home, then stopped. After 143 deep breaths – Roz counted – she heard the footsteps retreat and the door close once again. She waited for another 200 breaths before uncovering herself, enough to picture the intruders descending through the building and walking out.

It took all the energy she had to use her jelly-like limbs to pull herself out of the bath. She panted with relief when she found her home was truly empty, tears falling. She raced to Harsha's card on the coffee table only to find that now, a second one, in deep pink, lay right next to it.

Tapping Harsha's card twice, she ran to her bedroom, threw on clothes and stuffed some belongings into a bag. She could not stay here.

8

This Will All Make Sense in the Morning... Right?

"Right." Drake clapped his hands as both Olise and their unfortunate kidnappee stared at him with the same tired, unhappy expression. The spotlight they stood under in the corner of the dark warehouse now felt less like a threat and more like a stage on which he was a performing clown. "We've been played here. This is all one big misunderstanding, and for that, I'm very sorry, kid." He patted the boy on the shoulder, who flinched at the touch. "I say we all go get a beer and laugh about it. How does that sound? We'll meet up with our ship, then we'll take you anywhere you want to go, anywhere at all."

There was a long moment of silence.

"You're not going to kill me?" the waiter asked.

"No," he replied softly. "I'm not in the business of killing people, especially not when some woman set you up and threw you into danger. And," he added, "for the record, if you were the person we're after, we still wouldn't have killed you."

"Who was that woman? Were you hunting for her?"

"I'm not sure." Drake sighed and squatted on his haunches. "We were just... I don't even know what we were doing."

"Drake had a feeling," Olise said. He couldn't tell if she was making fun of him or not.

"Drake is getting paranoid in his old age," he replied. "We weren't expecting to find anything on the train. I was on edge. Thought it couldn't do any harm to investigate." He looked up at their prisoner and gave an apologetic smile. "Guess I was wrong."

"So, if you weren't searching for her and we, the train staff, weren't searching for her, why would she do something like that?"

"She must have had something to hide. And/or be super paranoid."

"And now we know her face," Olise added.

Their prisoner snapped to attention.

"Does that mean she's still on the train?"

Drake glanced at Olise.

"Probably," was his measured response. His stomach did knot at the thought.

"There's no news of any trouble on the train," Olise told them. "We don't know what her motive was. She might be on the run or in hiding or smuggling." Drake nodded along as she spoke.

"Or," he continued. "Someone was just messing with us altogether. Olise and I don't have many friends."

He unbound the kid, whose shoulders dropped in relief.

"I'm Drake. This is my partner in crime, Olise. We're bounty hunters. What's your name?"

"I'm Phin," he replied. "Waiter and physics student."

Drake offered him a hand to pull him to his feet.

"No hard feelings?"

"Sure," Phin replied, rubbing his head as if in a daze. He looked up at them, smiling lopsidedly. "If you buy the first round."

***

Two rounds of beer and a whole stack of snacks later, all of them could see the funny side of it. Drake and Phin sat around a small, round table, now covered in their empty cups and plates. All around them was a hearty chatter, crowds of people only half-lit by cheap spotlights. It was the same as a million bars Drake had been in before. There was comfort in that.

"So, this is what you do?" Phin asked. "Travel, harass people, get paid?"

"Usually we're a little more successful," Drake replied. "Plus, we're not getting paid until we achieve something useful."

Between them lay a rough sketch of the woman who had led them both astray. Drake frowned at it, wondering just who she was and what she'd gained from pitting them against Phin. Olise was sending the sketch and her description to their contacts as they spoke.

"How did you meet?" Phin asked. "Or how did you get started like this?"

"I grew up doing odd jobs," Drake replied simply. "Mafia family. Olise is ex-military. One day, we crossed paths, and she seemed lost. Said no one was watching out for her." Phin's face fell. "And I took that as a challenge. We've got each other now. I talk our way into places. She gets us out when things go tits up."

"Must be nice," was all Phin offered. "Having a partner like that."

Drake stared at him for a long moment.

"What about you, Phin?" he asked. "Will things be okay with your boss?"

Phin sucked in air through his teeth and shrugged.

"We'll make something up to cover you if that's useful. We were registered passengers on the train; we could say you needed to help us in the train station and missed your chance to board again?"

Phin turned his communicator over in his hands thoughtfully.

"Worth a try, I guess," he replied. "Not sure it will help, though."

"Where can we drop you off later? Home or somewhere else? You seem like a somewhere else kind of guy, but don't let me influence you."

"Home is..." he seemed to force the words out. "Probably for the best."

"People are waiting for you, huh?"

The kid did not reply. He looked like he'd be more at home under a massive hoodie than in a stiff, pressed uniform.

"We'll pay for you to get a change of clothes for the meantime, too," Drake offered. "That uniform doesn't look comfy."

Phin shrugged. There was a moment of silence before Olise returned to them.

"They'll let us know," was all she said.

They collectively glanced over the news again. It had become a habit. The airwaves were blissfully quiet. No attacks. Phin shook his head as the broadcast recapped what they already knew.

"Universe has gone mad," he said. "Must be a hell of a weapon to take out a Shangris *and* some of the others like Rugh-Cuwe."

Drake froze, glass pressed to his lips, eyes narrowed.

"What's that got to do with anything?" he asked, lowering his glass slowly.

Phin stared at him like he was dumb. Drake only leant in closer.

"Because traditional human weapons rely on a traditional human oxygen-based atmosphere to work. We're carbon-oxygen lifeforms like the Eozo. The Veqtris aren't. So their traditional weapons are different. It's why the first contact war fizzled out. We didn't have weapons to hurt them, and vice versa."

"Yeah, and now we have all the weapons. What's your point?" Drake felt a spark of adrenaline race through him. Could this be... after all their fumbling... a lead?

"We don't have a weapon that'll do both, though," he said. "And all the attacks appear the same. So this is something new. Something bad."

"How much do you know about this kind of thing?" Drake asked, tone level. He could tell from the way that Olise straightened up that she was thinking the same as him.

"Just bits and pieces from various laser and energy classes," Phin dismissed them.

"If you could see some readings from the explosions, could you tell us something about it?"

"Probably. *Maybe*," he corrected himself. "At the very least, I could find you someone who could."

Drake looked to Olise, who nodded.

"How would you feel about a little detour on the way home?" Drake asked.

Phin raised an eyebrow.

"Does it pay better than wait staff?"

9

AN EXISTENTIAL CRISIS IN A PUDDLE OF BLUE GOO

"I didn't touch it," Roz stood with her arms folded, bag packed, and hair still dripping wet. She and Harsha both stared at the pink card, which lay exactly where her intruders had left it. "In case I triggered it somehow."

She had stopped shaking before Harsha arrived, though she knew she wasn't fooling anyone. Around her, her apartment was in disarray, having been scoured by her intruders, herself, and now Harsha.

"A good idea," he replied. He pulled out some tweezers and picked it up, examining both sides. On one, there was a simple logo, a blinking outline of a triangle, and on the other was an address.

"Does your apartment have security cameras?" he asked.

"Yes, but I turned them off because I was home." She shifted uneasily. "Do you recognise it?"

"No," he said. "The only way to tell what this does is to take it apart. Or use it."

"Do you think it's something bad?" Roz asked.

"Will it kill us? No. Will it track us? Probably. Will it notify whoever those people were? Definitely." He pulled a small plastic bag out of his pocket and dropped it in.

"I'll have the tech guys look at it."

"What now?" she asked.

"First," he said, "let's make plans to get you somewhere safe. After that, there's one more test we'd like to run."

She nodded. The thought made her stomach churn, but Harsha had been nothing but helpful, she reminded herself.

"Where's safe?" she asked.

"It'll take a while to organise," he grumbled, rolling his eyes. "The paperwork for this kind of thing always does, but we have several safe houses in the city. With any luck, we'll get you into one of those."

He took out his communicator again, and she hugged herself, shifting from foot to foot. She scanned her apartment with tired eyes again, wondering if anything else had been left behind that they hadn't seen. Harsha frowned and pocketed his communicator.

"Why don't we go to the station, and we can organise things from there?" he offered. She nodded hastily.

A short taxi ride later and she was sitting in a small waiting room as Harsha spoke with his colleagues in another room. A collection of wooden chairs and one stained coffee table made the space cramped. A mixture of posters, some old recruitment drives and some much newer advertisements for local community programmes, plastered the walls. Roz had no desire to pull out her communicator and see her own paparazzi shots all over social media, so instead, she traced every line of the posters with her eyes. The room was warm, and as the adrenaline wore off, heaviness and sleepiness settled down on her. Her head nodded once, then twice, then she was asleep.

A gentle knock on the waiting room door woke her. She sighed heavily and looked blearily up. Harsha gave her a well-meaning smile.

"I'm glad you got a bit of rest," he told her. "My colleagues are preparing the safe house. In the meantime, it's time for the test."

She followed him out of the station, pausing only briefly to get a bottle of water and a snack. He beckoned her into a shuttle and they zipped through the streets of Revalin. Revived by crisp, cold water and a bit of food, she gazed out the window. They were in an area of the city Roz didn't know well, not that that was unusual. The shuttle stopped on an unassuming street, and Roz looked around as she got out. Harsha headed towards a building signed as a medical clinic. She frowned.

"What exactly is this test you want to run?" she asked, though she followed him.

"Everything you've told me is the truth, Roz, or at least you think it is. But there's one last possibility to explore." He held the door open for her, revealing an uncomfortably bright room with mint floors and white-panelled walls. To their right, in a spartan waiting area filled with pallid grey chairs, a few people lingered. One could not sit still, fidgeting and checking the time. None of them spared Roz or Harsha a second glance as they walked towards a reception desk.

As swiftly as they had entered, they were taken into a small room with one very large, scary machine. It was similar to the many medical devices she'd grown accustomed to when taking her mother to her appointments. It was a large doughnut shape with a chair in the middle. On the end of each armrest were two pools of blue gel. A blue visor surrounded the cushioned head of the chair inside the machine.

"So what remains?" he continued. "Memory alteration, memory erasure, memory replacement. They're uncommon and expensive but—" He shook his head. "It's an uncommon case. Something is off about all of this. These tests will tell us whether your memory was changed in any way."

The doctor pointed her to the chair within the machine. She guided Roz's hands into the two dishes on either side, filled with a cold gel, before placing circular tabs on her head.

"If you've had any work done before now," she said.

"Legal or otherwise," Harsha added.

"I need you to tell me now."

"I don't *think* so," Roz said.

"What about implants?" the doctor continued. She showed Roz a list. "Anything here?"

Roz scanned it. The first third of the list were all implants installed in the brain. They were niche but not uncommon in some professions and hobbies. The last two-thirds... Roz didn't know what most of them were, but the ones she recognised were heavily controlled or flat-out illegal. She shook her head again.

"I just have the standard ones," she offered, "plus a couple of radio ones for my job and hobby."

"'Standard' means different things to different people," the doctor replied. "Would you mind clarifying which?"

"Um, my identification," Roz began, "my financial accounts, and a translator."

The doctor nodded. Those were the implants that the vast majority of the population of the inner systems would get at birth or during their childhood. For some people, they would be the only implants they'd ever get. Everything beyond that was personal preference or job-related.

"My radio implants," she continued, "I have a receiver to let me pick and listen to things. I also have a manipulator to let me look at and deconstruct the sound waves. Both of those were off-the-shelf and I haven't modified them. The last one is one from my work, to help my implants and what I'm doing interface with their equipment." She'd have to get it removed if Radio Broadstrokes didn't take her back, she realised with a pang.

"Nothing that will interfere with the tests," the doctor said, looking to Harsha, who nodded. "This should go smoothly. Try to relax," she said, pushing her head gently into the chair and sliding the visor over her. She stepped back behind a small desk. With a wave of her hand, she brought up a holographic screen containing six different pulsing graphs and information that Roz couldn't begin to comprehend. A tingle ran across her body, starting at the contact points with the gel. The doctor nodded at the response on the screen. She did it again, this time stronger.

"Did that hurt?" Roz shook her head. "Please try not to move."

Another few zaps hit her, some long, some short, some close together, others far apart. Eventually, the machine around her began to hum and spin. A strange pattern began to appear on the inside of the visor and it made her woozy.

"You might want to shut your eyes," the doctor said. "This tends to give people motion sickness." Roz did as she was told, taking steady, deep breaths. After a few breaths, she barely felt the cold of the gel. The churn of both her stomach and her mind began to settle. In combination with the machine's humming, it was almost meditative. But her stomach and her mind continued to swirl. She was sick of it. She flinched when Harsha's phone began to ring.

"Sorry," he said. "I have to take this." Roz pursed her lips and squeaked in acknowledgement.

"Not much longer," the doctor assured her.

Either the doctor had lied, or the last few days had given Roz a different definition of long. When the visor finally came off again and the tingling died down, she crumpled in relief. The doctor stared at her screen intently. When she saw Roz get up out of the corner of her eye, she snapped to attention.

"I'll analyse the results, but it will take a while." Roz was surprised to find her heart didn't sink at the thought. More waiting was the opposite of what she wanted but... *Par for the course, at this point*, she thought. "You can wait outside for the detective. There's a coffee robot down the hall," she offered.

Roz didn't need telling twice. Leaving the oppressive room, she rolled her shoulders and headed back down the corridor to where a robot protruded from the wall serving drinks. She bought herself something sugary. Dutifully, the machine spluttered into life and slowly filled a paper cup. She took it, grateful for the warmth that seeped into her hands.

"Hey." Harsha caught up with her, making her jump and splash some of her drink on herself. "Everything alright?"

She nodded, cleaning splatters of her coffee off her shirt, but not before they stained. She sighed. Worse things were happening, but it was still inconvenient.

"Need to wait a little while for the result," she replied, taking a cautious sip. He avoided her gaze. "Everything alright with you?"

He nodded, ordering himself a coffee.

"The card was a tracker. The address on it seems to be a warehouse."

"A warehouse?" Roz frowned.

"I'm going to investigate later."

When he spoke again, he lowered his voice.

"Roz, you should make some preparations to go somewhere safe," he said. "A friend's. Your aunt's. Some distant planet you've always wanted to visit."

"Why?" she asked, chest tightening and lip trembling.

"The less guilty you seem, the less protection you'll get from law enforcement. It doesn't matter if we find you're innocent. A lot of the public has already decided that you're guilty. The police will decide you're not their problem." He shook his head. "It might happen. I might be able to convince them, I've..." He stopped, looking distant. "I've seen the system fail people like you before, Roz. So make a plan B, if you can. It wouldn't be forever. Just until things die down a bit."

Before she could respond, before she could process it, before she could even begin to regain the feeling in her body, he got another call and left her again. She watched him go, then returned to the waiting room and sank into a chair. She stared into her coffee as if it would explain anything.

With a sigh, she stood, deciding fresh air certainly couldn't make anything *worse*. She didn't go far, just out a side door to some steps she could sit on. Unlike the coffee, that did make her feel a bit better. As time went on, it became clear Harsha would be gone for a while.

The more time Roz spent outside the doctor's office counting lights in the city, the more she was reminded of her childhood. She swung her legs, trying to squash the knot in her stomach that accompanied the waiting. She was very good at it.

She dared not dream that these last couple of weeks were one big misunderstanding. It all felt so deliberate, and if it wasn't her, *someone* had destroyed five space stations. But that was why they were here, she supposed, to see if it was her. The knot came back.

Make a plan B, Harsha had said. The thought made the knot so tight she thought she might faint. Who could she turn to now? If she'd made more effort post-breakup, she could have kept some of her friends. If she'd made more effort after her move, maybe she could have asked. And even if she could ask, would they take her now, with accusations and press following her? She wouldn't have blamed them for saying no. But this was all hypothetical anyway, she reminded herself. She'd missed the first two steps. No friends. No Eva. She put her head in her hands.

Where was Aunt Alison now, she wondered? Too far away? Too busy? She was notoriously hard to contact, and Roz didn't even know where to begin looking for her now. Surely, if she'd seen the news, she would have found Roz. She sighed. Her aunt was a rock when she was around, but she was rarely around. No, she was alone, and she only had herself to blame.

Harsha appeared beside her.

"They'll see you again now," he said. "I need to call and give the results back to the precinct." He winked. "You'll be alright."

"Detective?" she said, lingering a moment more. "I thought about what you said. A hotel far away is the best I can do. I burned all my bridges." He hesitated, then nodded. Taking a deep breath, Roz rose and returned to the test room.

10

Rolling with the Punches

The Inter-Planet Express stopped at Revalin on every single one of Phin's shifts but until today, he had never set foot inside it. Despite its best efforts, it was unmistakably a space station. Not even the multitude of decorations, signs, and city clutter could pretty up the fact that everything he could see was made of the same utilitarian grey metal. The air tasted metallic too. From the amount of artificial sunlight and the carefully engineered plants to the traffic systems and block after block of straight buildings and streets, everything was just a little too exact. It was big, though, almost forget-you're-in-a-space-station big. Almost.

He kept a brisk pace behind Drake and Olise. It was good to stretch his legs, to work out some of his nervous energy, but as he looked from the city to the bounty hunters and back to the city, he shook his head. *What the hell am I doing here?* Part of him thought, but he shoved it down.

"How are you feeling, kid?" Drake paused and turned around to look at him. Phin had never been better... mostly.

"Oh, you know," he said, shrugging, though his voice threatened to break. "It's something a little bit different from the boring day-to-day."

"Good answer. We love a positive outlook, don't we, Lis?" Olise ignored him. In truth, Phin was riding a high of excitement, terror, and something else he couldn't quite put his finger on. Was he worried about being an accessory to a crime and risking his degree? Of course. If there was one thing his mother had managed to drill into him, it was to do the right thing, which didn't usually involve getting into trouble. But... in theory... Finding the cause of the terror attacks could count as that too, right? He had an *in* here. He'd already proven his physics background could be useful to Drake and Olise and so the question really became: if he went home now and watched events unfold from afar, watched more space stations with more people be destroyed, how would he feel? He felt the answer deep in his gut. He'd always wonder if there was something more he could have done.

Plus, he *needed* this. Needed a break from it all. Hell, he needed to be needed by someone, even if that someone was a questionable, yet very charming, pink-haired man. Though Drake's charming ways couldn't entirely quash the worrier his mother had created.

"What's the plan here, exactly?" he asked. Drake hummed and began walking again. Phin skipped to catch up and walk beside him.

"A few things," Drake said, holding up two fingers. "First, we need to grab our ship. The old piece of junk has been in for repairs. Second, there's all the rumours about this DJ being involved somehow?"

"Yeah, I've seen them," Phin said.

"We're going to see what those are all about. And finally, I was thinking," he said, turning to Olise and raising an eyebrow. "It might be time to pay Gren a visit. He's on Revalin these days, right?"

"What if we didn't do that?" Olise said, but even Phin could hear that it wasn't really a protest.

"I hear he's in Interpol," Drake continued. "Might be able to get us some more information about the attacks, like footage or the energy readings."

All information sent in the station's last moments, anything recorded by vessels or satellites nearby, had been immediately locked down by law enforcement.

"And if he can't?" Olise asked, folding her arms.

"He'll find a way." Drake said it with a quiet confidence. He was smiling, but Phin could hear the slight edge to his words. "He owes us a favour," he explained to Phin.

"More than a favour," Olise muttered.

"More than a favour," Drake echoed with a tired sigh.

"O-okay," Phin said. Maybe it was better not to ask questions he didn't want to know the answers to.

"But first," Drake said brightly, "ship."

"I'll catch up with you," Olise said. "I'll head to the bounty centre, see what I can find out." Drake nodded. "And while I'm at it, I'll find out where we can find Gren these days."

"Take care," Drake said as she split off down a side street. She gave him a half wave. Phin looked around. Was this what life was like for them? Taking whatever work they fancied and seeing where it took them? He couldn't say it was glamorous, but it certainly had its charms. Drake tapped his arm.

"This way," he said. Phin shoved his hands in his pockets and scurried to keep up, unable to take his eyes from the dizzyingly tall buildings. "Where are you from?" he asked.

"Next system over," Phin replied. "I grew up on the planet Dotu-8, but I'm studying on Staycery's biggest moon, which is why I work on the train."

"Enna?" Drake asked. "I've heard nice things. Proper green down there, right?"

Phin smiled, running his hands through the leaves of one of the space station's trees as they passed.

"Yeah," he said. "Proper green. Overgrown. Warm." He squinted up at the artificial sun above them. "Not quite the same as sunlight, is it?"

Drake smiled, too, and shook his head.

"Not when you've grown up with the real thing, no. I'm from Buse-a-Thes," he offered. "So not a million miles away, well, that's a poor choice of phrase, but you know what I mean."

"It's a big old universe," Phin agreed. "What's it like to travel it?" he asked after a moment.

"Lonely, dark, quiet," Drake replied. "Slow. When you go out far enough, sometimes you don't know if you'll reach the next fuel station or supply stop in time. And yet," he sighed, sounding content. "I can't wait to be on the move again. It's got its hooks in me. Don't know if I'll ever stop travelling. Not while I'm with Olise, anyway."

"Are you two—"

"In a romantic relationship? Nope, she's my best friend. You need someone like that, to help ward off the space-crazy, even if the pair of you drive each other crazy in different ways."

As they reached the end of the canyon of buildings and the city opened up into a plaza, Phin noticed he was not alone in taking a deep breath of relief. They were at the edge of the space station again, Phin realised. It was a small area, a few benches, a few troughs of grass and plants, and then the centrepiece: one long, tall window out into the vastness of space. The contrast was striking, and as Phin took a few steps into it and lingered, Drake let him. *You could get lost in it,* Phin thought, staring into the void. *You could get lost in it and it would wrap you up warm and safe.*

When he snapped out of his fervour, he turned to find Drake smiling.

"There's a lot out there to see," Drake told him. "Lots of different people and different places. A lot *more* new systems and planets to explore." He paused for a moment more. "Come on," he said, nodding at a building on the corner at the far end of the space. "Let's grab the ship."

Drake walked in first, and Phin snuck in behind him into a small, dark reception. They were immediately overwhelmed by loud music and the smell of hot metal. A man in mechanic's overalls polishing an intricate mechanical part jumped to attention as he saw them. He grinned and turned off the music with a wave of apology.

"Hey," Drake said. "I'm looking for Ciro."

The man's eyes lit up, and he wiped his hands on his overalls.

"You the owner of the Acar-Y8?" he asked. When Drake nodded, he pushed a button on the wall and said, "Ciro, your boy is here."

"Show him in. I'll be right down."

The man waved them through a door that opened into a large garage with what could only be Drake's ship at its centre. An upper mezzanine level ran around the top of the room. Phin knew enough about ships to know it was a good-looking one. A V-shaped front slid into a long glass windscreen, which melded into dark yellow metal. At its tallest and boxiest, the ship was perhaps two stories high, enough space for storage and basic living space, Phin guessed. Two broad, flat wings lay across its top. Two large rockets dominated the back third of the ship, and Phin screwed up his nose at the smell of their almost sweet-smelling fuel. Attached to the underbelly nestled a small, rectangle shuttle for short-range trips. It was simpler and underneath layers of graffiti, dirt, and what looked like posters, Phin thought it might be black. Covered in all the mess, it would have blended in on many city streets and been camouflaged in many alleys. Phin wondered if it was a happy accident or by design.

"She's a beaut," the mechanic said to Drake. "But she's not doing too well these days. She's going to need a pretty major retrofit in a year or two. I'm assuming you want to keep her." The man touched the nose of the ship affectionately.

"With the amount of flying we do, I can almost guarantee we'll be back in less than a year." Drake sighed. "I love her, but she's bleeding me dry." He nodded at the ship, then turned to the man. "What's the damage this time? How much do I owe you?"

"It's on the Family this time, Drake," a new voice called out. A second man, who looked uncannily like Drake but without the pink hair, jumped down from the upper level.

"Ciro!" Drake said, opening his arms to hug the man. "Good to see you."

"Good to see you too. Where's Olise?"

"Working hard," he replied. "What about you? Working hard or hardly working?"

"Working hard, Drake, of course." Ciro laughed. "At least, I was when I saw the state of your ship. Heard you're busy too."

"Yeah. It was good of Remo to pay for the repairs, considering."

"Listen, Drake," Ciro began. Then his gaze fell on Phin for the first time.

"This is Phin," Drake said. "Call him an intern."

Ciro gave him a look Phin couldn't read, and Drake nodded somewhat reluctantly.

"Max," Ciro said, "Why don't you take the kid outside?"

The mechanic nodded with an understanding Phin only wished to have. He knew he was being sent out for a reason, and probably a good one, but he couldn't help but strain his ears as Ciro spoke again in a lowered voice.

"Listen, Drake," Ciro said. "Sven has a lot of friends here. So watch your step and take care out there, okay?"

"Appreciate the head's up," he said, sounding so solemn Phin almost didn't recognise them. "We're only here for…"

As he and Max stepped outside, the words were lost. He glanced over his shoulder and felt Max tug him away and out of the building, back into the small park.

"You must be pretty new, huh?" he said, not unkindly. "It's Family business. Best to keep out of it when they ask. 'Specially if you're an intern." He sat on one of the benches, looking out the window. "Speaking of, I didn't realise Drake and Olise *hired*."

It took Phin a moment too long to realise he should respond.

"Well?" the man said, causing Phin to realise he needed to talk. "Do you speak?"

"Uh…" he began. "It's just a little detour on my way home. I'm helping them out a bit."

"Always another detour with them." He laughed, and Phin tried and failed to laugh with him. Max glanced over his shoulder in the direction of Drake and Ciro. "And some of the people they're in trouble with…" He trailed off. Phin's heart pounded, willing him to say more. He didn't. "Just try not to get swept up in it. You look like a good kid, not a bounty hunter," Max finished.

Phin thought again of the void outside the window, of the world Drake and Olise inhabited, and of the warning he'd overheard. Shivers ran down his spine. 'Out of his depth' didn't cover it. Not for the first time, Phin wondered what the hell he'd got himself into.

11

Ghosts

The knot in Roz's stomach accompanied her into the test room. The doctor tried to talk her through the results, but no matter how many times she explained it or how many diagrams she showed, Roz couldn't take in any information.

"So I didn't do it?" she asked. Her voice was small. The doctor shook her head. She started to talk again, but that was enough for Roz. Her hands were cold, and as they gripped the plastic of the medical bench, they almost didn't feel like hers. She must have looked like a ghost when she rejoined Harsha because he looked concerned, despite his own scowl.

"What's the long face for?" he asked, guiding her into a vehicle. "You did well, Roz," he told her, "and the safe house is ready, so you can get some rest while my department figures out the rest." She could only nod.

"It's been a long few days," she replied.

"Yes," he agreed. "I'm sure you'll be happy to see the back of it."

"Am I free then?" she asked him. He nodded. "Then what's with *your* long face?"

"Since you're no longer part of the case... they're not going to offer you any protection." He looked away. "This will be your only night in the safe house."

"I need to go... home?" Her voice wobbled. Her stomach dropped at the thought of going back to the apartment after the break-in.

"I'm sorry, Roz. I don't get it. If we made the investigation results public tomorrow, there would still be people out for your blood." Her throat tightened. He was right, she knew. Too right. But it wasn't *fair*. He shook his head. "I'm not going to let anyone hurt you," he said. "I promise you that."

"Don't get in trouble for me."

"Roz, this is something I need to do."

Her stomach became unsettled. Why? This wasn't going to be something weird, was it? She was basing everything on the idea she could trust this detective. Could she? She slipped his card out of her pocket and into the gap between the seats. She glanced at their destination and began to plan her escape.

"Why?" she asked. "It's not right, it's not fair, but I'll bet most of your other cases are the same. Why me?"

He gave a heavy sigh, staring out into the night.

"Most cases are the same," he agreed. "Your case is the same in a lot of ways as my daughter's. She was murdered. I just... I look at your situation, and it reminds me of the days before she was killed. I see you and I can't help but think that if someone had stepped up to help her, she might still be here." Roz covered her mouth with her hand, stifling a gasp.

"I'm so sorry," she said. "But you still don't have to put your job on the line for me."

"Trust me," he said. "There's nothing much to lose." He wrung his hands. As he looked down and his hat cast a shadow over his face, he was the picture of a detective from a black and white movie. "You may not think they'll miss you. You may not have left them on the best of terms, but your friends, your family, your ex? They *do not* want to wake up and see you reported dead on the news, alright? No matter how hard a reunion might be, how hard it would be to live apart, how awkward, you're going to live to grimace through it."

There was a long moment's silence.

"Thank you."

She watched the lights flicker by. Watched as one tall building bled into the next. Watched as the city she barely knew blurred into something much more familiar. Once, she'd been excited about moving here. Some days, it was hard to remind herself of that. It seemed like the wrong decision. One big mistake. She glanced over at Harsha. But maybe taking the wrong road could still be good. Maybe she could still reach her destination, whatever that was. She tugged his business card back out of its hiding spot and returned it to her pocket.

"So what's next for the investigation?" she said. "If you're allowed to tell me."

"The card left in your apartment..." Harsha replied, shaking his head. "It's *something*, but I don't know. You're beginning to seem like a distraction. From what, well, that's what I'd like to know."

A large part of her was relieved by the day's results, of course it was, but something still gnawed at her. Even if she wasn't guilty of terrorism, she was still involved. Even if she was a distraction, someone had chosen *her*. Even if this was the end of her part in the investigation, would she be able to move on while it remained unsolved? She straightened up again.

"Say, Harsha," she said, turning her face to the window. "If, hypothetically, someone could listen in on private radio streams as well as the usual public ones, could that be useful?"

Harsha raised an eyebrow.

"Hypothetically," he replied. "Yes."

"I've never used it for anything illegal," she said. "Promise."

"Then what do you use it for? And *why*?"

"It gets lonely travelling out in space," she replied. "And a girl's gotta have hobbies."

"Don't you want to forget about this? Try to go back to a normal life?"

"You said it yourself. Even if the results were published tomorrow, life won't be normal for me for a while."

"I'll go alone to the card's address tonight," he told her. "Then..." He nodded to himself. "Then, we'll see."

They arrived at a featureless tower block, where Harsha guided her to a small apartment. It appeared a perfectly normal home. A humble living room opened into a plain kitchen stocked with some basic ingredients. Behind two doors was a room taken up almost entirely by a bed and a bathroom. It was bordering on cramped, but something about that made her feel safer than the large open spaces of her own apartment.

"You'll be alone here," Harsha told her, "and no one will be watching you inside, but there will always be officers nearby if there's trouble. I'm sure I don't have to tell you, no more deliveries."

Her jaw tensed at the memory. When she nodded, it gave her a headache.

"I didn't bring Ambo, my AI assistant," she added quickly, "with me for that reason. I hadn't really considered... how much information it knew and shared about me."

Harsha nodded sympathetically. She looked around the apartment with a rising feeling of dread.

"Does it defeat the purpose of a safe house if I stretch my legs around the block?" she asked. "I don't think I can spend another day alone in a room, that's all," she added. "I know it's crazy. People broke into my home, after all, and my pictures are... everywhere."

"No, that isn't crazy," he replied. He looked thoughtful. "And you're not a prisoner. Get changed, preferably into something baggy. Cover your hair with a hat or a scarf. Put on some anti-reflection glasses..." He dug into his breast pocket and offered a pair of what appeared to be sunglasses. "It's not foolproof. If someone really wanted to find you," he stopped himself. Roz heard the unspoken words. *You couldn't stop them.*

"All the more reason to get out for a bit," she replied briskly. "Stop myself going *completely* insane." Even so, her hand hesitated above the offered glasses.

"I can come with you for a bit if it would help."

She nodded, picked up the glasses, and took her small bag of belongings into the bedroom. Like a child saying good night, before she shut the door between them, she whispered, "Thank you."

Soon enough, she was on the move again, but in a more relaxed way. The cold air outside forced her to focus on the here and now. People didn't spare her or Harsha a second glance on the busy streets, and the buildings that stretched above seemed to drown them all out. It was something Roz found comforting or used to, before she had become more than another small piece in the clockwork motion of the city.

The space station was split into multiple tiered levels, and the safe house was near the top. A short walk took them to a small park, a lookout point over the city. Puffs of Harsha's breath appeared before him and Roz tried not to marvel at them. The weather system here was so much more advanced than the one she'd grown up with, almost like a real planet, she was told. But you could expect nothing else from the "capital" of this star system.

"I guess one good thing about being a radio DJ," Harsha began, looking around them. "Before all of this started – is that most people don't really know your face. Not without specifically looking."

"My grandmother always said if you have to be a celebrity, it's the best kind."

"Is that why you started, then? I mean, I assume you love music too."

"It's not, actually. It's kind of unrelated. A footnote, I guess." She leant forward on the barrier, staring at the city below. She shuddered as drones zipped to and fro, hoping her glasses and scarf would be enough to stop any paparazzi drones from spotting her, hoping it would be enough to hide her from whoever had broken into her apartment. "I grew up lonely. My mum and I travelled about for work, and she was, well, working. Trying to keep us afloat as best she could. Radio kept me company on those long trips." She closed her eyes. She could almost remember the feeling of their beaten-down ship and the smell of her mother's god-awful cooking. "Hearing other people's stories, other people's music, other people's worlds. I... it was nice." She opened her eyes again, her smile slipping away. "I thought I could be that voice for someone else."

"Well, the consensus I've heard through this case is that you succeeded," he said.

"Are you allowed to tell me anything else about the investigation?" she asked, not sure whether she wanted the answer to be yes or no. He shook his head, and she felt nothing either way. "Am I allowed to buy you a coffee?" she asked instead. "I know you're doing your job, but you've helped put me at ease."

"Sure," he replied. "A coffee bribe wouldn't exactly help you cover up terrorism. Plus," he nudged her as he straightened up from the barrier. "I bet a trendy young person like yourself knows where to get a good one, too."

"I used to," she replied. "On Nonke. So if you fancy a road trip…"

"Maybe not." He began to lead her down the street. "I thought you'd been on Revalin a while?"

"Eh," she managed. "I have, but… turns out it's intimidating to come to this place all by yourself."

"All the more reason to go for coffee now, then." He checked his watch, nodding to himself.

"Not too late in the day for you?" she asked. "I'm not actually going to get a coffee. I'm having enough trouble sleeping as it is."

"I'm not sure there is such a thing as too late for me anymore," he replied.

"That busy, huh?"

"I would certainly try to claim that, but if I'm being honest, it's a bad habit."

They settled for the first coffee shop they came across. Its windows were steamed up but glowed warmly around the shadows of the people inside. Roz's heart ached as they stepped inside to find gentle music, lots of little nooks and crannies lit with fairy lights, and an overabundance of hanging plants. She almost expected to look around and see Eva sitting drawing, headphones on, and tea by her side. She stopped herself and forced herself to look at the menu. As a barista took notice and joined them, she said, "I haven't slept properly in days. What have you got that's not just caffeine-free but will actually knock me out?"

The barista laughed.

"Well, when my wife was pregnant, she swore by some warm milk with honey, Enna moon flower extract, and taizo spice."

"Sounds good to me," she said. "One large, please. And you?" She turned to Harsha and caught him wincing.

"My ex-wife used to love that too," he said to the barista with a forced smile. "Just black coffee, please. Extra shot."

As Roz swiped her hand to pay and the barista set about making their drinks, she looked up at Harsha with some sympathy and sighed.

"We both have ghosts, huh?"

"Hmm."

She left him to his thoughts, watching instead as the barista weighed out the coffee beans and ground them down exactly. It was a level of care that could be replicated by a machine these days, much like radio. Yet here she and the barista stood. Though chemical analysis and multiple human studies showed no tangible difference between the products of high-end coffee machines or DJ AI. It was the human connection, the intangible, that was in demand. Maybe their ghosts were a part of that, too. The fact Harsha remembered his ex-wife's order and Roz remembered Eva's. The way the baristas remembered their regular's orders and Roz recognised names of the frequent commenters on her shifts. It wasn't that robots took anything away; it was that humans *added* something, ghosts and all. She nodded to herself, collecting her drink when it was ready and watching a dusting of edible glitter and extra spice drift around the surface of her drink.

"If I can just drown everything else out," she said aloud, but not necessarily to Harsha, "maybe I'll actually get some sleep."

"Cheers to that," he replied softly.

It was a sedate afternoon and a welcome one. Even after a trek back to the safe house in the cold, she was desperately sleepy. Harsha left her with the same instructions as before, but this time, when he left, she tumbled straight into bed.

Before she so much as thought to take off her shoes or her makeup, she was asleep on top of the bed.

12

We Should Have Got a Phin Years Ago

Phin hovered at Drake's heels as they flew the ship from the garage to one of the docks nearby and registered it with the authorities. By the time the paperwork and small talk were done, through which Phin contributed nothing, Olise had walked to meet them.

They detached the shuttle from the underside to take around the city. The ship was their long-distance vehicle, and between its size and its emissions, there were limits on where they could take it in space stations.

"We got paid without issue this time," Olise told them, settling into her seat.

"Had to happen eventually," Drake replied.

"This is where you tell me the repairs are going to take all of it away," she said.

"Remo paid for them, actually. So you know, no pressure to get results or anything."

"You said it yourself, Drake," she replied. "We'll get results. One way or another."

Drake hummed in agreement.

"Ciro said Gren's back to his partying ways." She nodded.

"I heard the same. Four-day bender, as per fucking usual. Started last night in his penthouse over in East-Mid."

"Let me guess. In the biggest, shiniest tower. Same shit, different star system," Drake replied, though he did stroke his beard thoughtfully.

"If we can get invites…" Olise said. "We'll have him cornered."

"Cornered by social convention is my favourite kind," Drake said. He waved a hand. "He holds these things every few weeks. They're not exactly exclusive or special."

"So we're getting in by…?" Olise prompted.

"He won't say no to a Thaler."

"And if his guards do?"

"Well, then they should know better." He looked at her. "Come on, Lis. You know we'll get in. You know the drill by now. We'll grab our suits from the ship. No visible weapons, no major threats, lots of charm."

"What about him?" Olise pointed at Phin without looking. Drake glanced back, pausing.

"I'll wait in the shuttle," Phin offered reluctantly.

"Perfect – our getaway driver," Drake said before frowning. "Do you know how to fly?"

Phin nodded.

"Fantastic. Problem solved. We'll go along this evening."

"You have a plan for the meantime?" Olise said.

"The DJ," Phin suggested. Drake nodded.

"Kid's like a sponge," he said. "If this *was* an internship, you'd be doing great, kid." He sighed, sinking into a chair. "Even with everything that's going on, I'm not sure I'm prepared to stalk this poor girl," Drake said, looking at a picture of the DJ Roz on a screen. "Not as a first resort, at least," he conceded with a sigh. "Let's start by going to her work. The radio office is public knowledge, at least."

Even Phin thought he could read Olise's expression. *If going to her work was enough, someone else would have done something by now.*

"You never know," Drake mumbled.

"I think you're projecting quite a lot onto this girl," Olise said, taking her place back in the pilot's seat and punching Radio Broadstrokes into the navigation panel. "You need to prepare yourself for the possibility that she's involved in all this for a reason and not who you think she is."

"Nah," Drake said, but he was missing his characteristic grin. "I'm a great judge of character."

"How you and I met would suggest otherwise," Olise said with the smallest of smirks. "What about the detective on her case?" she asked. "We could stalk him. If she's hiding, he might know where."

Drake nodded.

"Ideally, information about both is good. If Phin and I deal with Roz, can you see what you can find about him?"

Olise nodded, seeming more comfortable with the plan.

Phin sat and bounced his leg as he watched the pair.

"So are you just going to walk in?" he asked the bounty hunters, nervously intertwining his fingers.

"Is there a problem with that?" Drake asked. Phin fell silent, heart pounding. *Just say it,* he snapped at himself internally.

"You—" he began, but no sooner than he'd started had his throat tensed, and he choked on his own breath. Drake spared him a sympathetic glance.

"What's wrong, kid?" he asked. "Apart from current events."

"I just..." He forced himself to take a shaky breath. "I think I should be the one to ask." He rushed all the words out in one breathless burst. "To ask them about Roz," he said.

"Okay, interesting," Drake said. He wasn't making fun of Phin, he could tell that much. "Why?"

"Because ultimately, they're a company, right? And they got bad press from this. They're going to be looking out for journalists and tabloids and stuff. Looking out for bounty hunters. Drake might pass as a reporter, but I don't think it will help. They'll have one statement to give."

"Get to the point, kid," Olise said softly.

"Nobody will think I'm either. I can pretend to be her friend." He shrugged. When he dared to look up at them, he found them looking at each other instead. "They might just give me the same statement, but... maybe not?"

"He makes a good point," Drake said. Phin watched him study Olise's face, wondering what he saw when he did so. Had anyone ever known him that well? He got the impression Drake could describe every detail about her. She nodded.

"There's nothing to lose," she said. "If he can't get information, then you can try. No danger in a corporate headquarters."

"Well," Drake said. "Not conventional danger. Enough businessmen to make up for it though."

They turned back to Phin.

"Are you sure about this?" Drake asked. "You're sweating."

"Like you said," Phin replied, "there's no danger. Just... social anxiety."

"Well, if the best lies are partly true, then it'll certainly sell the part," Drake said. "Try to take a deep breath, okay?"

Phin nodded, but his knuckles turned white as he clenched his hands, watching their dot edge closer and closer to their destination.

"Do you mind walking a block?" Olise asked. "So they don't see us come out the same shuttle."

Phin nodded. She brought them down. Without a word, before he could lose his courage, Phin wiped sweaty palms on his trousers and made the short jump out of the shuttle. Before he could walk away, Drake put a hand on his shoulder.

"We'll be right here," he assured him. "And no pressure, okay? This isn't the end of the world. It just would be nice."

Phin nodded, but his throat was too tight to speak.

"Okay," Drake said for him, pulling away.

Phin set off quickly, counting each street light he passed in an effort to keep calm. As he stopped in front of the skyscraper the radio station lived in, whatever calm he'd gained had drained away. But among the nerves was also a spark. Everyone in his family did something worthwhile; his mother was a doctor, his father was a repair technician on the front of the Maeh belt war, and his sister was building a new colony on a distant planet. He didn't have the stomach for medicine, the athleticism for zero-gravity engineering work, or the bravery to settle a new planet, but he was smart enough to help in this case. He could do this; he felt it in his gut.

The building seemed to stretch out above him. He steadied himself as a wave of dizziness washed over him and turned his head instead to fix his gaze straight ahead. Nodding to himself, Phin straightened and strode through the glass doors into a dark, neon-lit reception.

The man behind the counter had drawn his makeup in such harsh lines that he looked like something out of a comic book. It was striking, and the highlight across his cheekbones caught the light in an alluring way. When he looked up at Phin and smiled, Phin faltered and blushed.

"H-hi," he said lamely.

"Hi, what can I help you with today?" the receptionist asked.

"I'm a friend of Roz Dayne's?" he began. The receptionist became stiff. "I just wondered if she's here?"

"Ms Dayne is taking an extended break from work at the moment," the other man rattled off a script.

"Is there anyone who's in touch with her?" he asked with a gulp. "Anywhere I can reach her? She... hasn't been responding to my messages." He forced the words out. His stomach churned at the lie. "She helped me through some hard times. All I want is to know she's okay." At least that wasn't a lie, not technically, just withholding the fact that *she* did not know *him*.

The receptionist's gaze softened. His shoulders dropped. He nodded.

"I don't know," he admitted. He pulled open a drawer and took out a pink business card. "Someone left this for her," he said, offering it to him. Phin turned it over in his hands. Fumbling, he pulled his communicator from his pocket, almost dropping it in the process, then hastily took a picture of both sides of the card. "Do you recognise it?" the receptionist asked. Phin shook his head and gave it back.

"No, sorry." He straightened up and spared the reception one last glance. It was more than he had been expecting to get, anyway. "Thanks."

"I hope she gets back to you soon," the receptionist said.

"Yeah," Phin said hoarsely. "Me too."

Shoving his hands deep into his pockets, he turned on his heels and fled in the most controlled way he could. Back in the safety of the streets, he took a deep breath and then raced to the shuttle to find both bounty hunters watching him with a raised eyebrow.

"Any luck?" Drake said. Phin nodded, holding out his communicator. Obligingly, Drake tapped his own to it, allowing Phin to transfer him the pictures he'd taken.

"He gave me the press statement, but he also said someone left that there for her."

Drake hummed and nodded to himself as he examined them.

"Nice work," he said. "We should have got a Phin years ago," he joked to Olise. "Let's see who this belongs to, shall we?"

Phin's whole body sagged in relief. He sank back into a chair. Olise was watching a terminal of her own. Phin couldn't quite see what she was reading from his angle, but it appeared to be a news report.

As Drake set to work, Phin watched intensely. It didn't take long for the address to return a warehouse on the lower quadrant of the space station.

"That's a little strange for a business card," he said with satisfaction. "Doesn't look like much. Want to do your thing, Lis?"

Olise obliged and disappeared into the back of the shuttle, returning with a large briefcase. She laid it on the shuttle's seats and opened it to reveal a small drone. Dropping to a crouch next to it, she pulled out her communicator, tapped it to the drone's top, and began fiddling with the settings that appeared on her tile. After a few minutes, she stood, opened the shuttle door, and tossed the drone gently up into the air as if she were releasing a bird. It zoomed away down the street. She returned to the shuttle's main console and tapped her communicator to it. A video streamed by the drone appeared, showing blurred views of the city as it travelled. Within ten minutes, it had slowed down almost to a stop.

"Let's see what we can see," she said, almost to herself. She sent the drone backwards and forwards through the street, looking at every door, every branching path. It was nothing but a bland industrial street. She looked over her shoulder to Drake, who nodded.

"I'll set up motion alerts," Olise told them. "If a leaf blows by that door, we'll know about it."

"A warehouse to watch, a detective to stalk, and a party tonight," Drake said, clapping his hands together. "It's all coming together. Time to go back to the ship and prepare."

13

Background Noise

Roz's eyes flickered open, and in her half-awake daze, she saw night had fallen in the city. She leapt to her feet, almost slamming into a wall in the cramped bedroom, before remembering where she was. She wasn't late for work. She wasn't even at home. She was in the safe house. Groaning, she swept stray pieces of hair back as she rubbed her face.

"Ambo," she mumbled, "what time is it?"

The silence that followed was accompanied by a pang of guilt. Not only had she turned Ambo off, she'd left it behind. Despite the stillness without her synthetic companion, a cold feeling of certainty settled over Roz. The less people could find out about her, the better.

She checked the time herself and was surprised to see that it was barely past sunset. It was later than she'd typically wake up for work, true, but she had anticipated sleeping more after being awake so much of the day. Grateful she'd slept at all, she began wandering the apartment aimlessly. A quick check of her communicator showed no messages from Harsha and she was happy to keep avoiding everything else. She tossed her communicator onto the couch and continued to pace. She wondered what time Harsha would be investigating the warehouse, wondered when or if she'd get an update.

Chewing her nails, she paused by one of the apartment's windows and gazed outside. She needed something to do to pass the time. She was embarrassed to admit just how lost she felt without Ambo and without using her communicator. Going out again was a possibility, but the thought of doing so alone and in the dark made her feel sick. Under normal circumstances, she'd have listened to the radio, but normality felt like a lifetime ago.

She came to a stop, staring at the front door, and pressed the flats of her hands together, tips of her fingers touching her lips. Commercial public radio was out of the question, she was certain of that, but Harsha had said there was law enforcement nearby. To use the age-old phrase, maybe she could kill two birds with one stone: find something to distract her *and* hear how Harsha was getting on.

Long before she had ever been a professional radio presenter, Roz had been an avid hobbyist. Her mother had cottoned onto her love of radio on their long journeys, and, in Roz's mid-teens, had gifted her a small radio set capable of tuning into all sorts of channels. From that day, Roz had been fully gripped by the airwaves. She'd studied a technical apprenticeship with a radio station, which had led her to qualifications and, eventually, her first job at Nonke Radio 1 as a technician. Over time, both Roz and her employer had realised she wasn't just good at the technical side but the people side, too, and she'd been given a shot on the air. The rest was history.

The job did not stop her dabbling in her free time. Rather, it funded it. She'd saved up to move away from most physical equipment to the various implants common amongst hobbyist radio enthusiasts. They weren't required for her job, but Roz found the ability to change how she received and manipulated the various streams of information, interface with the hardware in the radio station, and customise her workflow to be a benefit in and out of work.

She settled into the couch and activated the implants. She did not bring up a visual display; instead, she closed her eyes to focus on the sounds. She wasn't looking to do anything fancy, just listen to what non-commercial or independent radio was currently floating through the station. Listening wasn't illegal – hobbyists did it all the time, and it was how Roz had learned in the beginning – acting on any private information was. If she found a police stream and heard an ongoing chase, it would be illegal to go out into the streets like a vigilante and help. If she overheard something juicy, it was illegal to report on it. Anything she could hear freely was fair game, but hacking and decoding anything she couldn't was also illegal.

She flicked slowly through channels by pinching the thumb and forefinger on her left hand – the fingers with the necessary component implants – and twisting slowly as if turning a dial. She found a hobbyist radio station run by what sounded like two young people, a station blasting an advert on repeat for a chain of shops she recognised, and some interesting folk music on instruments she couldn't identify. Species-specific radio stations were common, sometimes shared across the galaxy from their respective homeworlds. Organisations and religions sometimes had them too. Roz hummed and kept searching. There was always a lot out there to find.

She listened intently to one channel's monotone speaker before realising she was listening to a maintenance team in the engineering core discuss their work orders for the night shift. One to return to if she couldn't sleep, she thought with an eye roll.

For a while, there was gentle static where no one was broadcasting. She took a deep breath. Maybe she should just sit and listen to this and let it consume all of her worries, all of her thoughts. Her arms and fingers ached from all of her nervous clenching. She tried to relax her muscles now, but her thoughts swirled. What would Harsha's investigation uncover? What would tomorrow bring? How was she going to keep going? The thoughts were as much of a background noise as the static. She didn't know the answers. Thinking about them over and over again wouldn't give her answers. She focused on the static instead, letting it fill her mind.

She allowed herself a moment of rest, then pressed on. She found another channel solemnly giving out instructions attached to badge numbers. Could this be the local law enforcement? She listened a while longer. It would make sense, but much like the maintenance channel, it contained no interesting information. She lay back and stared at the ceiling. That was to be expected, she supposed. Of course, they would keep any sensitive case information private.

She got up and paced another lap of the room.

"It was worth trying," she told herself and checked the time, "if only to kill a little while."

She left the station playing in the background. It helped fill the small apartment, creating enough background noise to distract her from everything else. It may have been boring, but at least they weren't sharing the news.

14

Fun at Parties

Suited and booted, Drake entered the cockpit to find the kid squirming in the pilot's seat. He was watching the security feed of the warehouse and wringing the front of his hoodie in his hands. Drake put a hand on his shoulder and took a look for himself, frowning. Still unchanged. Had they already missed the action? Maybe after the party they'd be taking a trip there themselves. *Hmmm*. Phin looked at him expectantly.

"Right, kid," he said. "We're off. Sit tight, order yourself some pizza or something. We'll be on this comms channel if you need us." He tapped the communicator on the console of the ship.

"What should I do?" Phin asked.

"Keep an eye on the warehouse. Otherwise... just stay ready. We might need you to get us out of here quick if things go south." Phin nodded.

"Actually, I had a thought," Olise began. Drake turned to see her pulling a familiar metal pin out of her jacket's inner pocket. She held out her hand to Phin. "Give me your communicator."

He peered at the pin but did as he was told. Olise took the device and held it to the pin for a moment.

"What is it?" Phin asked.

"A tiny camera," she told him. "If you're gonna watch camera feeds, could you be the eyes on the back of my head?"

Phin nodded. Olise handed the pin to Drake, who dutifully pinned it to the back of her collar. At a glance, it looked like part of the design. Phin's communicator lit up with a notification that the device had connected. He tapped it, and a video feed began to play. He looked up at them and nodded.

"I can do that."

"Awesome, well." Drake adjusted his cuffs, making sure some Thaler cufflinks showed well. "Sorry to leave you behind, but the people in there are dangerous. Gren is going to give us what we want, but who knows who else is in there?"

Olise entered behind him in a suit of her own, with an open shirt. She looked like a normal guest, but he knew she had weapons concealed somewhere. He had a few of his own, just in case. She, too, bore the cufflinks – after all, she was family.

"Count?" Olise said, starting their familiar pre-mission routine as Phin watched, bemused.

"Three to four hundred people, maybe?" Drake said, peering at the building outside. "The penthouse is big, but it's still an apartment."

"Conditions?"

"Crowded, noisy. If there's a fight, there'll be collateral damage."

"We always find a way to cause collateral damage," Olise said with a shrug. "Complications?"

"Where to start? We don't know the count or conditions for certain and we don't know who's going to be up there."

Olise sighed. "My favourite type of job," she muttered.

"What kind of implants do you have?" Phin asked.

"A few," Olise said.

"The usual," Drake replied. "Plus a few bonuses," he added with a wink.

Phin shut his mouth and nodded.

"Shall we?" he said, offering her an arm that she ignored.

"No chit-chat, got it? We're in and out," she warned him. "We don't know who else is in there, and we don't need any distractions."

"You're the one with ex-girlfriends everywhere, not me," he replied. "But you're right." The warning Ciro had given him, and that he had passed onto Olise, about their old enemy Sven weighed heavily on them both. If anyone was going to keep him alive, it was Olise.

Giving Phin a quick nod, he stepped out into the Revalin evening. The air was crisp, clean, and cold, fresh after a short burst of sleet. Stepping gingerly over puddles, he walked towards the entrance of a large apartment building. The party would take up the top few penthouse floors. He joined a queue of people waiting to get in and scanned for familiar faces.

"It'll be fine," he told Olise again. "We'll get what we need one way or another. We always do."

"Let's just avoid making a scene." She slid her hand into her pocket and pulled out a drug stick. Drake swatted it out of her hand and into a puddle. She sighed but did not argue.

"Empty your pockets," he ordered. She pulled them out, revealing a slim pack of three more, which she handed over wordlessly. "Thank you."

Drake loved Olise more than any friend, lover, even more than any family member he'd ever had. Ever since he'd met her, it had been one addiction after another, but slowly, they were working their way down to less and less serious vices. Soon enough, she'd be addicted to little more than caffeine. And what a victory that would be, given how he'd met her and the things she'd suffered before then. She looked healthier, too. Her skin didn't look waxy anymore and her eyes were bright. He didn't have children and he didn't intend to, but he imagined this was what it felt like to be proud of one. He told her that. She did not reply, but he did see her expression soften.

They made it to the front as the sleet began again.

"Name?" a bodyguard asked. His eyes glowed blue in the telltale sign of computerised contacts. He would be seeing a screen while they saw almost nothing. It would be paired with implants in a hand to control it. Drake watched him for movement. Left-handed. He made a mental note of that for later. He held out a hand for the other man to shake, showing his cufflink subtly.

"Drake Thaler," he replied. "Good friend of Gren."

The man stared him down for a moment, no doubt sizing Drake up in the same way Drake looked at him – for identifiable features and potential issues. With pink hair, Drake wasn't trying to hide. That helped.

"And you?" he said eventually, turning to look at Olise.

"Olise Tsunoda." She nudged Drake. "I'm with him."

The bodyguard waved a hand, and the elevator door slid open.

"Have a good night."

"They've got some protection here," Olise noted under her breath. "He marked us."

Drake hummed in agreement.

"Well, we weren't invited explicitly. When the family opens doors, people tend to pay attention."

The elevator shot them upwards at a remarkable speed. As the lights of the city blurred into the vertical stream, Olise said again, "In and out."

Drake nodded, rolling his shoulders and trying to relax. *This is your element,* he told himself. *You are in control.*

"Chances some of Sven's friends are in there?" Drake asked in a low voice.

"Almost certainly."

"Chances they'll try anything?"

"In the party? Depends who else is there. Outside the party, we'll need to watch our backs more than we have been."

Drake nodded again. Trying to focus himself. In and out. Charming, swift, blend into the crowds. He couldn't shake the intrusive thoughts. "Cornered by social convention" was all very well and good, but if the host and some mutual friends with Sven thought there was a problem, well... It wouldn't be the first time Gren had sold them out, and it wouldn't be the first time he'd done it for Sven. It would be easy to walk away. All it would take was one word to Olise. But something deep inside him insisted that the space station data was their lead, their *in*, the key to this terrible mystery. There had to be something in the readings and recordings of the attacks, some piece of data, some *clue* that would blow the whole thing wide open. They had to get it from Gren. They had to get it *to* Phin. He grimaced and nodded to himself.

"I've got your back," Olise said as the doors slid open to reveal the top floor of the penthouse apartment.

"I've got yours," Drake agreed.

The floor was open plan, and he couldn't help but feel exposed. Polished stone floors reflected swarms of richly-dressed people. Glass windows from the floor to the ceiling gave a perfect view of the city below them and it *was* below them. The building was the tallest on the station, by at least five floors as far as Drake could see. He reached out to take a drink from a server carrying a tray, but Olise stopped him, shooting him a look he knew meant to focus. So, instead, he scanned the room, looking for familiar faces, good and bad.

"I don't see Gren here, do you?" Olise shook her head but nodded towards the corner.

"I do see some others I'd prefer to avoid, though."

Drake glanced where she was looking and saw a trio whispering and looking back. Drake and Olise were laid-back bounty hunters. They picked up jobs at their own pace and did what they could. Not everyone in the field shared the same view. They'd worked the same bounty as the trio a couple of years ago. Things had grown heated, and the whole thing became a race. When Drake and Olise had reached the bounty first, it hadn't gone down well.

"Ah," he said. "Shall we go downstairs?" They were calm and controlled as they moved with purpose through the crowds.

The comms channel crackled. Phin's voice sounded.

"There are three guys following you from the back of the room."

"We see them," Olise said, taking Drake's arm and pulling him through the crowds. "Thank you," she added after a moment.

They bobbed this way and that, like a boat on choppy seas. For the most part, the groups of chatting people paid them no heed. Olise tugged him behind a tall, decorative water feature, and in its brief shelter, they took stock of the situation.

"They're still looking for you, but I don't think they know exactly where you are," Phin reported. "Be careful."

They scanned the party, looking for anything or anyone to help them. When Drake spotted a large, colourfully dressed man watching them through the crowds, he smiled.

"Olise," Drake nodded towards the familiar face, "your best friend is here."

"What?" She spun. "Oh, for fuck's sake. Oji fucking Nasato."

At the sight of Olise, the jolly man beamed and gave them a short, quick wave. He pointed at the trio working their way through the crowd and gestured *well?* With a grimace, Olise nodded. Oji beamed and, with the musical swagger of a man on top of the world, intercepted the trio with a cry and a hug.

Oji had helped them several times now. As far as Drake was concerned, he was a lucky charm. They owed him a favour now, but the bounty-hunting world ran on favours, and it was always good to see a friendly face.

They made the most of the opportunity, making a more direct dash for the stairs.

"Who... was that?" Phin asked.

"Friend of the family," Drake said through a giggle. "Don't let Olise's demeanour fool you, Phin. They are actually friends. He's just a big, friendly dog and Olise is a particularly grumpy cat. He's on a quest to get her to relax and dance at a party."

"I can't picture that."

"You won't have to," Drake replied. "She owes him now, and next time, I'll take pictures."

"Hmmm," Olise replied.

"Well, the good news is I think you've lost them," Phin said.

Drake and Olise made the same dismissive noise. Not good enough. Not while they were still here.

From the stairs, it was easy to scan the room and spot their prey. With Olise close to him, he continued through the crowds, smiling and greeting new people as he went and, before Olise could stop him, swiping a glass of fizz from a server to blend in. Gren paled as he saw him. He excused himself from his current conversation, but before he could flee, Drake had put an arm around his shoulder and was holding him tight.

"Gren!" he said loudly. "My friend, it's been a while, hasn't it? Not since that business on Rulmar's moon, I think."

"T-terrible turn of events," the man replied, visibly sweating.

"It was." Drake put on a fierce, toothy grin. This man had sold them out and they had almost died. Worse than that, it had caused a shit storm with Sven that he and Olise were still hiding from. Now, they were here to collect a debt, just not in the way the weasel expected. "I hear you're in Interpol these days."

Cogs began to turn behind Gren's eyes. He relaxed a little.

"Yes," he agreed. "Busy at the moment, as you can imagine."

"Is it?" Drake mused. "You know me. I only take a passing interest in current events. I do have a friend, though. They're *fascinated* by the whole thing. They'd love to learn more."

"Mm-hmm?" The man nodded along.

"We're looking for some readings. And I just thought that, seeing as you and I are old friends, we could come to some kind of agreement where you send them over."

"I-I'm sure you and I can come to an agreement. As old friends." He glanced at Olise, who loomed behind Drake. "Why don't we go to my office and—"

"No," Olise said.

"We don't want to pull you away from the party," Drake said sweetly. *We're not going to corner ourselves for you,* Drake thought.

"So thoughtful, ahaha," Gren replied. "Silly me, I forgot I have some here" – he pulled out his communicator from a suit pocket and held it up feebly – "that I was perusing earlier." He looked between Drake and Olise with a slimy smile.

"Let me—" With a flick of his fingers, he moved through his communicator's menus. He held it for them both to see, and Drake kept an eye on what he did. Thankfully, the man knew better than to betray them here and now. After a moment, he held out his device expectantly and Drake touched his own communicator to Gren's, receiving the information. Drake gave a smile and for the first time, it was almost real. Gren seemed to realise that.

"A-are-are we ...?" Gren made a motion with his hand that Drake did not understand, but he thought he caught his drift.

"Even for now," he said. "I'm sure we'll cross paths again." He released the man and clinked his glass against Gren's. "Enjoy your party."

Olise watched them through narrowed eyes. Drake offered her his arm and said, "Shall we?"

"Sven's going to come for you, you know." Gren was trying to sound like a big man, but the way he rushed his words out betrayed his fear. "They all are. Your days are numbered."

Drake looked back at him, over his shoulder. He did not smile. The small man puffed up his chest, but it quickly deflated as Olise spun on her heels to face him. Drake nodded.

"I know," was all he said. Shrugging his shoulders, though he could feel the weight bearing down on them, he walked back through the party, feeling more than one set of eyes upon him. Olise lingered with Gren for a moment, no doubt non-verbally threatening him, and caught up as the elevator arrived to meet him. They stepped in and let the doors shut in silence.

"Kid," Olise said to Phin, "get that engine running."

Cold dread settled over them like a layer of snow. Olise looked from the door to Drake, to the door again. As they reached the bottom, Drake said, "I miss the good old days of dancing and drunken fights."

To his surprise, Olise offered him her arm. He took it and they stepped out together.

"Yeah," she said. "Me too."

15

Where is She?

It was a dark and stormy night when Harsha approached the card's address, and he thanked the random machine algorithm that had chosen it. Nothing ever quite made him feel like a detective more than walking towards an unknown location with his collar up and his hat brim down in poor weather. This was a serious situation, he knew it was, but there was something so cathartic about it. For the first time in almost two years, Harsha felt alive. For the first time in two years, he had hope.

He was deep in Lower-West's industrial district. Tall lampposts lit eerily empty streets lined with warehouses, factories, and complexes that had closed hours ago. There would be a million security devices around here, each protecting their own space, but would any of them record anything useful for him? He grimaced. And how much would they have to pay the corporations to see it?

Even before checking the number, Harsha could guess which building he was heading for. In the whole street, only one entryway was lit. The door was unmanned, but a blue panel lit up as he approached. In one smooth motion, he pulled the calling card from his pocket and tapped it against the panel. A circle spun for a second, and then, with a click, the door unlocked.

The room was dark and silent, but Harsha had been on the force too long to be deceived. He drew his gun, activated some tactical vision implants, and stepped inside.

"I'm a friend of Roz Dayne, here on her behalf," he called out.

Footsteps of heavy boots on metal sounded, echoing around the room in a way that made them hard to place and impossible to count. Maybe there were multiple people, and he was about to be surrounded. When a voice replied, it was not distorted, but that did not mean it wasn't disguised.

"And what makes her believe she's too important to come?"

"You're threatening an innocent woman," he replied, edging further in. His vision blurred momentarily as his tactical implants adjusted the contact lenses in his eyes. The change made the room visible as if it was broad daylight, but there was no one to be seen. The processor behind the implants would search for and highlight any signs of movement. "Nobody with half their wits would come here alone."

"So what does that make you?" the voice jeered.

"A man with half his wits, nothing to lose, and everything to gain."

The voice laughed.

"What do you want from her?" he pressed.

"The truth."

"She hasn't got anything to do with the attacks," he said. "We can prove that now."

"*She* didn't."

So there was something more. The hairs on his neck stood up just a moment too late. A cold gun barrel was placed at the back of his skull and another one was shoved into his lower back. *Better me than Roz* was his only thought. What did *that* say about him? *That I won't fail again.*

"Drop your weapon."

Harsha did as he was told.

"Walk with me."

As the person shoved him, Harsha began walking.

"Where is Roz Dayne?" they asked.

"I'm not telling you." He heard one of the guns click in the telltale sound of the safety being released.

"Where is Sabine Coren?"

Harsha stopped, only for a moment, but a rough shove made him move again.

"I don't know who that is."

The second gun's safety was released.

"Are you afraid to die?" the voice asked. Harsha did not respond, mentally searching for a way to get the upper hand. He was out of his depth, that was for sure. There was a long moment of silence.

"The target is on the move," a second, new voice announced. Harsha closed his eyes and said a wordless prayer. The next thing he knew, he was sprawled on the floor, the back of his head pounding. As he raised his head, vision blurry, he saw figures dressed in black leaving the building. There were at least eight of them, and the calmness with which they walked made shivers run down his spine. They'd been toying with him. He could have died, probably would have if things had gone on any longer. But more than anything else, he was glad that it was him, not Roz, who now lay on the dirty floor. As he scrambled to his feet, they turned on the building's lights. His eyes watered as his implants turned off and his eyes and implants readjusted.

Nevertheless, he staggered after them. The target is on the move, they'd said. Were they tracking Roz? How could they know she was in the safe house? Only one thing was certain: he had to get there first.

Though his head still spun, he broke into a messy run. None of the strange group paid him any heed. Across the street, they stepped into two black, featureless vehicles. Feeling more and more queasy as he went, he forced his camera add-on to turn on just in time to blink twice and capture one of the licence plates. He called his work before he'd caught his breath.

"I need you to track these vehicles," he ordered. "Harsha Sobol. *Now*," he stressed, though his legs finally gave into the dizziness and he tumbled into a puddle.

It must have been only a few moments later that a stranger helped him to his feet and asked a lot of questions he could not answer. With a wave of thanks, he stumbled through a few blocks to the nearest convenience store and to the medical shelves. He grabbed a jelly anti-concussion patch and slapped it on the sore part of his head before his payment had even finished. The cashier watched him in concern, as across the next few minutes, the world came back into focus.

"You alright, mister?" he asked. Harsha brought up his badge.

"I need a cab," was all he said.

Soon enough, he had that too, though the wait was long, cold, and filled with adrenaline. He tried to call Roz. She did not answer.

His thoughts spiralled. He envisioned Roz being found, though he knew she had to be safe. He remembered his daughter and how he'd thought the same about her the night before she died.

"This is not the same," he growled.

"Mister?" the cashier said, too young, too underpaid to be dealing with Harsha's shit. "Is everything alright?"

"It will be."

As the cab arrived, Harsha entered with no directions, a promise of a hefty payment, and a flash of his police badge, waiting for the location of the strangers from his colleagues. He was not the man who had failed his daughter, only one small part of a large problem, and he was not going to stop until Roz was safe.

He perched on the edge of his seat, ready to leap out at a moment's notice. He patted himself down, feeling everything in its place. He was as ready as he'd ever be.

Harsha almost dismissed the notification that popped up in front of his eyes until, at the very last second, his brain registered what it was. Roz's card. She'd tapped it. And she was on the move.

"Turn around!" he snapped at the cab driver. The poor man was shaking but nodded and did as he was told. Harsha pulled up the map that showed the card's location and forced it in front of the driver's own map of the city. "Follow that dot. Please," he added after a moment. He pinched his nose. "I promise I'll tip you well for this."

It did not ease the man's nerves. Harsha couldn't blame him. He watched Roz's dot on his map anxiously. It had finally come to a stop in a warehouse on the edge of town. It was hardly comforting, especially now he had a measure of who was after her. The only thing that remained was why? Why was anyone after this DJ from the middle of nowhere who was fully, undeniably telling the truth? Who was Sabine Coren, and why were they dragging Roz into this?

He didn't care if he never found answers, so long as he found Roz alive and well. So he raced through the streets, unaware, uncaring of who might be following him.

16

Not Like This

Roz flopped onto her bed with no small amount of tension. The unfamiliar setting was comforting. There was no way of anyone knowing where she was or who she was. Here, of all places, she should be safe.

She gazed out of the window at a city she barely knew and prayed that Harsha's expedition would bear some fruit and he would return safely. More than anything, Roz just wanted things to go back to normal. But even that seemed too much to ask for.

What even was normal these days, anyway? A glossy job and an empty apartment? A city she didn't know, her first friend, a man old enough to be her father? No, what she wanted was to rewind the clock, and that was an even bigger ask. She closed her eyes, a headache throbbing against the inside of her forehead. When her communicator buzzed, she ignored it. When it buzzed again, she winced. The noise made her feel sick. Could anyone understand how it felt to wake up one day to a communicator gone crazy and a conspiracy theory calling her a terrorist going crazier? So when it went off a third time, she sat up and grabbed it, ready to throw the thing out of the room. She faltered. It was the usual torrent of reporters, but Eva's message still hung above them all. One of these days, she was going to have to work up the courage to read it. She stared at it for a long moment. Why not now? She held her breath and opened the message.

How are you doing? This is crazy.

"It sure is," Roz murmured. Her mouth hung open. Her hands shook too much to even *think* of responding. A message from Eva. *Eva* had reached out. What did it mean? How should she respond? Her headache grew worse and she squeezed her eyes shut. But with her eyes closed, she saw only Eva, so she forced them open again. No, Eva was not waiting for her. That future was gone. She had made sure of that. She stifled a sob and blinked away tears hastily. This was all one big mistake. The case, her job, her breakup. *And there's nothing you can do about it now. There's no one left to help you and no one to miss you when you're gone.*

When she heard a knock on the door, her whole body tensed in an unpleasant way and her skin turned cold. She took a deep breath and tried to ignore it when it came again. A message bot could wait. A person at the wrong door would realise their mistake. Anything else... She gulped. Was unlikely. She was safe. Still, she strained her ears, desperate not to hear anything, but... unlikely was forcing the door open somehow. She heard it open, then close.

In that moment, she could have screamed. She threw herself out of bed and urged herself to open the door. Your imagination, she told herself. Your anxiety. The room next door. The wind. She grabbed the only thing available to her – a crap hairdryer – and kicked the door open, dryer held high.

It immediately fell to the ground as Roz gasped. It wasn't a masked stranger, wasn't a police officer, wasn't anyone who meant her harm. It was a middle-aged woman, familiar braids piled haphazardly on her head but bleached a violent blonde, in clothes that didn't fit right. The double of her late mother.

"Aunt Alison?" she stammered. "But how? Why? What are you doing here?"

"There's no time, Roz," her aunt said, grabbing her shoulders. "We need to leave."

"B-but," she insisted, but all air was gone from her lungs.

"They're not far behind us," Alison replied as if that explained anything.

"Who? The people who are after me?" She squeezed her eyes shut. "What's going *on*?"

Alison hurried her along, tossing clothes towards her and shoving any belongings she could find into a bag. When she looked up at Roz, frozen in place, their eyes met for one long moment.

"I will explain everything when we're safe," her aunt pleaded. "I promise."

I don't trust you, Roz's gut screamed. *Not like this*. Still, what choice did she have? She wanted answers, wanted safety. She pulled on her jacket, but when her hand found Harsha's card in her pocket, she did not hesitate to tap it twice.

With her life packed into a bag once more and, with it, any illusion of peace, Roz picked up her communicator and saw the message from Eva again.

The more the whole thing dragged on, the more the anxiety gave way to anger.

She deflated. "Why? Why now?" Hot tears came to her eyes. "Where the *hell* have you been?" She dismissed the notification, putting her head in her arms and suppressing a sob. "You couldn't have *called*? Couldn't have sent a tiny message? *Anything*?"

"It wasn't safe, Roz," her aunt said, her voice strained. "I had to get here, in person. I came as fast as I could but—" She gulped. "Roz, *please,*" her aunt begged, looking back at her with what Roz thought might actually be genuine *fear* in her eyes. "We need to move."

Why her? Why now? Why Eva? Why Alison? Why any of this?

It was all too much. So, in a reality that didn't make sense, she let herself be dragged into the night.

17

BURNING HOT AND HARD AND OUT

DRAKE WAS AWARE HE was uncharacteristically quiet. He could see it on Phin and Olise's faces as Phin flew them away from the party into the darkness of the rainy night.

Shaking rain out of his hair, he took a deep breath and said, "Well, all things considered, it could have gone a lot worse. We got what we needed, anyway."

Olise did not reply. Phin laughed nervously.

"Am I allowed to ask?" Phin ventured. "About... Sven."

"No," Olise replied.

"Yes," Drake said in unison.

Olise tutted and rolled her eyes.

It was one of the few arguments Drake and Olise had, and one they couldn't seem to shake. Drake always shared more information about their jobs, about themselves, than Olise was comfortable with. In Drake's experience, information begot more information, and so did the appearance of trust, as long as you were careful enough about who you told what. Olise didn't believe he was careful enough. In her experience, the information they gave away was a risk to them and their work. He could accept she had a point, but he maintained he did too. They tried to find a balance.

"What?" Drake said. "If the kid is travelling with us, doesn't he deserve to know?"

"Sure," Olise relented.

"Who is Sven?" Phin asked as if all of his energy had burst out of him.

"Sven is..." Drake began. "Not our friend." He sighed. "When we were young and stupid and felt like we didn't have many options... Sven," he began again, "is a very bad man that we may or may not have *accidentally* fucked over" – he sucked in air through his teeth – "quite severely."

"So he's coming for revenge?" Phin ventured. Olise nodded sharply. She looked like a tightly wound coil, arms crossed and body stiff.

"We're outnumbered and outmatched," she said, mouth twisted into a grimace. "So we've run... and run."

"He has more friends than we do," Drake sighed. "We only really have each other."

"But you two seem unstoppable." They flinched.

"Not really," Drake said. "Sven's a big name, kid. The Family can't help us and no sane person would go up against him for money. If we even had the money to offer."

"I'll be your friend," Phin offered in a tiny voice.

"Not in this case, Phin," Drake said with a weak smile. "Being our friend will just get you shot."

They fell into an uncomfortable silence. Drake watched as Phin opened and closed his mouth several times without saying anything, concern, frustration, and curiosity all washing across his face, though he did not ask anything more.

"I'll take over from here," Olise said, nudging Phin out of the pilot's seat.

"What? I was doing a good job."

His face flushed. Drake offered him an encouraging nod.

"You were," Olise agreed. Her tone wasn't soft and encouraging, but Drake knew it was the best Olise could do. "But now you need to look at this data."

"Oh," Phin said. As he settled back into his seat in the corner, Drake waved a hand to transfer the data to him. He looked at it for only a moment before saying, "Hypothetically, if I used some... lesser-known ways of getting some information to compare it to, you wouldn't tell on me, right?"

Drake grinned and slapped him on the shoulder.

"Don't give us any reason to," he said with a wink.

Phin paled a little but set to work, surrounding himself with blue holographic screens that cast sickly shadows on his face.

Olise pulled them up from where they'd been hovering, hiding in the depths of the streets between the colossal skyscrapers and into what classed as the sky in the station. Drake had never quite grown used to space stations. He'd grown up on a planet where a city had naturally sprawled out. The rigidity and efficiency with which the buildings and grid-like streets were packed into the station made him almost claustrophobic.

He glanced at Phin and wondered how he was doing. The kid *had* wanted to come, he reminded himself, but even so... *He's nervous,* he thought, *and not about the attacks.*

"What made you study physics, Phin?" Drake asked, but the boy was buried in the info. He repeated himself, but the words seemed to wash over Phin with no effect.

"Let him work," Olise said. Drake nodded and settled into the seat next to her.

"How are you, Lis?" he asked.

"Me? I'm driving."

"No, I mean, how are you feeling about all this?" he gestured vaguely.

"I don't feel fantastic about being on a space station when it's space stations that are being targeted."

Drake clasped his hand in his lap, watching out the front window.

"Tell me about it," he muttered. Space stations were quickly becoming home to a significant percentage of the galaxy's inhabitants. Every star system in the inner systems had at least one space station now. Not only could they be built anywhere, providing more housing and jobs in the already heavily populated inner systems, but they were places where the interstellar community, and its people of all species and backgrounds, could come together most easily. Drake suspected most species had been touched by the attacks.

"We'll be off soon, though," he continued.

He rapped his knuckles gently against the screen, showing the mystery warehouse, and glanced back at Phin.

"One way or another."

They returned the shuttle to their ship and fell into an easy routine. As Olise did security checks, making sure no one from the party had followed them, Drake did checks of his own. Checking the news, checking the bounty hunter network, checking the Family's web of contacts. There was endless chatter but no real information about the attacks or Sven. Thinking of the latter left a bitter taste in his mouth, so he turned back to the video feed of the warehouse. Still nothing. He hummed to himself, watching every speck of dirt that passed in front of the lens. After another while, Drake had hit his limit. Aware of Phin and Olise still working, he closed his eyes and rested his head back in his chair. Even then, he couldn't rest. The different elements of the case floated round and round his mind, slowed only by the creeping dread of Gren's warning about Sven.

Finally appearing satisfied, Olise sighed and leant back in her seat. Drake opened his eyes, sat up, and ran his hand through his hair.

"Where to?" she asked.

Drake's stomach grumbled.

"How about some food?" he said. "You know I like some fast food when I've been drinking." He nudged her jokingly.

"You *held* a glass of sparkling wine," Olise said, but she did smirk.

"Yeah, but I'm hungry, and I want fast food."

Olise relented, pulling the ship from where they'd been docked above the city and down to the top level of the colossal skyscrapers. They pulled into one of the many levels of a fast-food chain's drive-through and began to order.

"What do you want?" Drake called over his shoulder. Phin did not respond. "Phin."

It still took a moment for the student to peel himself away from the screen.

"Huh?"

"Food. What do you want?"

"The meal deal things. Burger, chips, I don't care about the drink."

"A man of fine tastes," Drake began to joke, but Phin was already lost in the screen again. "Actually," he said to the worker, "can we take this to sit in?" He got up and tapped Phin. "Come on, bud, you're taking a break."

Phin waved a hand.

"I can take a break when I'm done."

"You know, for one so young, you have a lot of bad habits."

He looked to Olise for support and found none. "Honestly, the pair of you," he sighed, shaking his head. "How many bad habits do I need to break?" Olise docked the ship, and he pulled Phin to his feet and out the dock door into the establishment. When they sat, food in front of them in a sticky leather booth Drake knew better than to examine, he took a breath. Obnoxiously cheery music echoed around them.

"Now isn't this nice," he said. "Sitting down together to eat?"

Olise snorted. Phin looked vacant. Drake snapped his fingers.

"Hey, kid, what's up?"

"I—" Phin sighed, looking away. He was restless in his seat. What Drake had mistaken for nerves, he could see now, was frustration. He lowered his voice. "I'm confused," he admitted.

Drake glanced around them. There were other people dotted around the brightly lit, colourful chain restaurant, but none of them had any interest in them.

"About what?" Drake leant closer and Olise followed suit.

"It doesn't seem like a... a..." He dropped again to a hushed whisper. "I ran it against some known attack methods – it's not even close."

"Not a weapon?" Drake echoed.

"But it's also not a power fault, no fuel explosion or anything like that to match up with the space stations, as far as I can tell."

"That..." Drake began. "That's weird."

Phin nodded, turning back to stare at his burger.

"I'm scared," he said after a long moment.

"Yeah, me too," Drake agreed. "Look, you've done a lot for us. We really appreciate it. If you want us to take you home—"

"No," Phin said firmly, looking him dead in the eyes with an intensity Drake only knew from Olise. Drake straightened up. "I'm not going to sleep easy until we find out what it is and, preferably, how it can be stopped."

"Someone you care about from a space station?"

Phin shook his head.

"I don't want to see it on the news and wonder if I could have done something."

He took a long drink.

"I'm going to get another. Do you want anything?"

They shook their heads and watched him go.

"He scares me, Lis," he admitted. "Just like you do."

Olise did not reply. *Like a star*, he thought, *burning so hot and so hard*. "Do you think you guys are secretly related?" he said, trying to lighten the mood. "Like a long-lost sibling?"

She punched him playfully, and he saw the slightest smile creep over her lips. He sighed and sank again.

"I don't know where this leaves us," he said. "I'll feed this back to the family, see what the web knows."

Phin returned, looking tired.

"Break time's over," Drake told him. "Let's head back to the ship."

Once there, Drake slumped back into his seat sluggishly. What a day. What a couple of days. He glanced at the screen showing the warehouse, then did a double-take.

"Wait a second," he said. "That's changed!"

He jabbed a finger at the screen, where the warehouse door hung open. Olise sprang to his side, rewinding the feed. Sure enough, people blurred past. It was only a few minutes of footage total, but Drake felt his hopes rising. She started it again as a shadowy figure approached the door, presented something, and then walked in.

"He looked around before he went in," Drake said, feeling giddy. "Let's see if we can catch his face."

Olise nodded. She paused the video precisely, pointing straight at the man's half-shrouded face. She brought her other screen up alongside it. The same hat. The same coat. The same face, though partly in shadow.

"Huh," she said.

"Well, what do you know?" Drake said. "We're on the same path as our detective. Let's see how far we can follow him."

"Sending the drone to try and find them again," Olise stated.

As she started up the engine, Drake turned to leave the cockpit.

"I'm going to open up the toy box," he said over his shoulder. "Usual, Lis?"

"Yup," came the curt response.

Drake strode down the hallway, aware Phin was following him. He unlocked a door and ducked inside. The lights flickered on automatically, revealing shelves and shelves of weapons, tools, and pretty much anything else a bounty hunter could ask for. He glanced at Phin. The kid's mouth hung open.

"Whoa," was all he said.

"I know we don't always put our best foot forward," Drake said. "But we *are* professionals."

"Is this all legal?" Phin asked, reaching out to touch a long rifle on the wall. Olise's favoured weapon, when they weren't in close quarters.

"You'd be surprised what you can get with the right training and licences, though a lot of it is situational," Drake replied. He nodded at the rifle. "Can't use that on space stations, for example. Some of these guns could cause a hull breach. Approved for planet and moons only."

Phin withdrew his hand, turning instead to a small, open box of spherical devices.

"And these?" Phin asked. Drake waved a hand dismissively.

"Those are basically toys. They're for distractions. They make a lot of noise, flash some lights, and spit out some harmless smoke." Phin hummed and nodded as he continued looking around. "Bounty hunting *is* a legal profession if you follow the rules."

"So it's all legal?"

Drake cracked a smile.

"I didn't say that," he corrected. "We have one or two *gifts* from the family. But they're not here, out in the open. Docks officials and law enforcement do have the right to search us whenever."

"Sounds like a lot to manage," Phin finished, turning to watch Drake, who shrugged.

"Every job has its downsides. I'm not sure we could ever escape filling in forms and paperwork."

Phin looked thoughtful. Drake picked out a few items and handed them to him. For a moment, Phin's eyes grew wide.

"Not for you, kid," he said with a chuckle. "Take those through to Olise."

As Phin left, Drake looked around the room again, considering his own situation. Swiftly, from memory, he filled the pockets in his jacket and trousers with his normal loadout: his ever-handy multi-purpose tool, the spheres for causing distractions, and plenty of ammunition. He counted out the equipment with care, updating the ship's list of what it had on board. It paid to be prepared now, but they never knew when they'd have to leave somewhere in a hurry without restocking. His heart pounded at the thought of conflict, but if it meant a break in this case... He nodded to himself. It was time to show Revalin what he and Olise could do.

18

Poor Decisions

As Detective Harsha Sobol leapt from his taxi, Drake, Olise, and Phin were not far behind. Olise brought the shuttle to a quick and quiet stop at the end of the block. They were outside a warehouse in another of Revalin's industrial estates. Drake wasn't sure what part the detective played in all of this, what it meant, but as he surveyed the building, Drake became increasingly convinced he would lead them to Roz. They lingered in the shadow, half-hidden by the shuttle. They couldn't risk being spotted now.

"I hope you're not involved, Roz," he said under his breath as he stepped out into the night. "You seem too nice to kill people."

"What?" Phin asked, looking at him. He had insisted on joining them again, and as much as Drake didn't want to see the kid get hurt, knowing what might happen to the space station, knowing they'd brought him into all this, away from his home, how could he say no? He shook his head.

"Nothing," he replied. "I just hope this turns out to be another big misunderstanding."

"Yeah," he replied quietly. "Me too."

Drake could see the look in Olise's eyes. He knew what she thought: they'd blown all their luck already. She led their pack, gun ready, and eyes lit up a brilliant blue from the contact lenses of her tactical implants. He had a gun, too, though it felt heavy in his hands. He wasn't ready for whatever came next. He could feel it in his stomach. He followed her lead and activated his own tactical implants, feeling momentarily queasy as the implant's contact lenses changed. Still, better to feel queasy now and adjust than apply them in a hurry during a fight.

Phin wrung his hands. He'd refused a weapon, saying he was more a danger to them with than without it, which Drake couldn't help but agree with, and that he was less likely to be a target without it, which he did not. He said nothing. Olise said nothing. He wouldn't call it coddling, more just... taking responsibility.

As the detective drew his weapon, peered inside the warehouse, and entered, they began moving towards it. Olise scanned the warehouse and then said, "There are stairs on the left of the building." Drake nodded. From where they stood approaching the right side, he couldn't see what she was talking about, but that was the beauty of implants.

"What are you thinking? Split up? Upstairs and down?"

"No," she said, with a firmness that made him look at her. "We'll stick together and go up." He met her gaze, and realisation hit him in the chest. Oh *god*. Olise was *afraid*. That was rare. Rare and a kind of bone-chilling terrifying. All at once, the risks began to sink in. If this truly was going to lead them to whatever was behind these attacks, then there was a real risk that here was next. This might be where they die. All of this was communicated in a look between them. If that was true, then... He nodded.

"Yeah, you're right." He motioned to the staircase. "Lead the way."

He gestured for Phin to follow. Better for him to be in the middle of the pack. The stairs creaked under them, and Drake winced with every step, but when Olise jimmied open the door, nothing but darkness greeted them. Somehow, that was not comforting. Distantly, Drake could hear a woman crying. Olise led them along an upper level – just a walkway above the ground floor. Beneath them was a maze of shipping boxes. In the far corner of the warehouse, there was a small bubble of light.

"Not many people here," he whispered to Olise.

"But that detective has probably called for reinforcements."

"He's lost down there," Phin stated.

"We need to be careful," Olise warned them. "Keep your eyes open."

As they drew close to the light, Drake saw one woman, dressed in oversized clothes with long braids of hair piled lopsidedly on her head, hunched over a table with machine parts and tools strewn everywhere. She seemed familiar somehow. He leant forward, activating a zooming function in his visual implant to try to get a better look. He put one hand on the walkway's railing to steady himself as an element within his contact lenses moved, blurring the edges of his vision, and the scene below came into view. He grabbed Phin's arm.

"It's the woman from the train," he said. "The one who duped us."

The second woman stood to the side, hand over her mouth to stifle her tears. Drake squinted, scanning for anyone else, but saw no one. What had they stumbled into?

The first woman stood up straight and moved as if listening. Beside him, Phin gasped. Olise lunged to cover his mouth, but he swatted her hand away.

"That's it," he said, rushing his words out. "How could I have been so stupid?"

"The not-weapon," Drake pressed. He squinted at the table, but no eye implants could help him make heads or tails of the device.

"A teleporter."

"But teleporters don't exist," Olise said. "Not in practice."

"I don't think it's working in practice," Phin said. "I think that's the whole problem. It would explain the massive energy readings of the attacks, it would—"

"We're not alone," the strange woman's words cut through the empty warehouse and the trio froze, but she was not looking at them, and the detective was nowhere to be seen, still lost in the maze. Olise went stiff.

"She's right. There are people outside. Lots of people."

Drake turned off the zoom implant and waited for his eyes and brain to readjust.

"Police? Bounty hunters? Something else?" he asked Olise. It hardly mattered, not if this woman intended to use the machine again.

"Time to go, Roz," the woman called as the doors banged open and men started flooding in. She grabbed the second woman's arm and pulled her to the device.

"Roz, I'm coming," an unknown voice, presumably the detective, called out. As the scientist began fiddling with the buttons on the device, Drake leapt over the barrier, down onto a shipping container, and started running.

"Drake, no!" Olise called out, but he did not stop.

"You can't do this," Drake called. "You'll kill us all!"

Roz turned pale at the sight of him while the other woman drew a gun.

"Come any closer, and I'll shoot," she warned without taking her eyes off the device. Drake jumped down off the shipping container and kept running. She shot him, hitting him in the thigh. He tumbled to the ground only a few feet away from them, gun slipping from his grip. He grunted as the air was knocked from his chest. Through dizziness, he saw the woman turn frantically back to her device. Hot tears pierced his eyes as frustration boiled inside him. They were so close. *He* was so close. His leg burned and throbbed, but he dragged himself up onto his elbows and threw himself forward to grab his gun. Before he could fire, the woman had slammed her hand down on one of the device's buttons.

Prickles raced across Drake's skin as he watched the woman's hair begin to stand up on end. A strange metallic, but not bloody, smell filled the air. Drake's ears popped, and he tried to shake away the feeling. Distantly, he heard Olise shout his name again and jump down after him. The device glowed a vibrant blue. Soon, it was so intense Drake couldn't bear to look at it. The world began to blur in front of him. His breath hitched in his throat.

Was this how it all ended?

Everything went white.

19

A Crisis of Character

"No, no, no, *no*!"

Phin's head spun. His chest ached. And through it all, as the world slowly came back into focus, Olise screeched. The warehouse floor was empty. Drake and the two women were gone.

"What the *fuck* was that?" She was already on her feet, though she swayed dangerously. As Phin pushed himself up onto his elbows, feeling queasy, he watched her jump down into the area where Drake and the two women had been. There was blood. Lots of blood.

"Where the fuck did they go?"

The detective groaned, clutching his side as he stumbled into the clearing. On spotting Olise, armed and angry, he pointed his weapon at her.

"Who are you?" he demanded. "What do you want with Roz?"

"We just want to find out what was causing the attacks." Phin rushed the words out before Olise could say anything. "You are too, right? Maybe we can help each other."

Neither moved. He wanted to jump between them, but at the sight of their guns, his legs refused to move.

"Olise," Phin pressed. "There's no need to point a gun at him."

The rumble of approaching people grew stronger.

"We need to run, not fight."

After a long moment, the detective relented.

"We need to move," he agreed. "My way out is blocked. How did you get in?"

Olise looked from Phin to the detective to the direction the men were coming from.

"Follow me," she growled, "but don't think we trust you."

The detective held up his hands in resignation. Wary eyes glanced around at the source of the footsteps. He was uneasy. Could they help each other? Phin wondered, or was this doomed to end badly?

Olise led the charge up onto the containers and over the barrier. She held the door open with her foot for them as she looked back, pointing her gun. No one seemed to have spotted them. Phin's heart still pounded as they ran through the streets. He jumped at every shadow, winced at every sound. Harsha took the rear, both he and Olise checking around every corner. Dark streets stretched out above them and dark alleys stretched ahead. Phin panted. *I'm not built for this*, he thought as his stomach churned.

As soon as they reached the relative safety of a graffiti-covered alley far from the warehouse and, Phin noted, their shuttle, he sagged, leaning against a wall. He wiped his forehead, watching Olise and the detective warily. The detective took issue with Olise's treatment and said, "Now then, who the hell are you?"

"What's it to you?" Olise replied. Her knuckles were white around her gun. "We're not with the people doing this. We're against them."

"Oh? Can you prove it?"

"Can *you*?"

"I'm an officer of the law."

"And, of course, you're a holy saviour."

The detective groaned.

"Look," he said. "I was helping Roz because I cared, not just because of my job. Your friend went up in smoke too. Now, we can probably help each other."

"What makes you so sure?"

"You stink of being some kind of merc and you have Thaler cufflinks, meaning you came at this from a... shall we politely say, different angle."

Olise did not say anything.

"We know it's not a weapon," Phin said. Olise glowered.

"*Kid*—" she began.

"So they're not dead?"

"They're gone," Phin agreed. "Teleported, hopefully, but we don't know where. The other woman. She tricked me, Drake, and Olise earlier," he continued. "We were following a lead that someone involved was on the Inter-Planet Express. She pointed us at each other to throw us off the scent."

"So she's one part of the puzzle," Harsha said. "But not all of it."

The detective paused.

"I think her name might be Sabine Coren. Men who wanted Roz were asking where Sabine Coren was, like Roz would know who that was. I don't know what her relationship is to Roz, but I do know Roz is innocent in whatever this is; she had no idea about the attacks or any involvement."

"That adds up," Olise said to Phin. "Drake said the name Sabine Coren flagged in a system three weeks away and was then flagged on the train."

Realisation dawned on Phin.

"She *teleported*."

"And the people who stormed the place?" Olise continued, looking at the detective. The detective stared at her for a long moment. He looked like he was biting back a remark.

"I have this." He held up the same pink business card that the radio receptionist had shown Phin.

"We saw that too," Phin said. "That's how we found you."

"The owners of it are after Roz and that woman," he continued. He ran a hand through his hair, slicking it back. "Trying to fit these pieces together, I'd wager Ms Coren is involved with the teleporter somehow, and for some reason, by extension, Roz is a target. I don't think they're police. Even if I hadn't been told about it, they wouldn't have... They attacked me earlier."

"But they are highly trained," Olise said. "And organised. And there's more of them."

"And I'm willing to bet they have a fuller picture."

He held out a hand to Olise.

"You have your friends. I have mine. With our resources combined..."

Olise stared at his hand, stared at *him*, then closed her eyes and sighed. The events in the warehouse had made it clear they were all out of their depth. They were running out of options and running out of time. Grimacing, she shook the detective's hand.

"Let's find them and get to the bottom of this," she agreed. "Before the next station blows."

20

Something to Lose

Roz hit the ground hard. Her back arched as she choked to catch her breath in air she couldn't breathe. Tingling started in her fingers and began spreading up her palms. A world with a beautiful purple and orange sky faded in and out of view as she gasped, throat dry and raw. In the creeping coldness, in the creeping dark, she thought only of Eva and the life she had left behind. The life she would never return to now. Tears ran unfettered down the side of her face. As her eyes slipped shut, she could have sworn she saw in the purple light the shadow of Eva crouched on a windowsill, drinking tea and humming a soft, familiar tune.

Even in death, she was not allowed peace. She was wrenched from her dreams by someone hammering something onto her chest, and a sudden rush of oxygen returned to her. Still sobbing, still choking, and freshly in pain, Roz sat bolt upright, head-butting her aunt, who crouched over her.

She put her hands to her throat, finding she could breathe freely. There was a translucent bubble coming from a token pressed into her chest. Her aunt nodded and climbed off her. She had a similar bubble, her face pale and haggard.

"Really rolled the dice on that one, huh?" a male voice growled. It was the pink and blonde man who had tried to intervene. He had a bubble of his own, different from theirs, she noted, but who was he and— A sob caught in her throat as she looked him up and down for the first time and saw blood from more injuries than her aunt's gunshot.

"What happened?" When she spoke, her voice was hoarse. Her aunt turned her back on them, surveying the world around them. Long green-grey strands of grass came up to their shoulders on all sides. There were mountains behind them and ahead of them... a little hint of artificial light.

"Well, that's what he gets for piggybacking on our exit." She spared him only a glance. "He wasn't in range, but he wasn't quite out of range either."

"W-we teleported?" Roz asked. Alison nodded. Roz continued, "We weren't meant to end up here. Not in this air, not in this..." She waved her hands. As quickly as feeling had come back to her extremities, it was fading again due to the bitter cold. Alison did not respond.

"Still got some kinks to work out, have we?" the man continued. He tried to sit up but fainted backwards. Roz tumbled to his side, pressing numb hands onto his wounds. It looked as if his wound had burst outwards in places.

"I always said you sounded like a nice person, Roz," he said weakly. It took Roz a moment to remember that she was, in fact, a celebrity, and this man was not a stalker. Maybe not a stalker, anyway. There was still the question of who the hell he was and how he had ended up in that warehouse. Even more questions to add to the pile. She glanced at Alison, feeling her stomach flip. Even more questions she wasn't sure she wanted to know the answer to.

"Leave him, Roz," Alison said shortly. "We need to find some shelter before night falls and it gets any colder."

"We can't," Roz pressed.

"What shelter?" the man said at the same time. "Seems to me like we're on Agh-Ab-2. We won't find any friends here."

"I see a settlement over there," Alison continued.

"And how are you going to explain how a group of humans ended up here?"

"Please stop moving," Roz begged. Every time he spoke, the movement of his chest pushed blood through her fingers.

He continued anyway.

"At worst, they'll think we're spies or that they're being attacked. At best, they'll take your new toy from you."

Roz saw her aunt's shoulders sink. When she turned again, she looked down at them with some mix of reluctance and disgust.

"You need someone with, say, a smuggling background," the pink-haired man continued. "A pilot who can fly anything. A person with lots of... convenient friends."

"A person like you," Alison said flatly.

"A person like me," he agreed. "Alive, preferably."

Alison looked from him to Roz to the settlement on the horizon.

"You almost killed Roz once," he said. "Don't do it again."

21

WHAT WOULD DRAKE DO?

YOUR PLACE OR MINE? Olise thought sarcastically as she stared the detective down. She hated the idea of taking the detective back to their shuttle, let alone their ship, but she hated the idea of following *him* anywhere, too. A neutral space was what they needed. A *private* one. But since they were new here and Revalin was his home turf, that didn't feel good either. *What would Drake do?* She had never agreed with the amount of information he was willing to share with strangers. She was certain he would trust the detective, at least trust him *enough* for now. Then again, Drake usually got them *into* trouble, and Olise was the one to get them out. The part of her that Drake had influenced said *that settles it then. You work with him, and if there's trouble, you'll get yourself and the kid out.* She sneered. Even when he wasn't here, he was right.

Reluctantly, Olise took them back to the shuttle. Phin was silent, staring intensely into nothing. Olise could almost see his mind racing. When they were safely in the shuttle, terse introductions behind them, she said, "What are you thinking, kid?"

He made a holographic screen visible to them.

"Energy can be neither created nor destroyed," Phin said, not taking his eyes off his screen. Olise nodded along, eyes heavy and fists clenched. "There has to have been a lot of energy with that. It was all here, and then it wasn't. We'll have to spot it cropping up elsewhere."

The detective clapped him on the shoulder.

"So you can find it?"

Olise's stomach lurched as she saw Phin freeze. She was aware of the pressure they were putting on him, just as he was aware of the severity of the situation. She prowled around the shuttle, eyes fixed on the detective.

"The energy will likely fade fast," Phin explained. The way the light reflected in his eyes made them look hollow. "I can start a scan, but if it's too far away, it will have faded. And yes, there would be records of surges like that near civilised places, but that's an awful lot to search and aside from not knowing where this woman might have taken them..." Phin gulped. "I think we have to consider the possibility that they didn't end up where they were aiming."

There was a hard moment's silence and a bitter taste in Olise's mouth. The woman *had* still been working on it and she had left it to the very last second to activate it.

"I don't like these odds," Olise eventually mustered. "The ratio of the vacuum of space to land isn't great and the ratio of land to habitable land is worse."

"They weren't wearing space suits," Harsha offered. "That woman wanted Roz for a reason. If there was a big risk of getting it wrong, I'm sure she would have taken precautions."

Phin sighed with relief. Olise did not. She had seen people do one too many strange things under pressure. She would have loved to believe that, but she couldn't contact Drake and that in itself was a reason to worry. Like her, he always gave a signal, any signal that he was okay, but every message and every call she'd tried to reach him with had not gone through. He was out of contact range, or his communicator had broken, or the woman had done something to him or it. He would cobble together something if he had to but... how long should she wait?

"What—" she began, then stopped herself. She looked at the detective warily, weighing up her options, then her gaze fell to Phin once more. "What were you talking about in the warehouse? About the teleporter?" she asked. "How did you know it was a teleporter? What made you think it wasn't working?"

Phin flushed.

"Well, we're still alive and Revalin's still here, so I might be wrong," he admitted.

"But?" Olise prompted.

"We thought the thing causing the attacks wasn't a weapon," he explained to Harsha, who nodded.

"So did we," he said.

"And I study physics. And everyone in physics thinks teleportation, or something like it, some kind of warp speed, will be the next big breakthrough. I have an interest in it. We *all* do." He took a breath. "I recognised some of the design from Markal's theory of teleportation. The conclusion of Markal's research, and everybody's research since, is that it'd leave too much energy behind in the place it left. A dangerous amount of energy. No one could figure out how to control it safely, so it's never been built. But when I saw it in the warehouse... The attacks had such a crazy amount of energy in one massive burst, so... teleporter."

Harsha held his lower face in his hand, brow furrowed. Olise pursed her lips, turning the information over and over in her mind.

"It's the best explanation I've heard so far," the detective concluded after a moment. "But it still leaves a hell of a list of questions."

"How fast would the energy destroy a space station?" Olise asked. "Is it time to run?"

Phin shook his head.

"No," he said firmly. "If it was going to destroy Revalin, it would have been pretty instant."

Cold shivers ran down Olise's back.

"So that woman found a way to use her teleporter safely," Harsha continued. Phin nodded. "But why did four space stations have to be destroyed? The first could have been an accident, if they thought they could contain the energy. But why keep going after the first destruction?"

"Let's track down Drake, Roz, and that woman and grill her for answers," Olise stated.

"So Phin's starting a scan for the teleporter," Harsha continued. "It'll take a while, I assume?" Phin nodded. "So we can explore other avenues in the meantime. For starters, we can get people looking for Drake and Roz. The two of them are distinctive, so there's that. I can put out a call," he nodded at Olise. "You should do the same with your people."

"I can ask a few trusted Thalers to make some subtle enquiries. We don't want to put out a large search unless it's a last resort." There was a pause. The detective's face hardened. She felt compelled to fill the silence.

"I've never been the people person of the duo." The detective opened his mouth to interrupt, but she talked over him. "And we *are* a duo. If I ask for help, it will raise questions of where Drake is and we need to avoid that right now." The warning Ciro had given Drake weighed heavily on her. She felt exposed, *visible*. She'd found and watched the detective easily enough. It stood to reason someone could do the same to her.

"Phin," the detective said, though he didn't look at the kid, and Phin did not look up from his screen. "Once you've got that scan running, see what you can find out about Sabine Coren."

"Yeah," was the only response. Harsha nodded, pulling Olise a few steps away. They stared each other down. Olise was taller and younger, but she knew better than to underestimate the detective. In his eyes was steel that came from more than a desk job.

"You realise that this kid has his whole future ahead of him?"

"I do," Olise agreed, "but he's determined to stay."

"So? Where the hell did you pick him up? He clearly doesn't have any experience with this."

"Do *you* have experience with a new technology that's killed five space stations?"

"You know fine well what I mean. The pressure. The fear. He's just a kid. Whatever's coming, he isn't ready for it."

"We're never ready," she replied. "You know that."

"And if it comes to it? Will you protect him?"

"Yes."

"It's running," Phin called, interrupting them. Harsha moved to return to him, but Olise grabbed his arm.

"He's been dragged into this. Can you blame him for wanting to see it through? To put some meaning to it all?"

"You know as well as I do that he may not find it."

"I won't let him make the same mistakes I did," Olise said. Anger bubbled up inside her. What couldn't he understand? Drake would have understood. She was trying her best, whatever that may be.

"Okay, then," Harsha said after a moment and pulled free. Olise watched as he spoke to Phin and then made some calls of his own. Olise settled into the pilot's chair, the chair Drake was supposed to be in, and checked her communications again. Her heart was racing. This whole thing was… worse than a nightmare. She didn't want to be Harsha's enemy. She didn't want to be his friend. She didn't want to be on his radar at all. She didn't want to be apart from Drake, either, but there was very little she could do about any of those things now.

"We need to take a short trip across this system," Olise said. "To Buse-a-Thes. If we want my contact's help," she added.

"Seems to me that the case has left Revalin anyway," the detective replied. "Phin?"

Phin shrugged.

It stung to return to the ship and find that Drake was not there. It stung even more to pack up, to leave, doing his work and her own. Harsha and Phin followed her like two puppies as she strode up and down the top floor of the ship, securing any loose items in the three cabins, kitchen, bathroom, and armoury.

"Phin's already taken the spare room," Olise told Harsha. "But we're not carrying any cargo right now, so there's room down below." She ducked into the large cupboard that served as the top floor's mechanical room, opened a hatch in the floor, and climbed down to the bottom floor of the ship.

The open space was always warm, the back half dominated by the sealed-off engine. Several storage lockers were bolted to the walls, containing some of their lesser-used gear. A treadmill, some weights, and a pull-up bar gave her and Drake a way to stay fit and sane on long journeys. Beyond that, the room was empty, waiting for cargo. Olise opened one of the lockers, pulled out a padded mat and sleeping bag from some camping gear, and held it out to the detective. He took them without saying anything.

"Five minutes until take-off," she told them. "Be in the cockpit and belted up by then."

They nodded, and she climbed up to the top floor once more and finished her preparations to put Revalin behind them.

She settled into the cockpit and plotted a course, then checked her communications again. Still nothing. The kid and the detective followed her instructions at least, trickled into the cockpit, and secured themselves into its seats behind her. Phin returned to staring at his screen, and the detective looked slowly around the ship with the telltale blue glow of implants in his eyes. She grimaced, feeling uncomfortable in her own home. Even with two other people, it felt empty without Drake. It felt... *scary* without Drake. She thought again of Sven, of Ciro's warning and Gren's boasting. He was the shadow that followed them wherever they went. They hadn't physically crossed paths in years, but whenever Drake and Olise were on a high-profile job, whenever they were in the inner systems, there were signs and warnings that Sven was there. They were both things now, she thought grimly, high-profile, in the inner systems, *and* they were apart. It was hard not to feel like their time was running out before they'd cross paths again. She checked the ship's external cameras, then checked them again. Traffic flooded slowly in and out of Revalin. That was the other problem with the inner systems; they were so busy that you could never tell if anyone was following you or simply travelling the same crowded route. She would keep an eye on the cameras, for what little good they'd do her.

What was she supposed to do on this trip other than drive herself insane waiting for a message, *any* message? Her hands searched for a Twist but didn't find one. Drake knew all her hiding spots and no doubt had thrown them out an airlock when she wasn't around. The thought brought rare tears to her eyes, but she squeezed them shut.

She dozed, arms and legs crossed, feet up on the console, and awoke to a vibrant green clock telling her it was the wee few hours of the morning. The detective sat upright, arms folded, and snoring. Across the cockpit from him, a weary Phin sat hunched, typing away. She should have guessed as much. The more time went on, the more Olise saw Drake's point. Phin *was* like her, too much so.

"Hey, kid," she said, sauntering over, stretching her neck and shoulders as she went. "Take a break." He shook his head.

"I've got nothing to show yet," he replied. "Nothing back from the scan and nothing, *nothing* on Sabine Coren. It's like she's a ghost or something."

"A woman with a double life and second name is a bit more likely," she said in the gentlest tone she could manage.

"We're against the clock, against a whole bunch of people we don't know. We *saw* her, the woman from the train. We know her face. We know she's involved. But it all being in my head doesn't help us. I can't *stop*. I can't just go home and forget about all of this. I want to see it through. I want to figure it all out."

It took Olise a moment to formulate a response, the inherent problem being that she understood him and would have been doing the same in his situation. She was hit with the uncomfortable realisation that she had to be a role model now. *What would Drake do?* She wracked her brains. *What would he say?*

"Look, kid, I won't lie to you." She sighed. "I agree. I don't want to stop. But..." She looked away and shifted from side to side. "There's a reason that one of us has a university scholarship and a bright future, and the other has scars, enemies and addictions. This isn't your responsibility. You're doing all you can."

"What if it's not enough? What if I stop a little too early and miss something?"

"That's life," she said with a heavy sigh. "This is the real world, not a test that you can pass if you try hard enough or study more. You need to find a way to make peace with that. You're going to get things wrong. You're going to make mistakes. That still doesn't make anything that's happening or anything that will happen your fault."

She leaned close. "You want to find Drake? So do I. You're not going to find him in the state you're currently in. Go to bed. I'll take the night shift."

"Will you—" he began.

"Wake you if something happens?" She nodded. *Believe me, kid,* she almost said, *either nothing is going to happen or everything will, and you'll be awake before I can get to you.* He relented and stood up. When she slipped into his place, she found the detective watching. She looked pointedly away, and after a moment, he did too.

22

A VOICE IN THE DARK

DRAKE WAS AWARE HE was dreaming. Still, as his limbs were pulled in all directions, he fought against them, only to be dragged deeper into the unwaking world. His thoughts swirled like a piece of debris in a rushing river. Coherent thoughts rushed past, always out of his reach. The specifics of the dream were just beyond his grasp, the whole thing alight with panic. He heard Sven's voice, and ice ran through his veins. He heard Olise, and he tried in vain to cry out.

He chastised himself. He needed to calm down. He needed to wake himself up. He needed to fight until he was back at Olise's side. But this was a fight he couldn't win. The dream pummelled him for what felt like hours, playing Drake's nerves like a violin.

When he finally awoke to an unfamiliar sky above him, he was exhausted and covered in cold sweat. He took a deep breath and felt a small amount of tension leave his body. He sat up slowly, felt the aches of his injuries, and allowed himself a moment with his head in his hands to recap and feel sorry for himself. The waking world was not much better than the nightmare, but it was, at least, a situation he felt he could get himself out of. Out of habit, he pulled his communicator from his pocket to check it, but it was no use. The tile did not respond. Something about the teleporter had knocked out all of their communicators.

He longed to contact Olise to check if she was okay, to let her know that *he* was okay. That would have to wait.

Woozy from painkillers taken for his injuries but patched up and calming down by the minute, Drake leant back against the rocky outcrop they were making camp behind. They were hiding amongst the terrain and long reeds. So they hoped. The woman Roz called Alison was insistent that they could not light a fire, so Drake shivered in damp clothes and tried to think of warmer climes. The outcrop shielded them from the worst of the winds, at least. Roz sat nearby with her knees to her chest and her arms hooked around them, staring into nothing. She snapped to attention as he sat up.

"How long was I asleep?" he asked, stretching as much as his injuries would allow. They throbbed and a wave of queasiness washed over him.

"Not long," Roz replied. "An hour or two maybe. It's hard to tell here, and my communicator isn't working."

He nodded.

"Well, thanks for not abandoning me out here," he told her.

"I think Alison believes we need your help to escape. She said the teleporter is broken but won't say how or if she can fix it," Roz said, bitterness creeping in. "She's scouting, apparently," she offered as an explanation. Her eyes were puffy. She unfurled and straightened up. "How do you feel?"

"I've been better," Drake said with a long sigh, "but I've also been worse so…"

"Alison left this." Roz patted a large backpack next to her, "She said there were some supplies inside. You look like you could do with something to eat."

"Please."

She rummaged through Alison's backpack and took out familiar provisions that he'd wished he'd never see again. He pulled a face.

"You've had these before?" Roz asked, the hint of a smile passing across her lips. The ration was a small, thick disk. Roz twisted the top and clicked a button before handing it to him. It began to swell and heat up as the contents rehydrated. He warmed his hands on it.

"Unfortunately, yes," he replied. "They're not far off prison rations. Better than going cold and hungry though."

"Yeah, I bet." She sat back, taking a cylinder of her own. "You said you thought you knew where we were," she said.

"Agh-Ab-2, yeah."

"How…" She took a shaky breath. "Exactly how far away are we from Revalin?"

Drake closed his eyes and tried to visualise it on his ship's console, tried to remember when he and Olise had last risked a trip out this way. Trouble was, they rarely travelled in a straight line.

"Not crazy far," he began, to comfort her, "not most-of-your-life far, but it's not exactly close. A month on your average ship, maybe?"

Roz nodded. It was hard to tell if she was relieved by that or not.

"We'll get back," he added. "We will."

There was a pause as they began eating. Drake knew where he wanted to lead the conversation, but Roz seemed… tired. *You may not get a better opportunity*, he told himself. Alison was still out of sight, and they were, as yet, undetected by the planet's inhabitants. Tomorrow, they'd be trying to steal a ship and get off this rock. There was no other chance.

"Be honest with me, Roz," he said softly, gazing at her through the dying light. "Do you trust her?" Her face was so gentle, so genuine. Though he'd never known what she looked like before now, it matched her voice perfectly. He almost felt guilty when her face screwed up. Almost.

"I..." She stopped. "I believe that she is trying to keep me safe, I do... but how and *why*... If I'm being honest, I'm scared of it all. I don't think any of this has gone how she planned," she added after a long moment. Drake nodded. She blinked away tears. "She's all I have left. If I don't trust her, what does that mean?"

"I understand. I..." He sighed. "I have a big, messy family, and I've lost a lot of people over the years. I'm grateful that my extended family looks out for me, but... things are tricky. But they're family." He shrugged. She nodded.

"In a similar vein," she said, opening her meal. "Why do you trust me? We don't know each other."

"You don't know *me*," he corrected, prodding the contents of his meal. It was all the same beige-green colour in different shapes. "I've listened to you on the radio for years. Maybe it's all just an act" – he shrugged – "but it doesn't seem that way. You seem normal. I think that's why people resonate with your radio show." He smiled at her. "Plus, you know, you advocated to save my life back there despite not knowing me. That'll always endear you to people. If I'm being honest, and I think it's my turn, I think you're caught up in this mistakenly, like Phin."

"Who's Phin?"

"Some kid who was in the right place at the wrong time. Now that he knows the case, he won't let go. I'm worried about him."

"I am caught up in this," she admitted. It was surprising how easily she opened up. He'd always been good at getting people to talk. He was a natural charmer, but he wasn't sure a threatening, blood-covered stranger was charming regardless of what he did. He was just being honest, just being himself. Maybe Roz liked that about him in the same way he liked it about her. Maybe she'd been caught up in it so long, been so scared, so lonely, that she just needed someone to talk to. "I don't know anything about the attacks," she continued, "and my memory wasn't altered."

She paused, mouth open, as if she was going to speak again. Drake waited.

"But my aunt is involved somehow, isn't she?"

"Seems that way," he said. He couldn't lie to her. "The teleporter *definitely* is. Phin's a physics student and he was helping us analyse the attacks. He's confident the space stations weren't destroyed by a known weapon. In the warehouse, when he saw the teleporter, he seemed to think it was related." Drake thought of his communicator again with a pang of frustration. "I wish I could ask him in more detail." He sighed.

"She said it wasn't ready," Roz admitted. "You did too. But surely those attacks... killed everyone."

"I don't know how it all fits together yet," he agreed. "I..." He trailed off, wondering how much to say. "I crossed paths with your aunt on a train. I think she was using a fake name – Sabine Coren. It popped up on some checks I was doing. Sabine Coren had travelled several star systems in a day. I thought it was a ruse, but now... I wonder if she teleported." He turned the thought over in his mind, piecing it all together for the first time. "There weren't any attacks in either area, so... I don't think it's her teleporter that's the problem." He paused, aware she was staring at him intensely. "I don't know who those people after you in the warehouse are. We only put the teleporter dots together seconds before I jumped down. There was a detective after you there, too, by the way. It's how we found you."

"He came after me?" She pursed her lips. "Do you think they're okay? You got hurt being nearby. He gave me a business card to tap if I was in trouble, but it's not working. Maybe the people in the warehouse have another teleporter... Maybe it wasn't ready yet. Maybe Revalin is up in smoke too."

"We don't know enough about that, and we've got no way of finding out, so let's not worry for now." Though, in truth, there was a knot in his stomach. He and Olise would always contact each other. Even without his communicator, he would get to a spaceport or a space station and find a way to get a message to her... if Revalin still existed. "If our communicators aren't working, maybe the card is broken for the same reason. Maybe it's us, not them."

Roz bit her lip but nodded. She looked off into the distance and squeezed her eyes shut.

"When she comes back," her voice started out strong but faded away as she spoke, "I'm going to try and get some answers." She looked up at him, and he nodded grimly.

"How did you get caught up in all this?" she asked.

"I wouldn't say caught up, exactly." He rubbed the back of his head. "I'm here by choice. I had some family die in the attacks, so I'm here to find out what happened. Wasn't expecting this, though."

"How could you?"

"My friend Olise and I are bounty hunters," he continued. "We picked up Phin along the way and followed the trail to you."

"You meet a lot of people bounty hunting?"

"Loads. See a bunch of places, too. Spend a lot of time in transit listening to the radio." He grinned. "Hundreds of years and millions of miles from Earth, and we still have radio, of a sort. Why do you think that is?"

"I think space has always intimidated us," she said without missing a beat. "As alluring and exciting as it is, suddenly, we're faced with the fact that we're very, very small and very, very mortal. It's why most people don't travel. Radio still exists because when you're out in the middle of the vast nothingness, it's nice to have a voice in the dark telling us we're not alone."

Drake leant back, staring at a sky filled with unfamiliar stars. He felt a pang of homesickness but smiled anyway.

"You're the kind of person I can get along with, Roz. My grandma used to say that we're all spaceships passing in the night. That we can choose to be a light in the dark if we'd like. That's what you do, right?"

"Yeah," she replied. "Yeah. I try."

"You succeed," he told her. "Can I ask you something?"

"Mhm."

"You help so many people, you tell so many nice stories, share nice messages and requests, give good advice. You keep everyone company, but you sound so lonely." Roz did not respond. "I know you moved from Nonke to Revalin. That's a big jump. Did you leave someone behind?"

Roz sighed, and the atmosphere changed. He'd struck a nerve.

"You don't have to answer," he assured her. "I chat shit to fill the space."

"It is a long way," she agreed. Her voice was soft but strained. "A long way and the Maeh belt resource war between us. It was my girlfriend, Eva. I didn't want her to die coming to see me and vice versa. I—" Drake sat up again, watching as she rubbed her face. "I miss her, but I was always going to miss her, miss our home, our friends, but... today, while I was choking on this air, when I thought I was going to die..." Her voice cracked. "It was a mistake, Drake. A big mistake."

He heard a gentle sob. She hid her face behind the meal in her hands.

"I know life wasn't perfect. Night shifts put a strain on us. Sometimes, we drove each other crazy. But I was actually happy and safe and loved." She hiccupped. "I just feel like that decision was the start of this all. And everything that's happened after is my fault."

"Listen, Roz." He shuffled towards her and put an awkward hand on her shoulder. "If it's not working, don't anchor yourself to it."

"I thought I burned all my bridges b-but..." Her lip trembled. "S-she did message me. Before we, uh, left." She wiped red eyes roughly on the sleeve of her coat. "But I don't deserve that. For her to reach out after everything."

"Things ended in a bad way," he said, leaning forward. "But you still care about her. And her reaching out proves she still cares about you too, in some way. Roz, after all this, you deserve to be happy. Whatever that means to you, follow it. You want to speak to her, now, she's reached out. Maybe you won't get back together, but don't you want to try? At the very least, you could go back to your home station and see friends." Roz nodded, crying more and more.

"I don't think life is ever going to go back to normal."

"What even is normal?" he replied. "Life's just a series of steps, one after the other. Alright, this feels like you've been dropped in a pit, but you can still get out. You just need to focus on smaller steps. Not 'get out of pit' or 'go back to the way life used to be' but 'survive until tomorrow' and, when you're ready, maybe 'message Eva'."

"Do you think she still listens to the radio sometimes?"

"There's only one way to find out." Drake paused. "How's this for a small step: let's keep in touch. When all of this is over, I'll come to your space station. We can go out to some secret, chic cafe or whatever cool radio DJs do and trade stories. I'll check in. You don't have to take your steps alone."

Roz's teary face wobbled into a smile.

"That would be nice."

***

Roz watched from their makeshift camp as Alison trekked back into view and sat a distance away. She sat in the long grass alone, leaning forward with her legs crossed, her elbows on her knees, and her hands clasped. The teleporter sat in her lap. Roz took a deep breath and tried to steady herself. *You have to do this*, she told herself firmly, pushing down her nerves. *You need to ask her.* She strode out to her aunt with purpose but lost momentum as she drew closer and Alison turned to face her. Roz didn't sit, just stood over her.

"I need you to tell me what's going on," Roz tried to say firmly, though her voice wavered. "Why did you suddenly turn up on Revalin? I haven't heard from you in *months*. I needed—" She stopped herself, but Alison winced as if she had finished.

"I was trying to come get you, from the moment I heard about the first station being destroyed, I—" Alison put the teleporter down, stood, and held out her hands. When Roz didn't take them, she let them drop to her side. "I'm just trying to protect you. I will tell you *everything* when we're safe. I need you to trust me."

Roz pursed her lips and glanced back at their makeshift camp.

"I'm not sure I can," she said honestly. "Not until I know more. Why are you over here by yourself? Isn't there safety in numbers?"

"Roz." Alison's voice was soft, but her tone approached condescending. "What is it about that man that makes you trust him so much, so immediately?"

"W-what?" Roz stammered.

"He doesn't *seem* threatening?" Alison continued. "He's very charismatic, I'll give you that. But he's a self-admitted bounty hunter who *says* he's working for the right people. We have no way of verifying that. Would you tell the truth if I pointed a gun at you?"

"I would if I thought the truth would stop you *shooting* me," Roz stressed.

"There are people after us, Roz," Alison said dismissively, "and it won't necessarily be obvious who they are. It's not a movie."

"Don't speak to me like a child," Roz snapped. "He could have shot us in that warehouse." Roz paused. "If he wanted the teleporter, he could have shot us and taken it. Instead, he yelled for you to stop. He wanted to talk."

"Why do you trust him?" Alison demanded again. "What actual, tangible reason has he given you? He's a *bounty hunter*. Even if, hypothetically, he's working for the 'right people' now, he could sell us out for a lot more money than he'll get from helping us. It's just a matter of time until someone makes him a better offer." Alison did not give her a chance to respond, quickly following up with, "Why can you trust him but not me?"

Roz felt like she had been punched in the chest. Her lip curled into a sneer.

"And that's the *real* root of the problem here, isn't it?" she spat. "So, I'll ask you all the same questions. What actual, *tangible* reason have you given me recently? You disappear for months on end, then you turn up in the most insane period of my life and expect nothing to have changed. Why don't *you* trust *me*?"

"I do—"

"Then *talk* to me," Roz shouted. Alison recoiled. Roz's cheeks burned. She swallowed a lump in her throat. "Explain what's going on," she said more softly, voice cracking. "I need *something*, Alison."

Alison closed her eyes, and for a long moment, Roz thought that her aunt wouldn't answer.

"We need to keep moving—" Alison began. Roz tutted and spun on her heels to leave, but Alison grabbed her arm. "*Because* some very dangerous people are after the teleporter and they can't be allowed to have it. They will never willingly make this new invention public, and they will use it for terrible things as the rest of the galaxy scrambles to figure out how they're doing it." She spoke quickly but steadily. When Roz turned back, cold shivers ran down her spine at her aunt's steely eyes.

"With the teleporter," Alison continued, "suddenly assassins can get in and out of the galaxy's most secured areas in moments. Suddenly, thieves can access information and resources that are locked away. Can you imagine the impact on the war in the Maeh asteroid belt if a third party could teleport in and steal all the resources out from under everyone? If that same third party could pick a side and assassinate the leader of the other?"

Roz gulped and nodded.

"This teleporter" – Alison pointed at the device lying by her feet – "*my* teleporter is the most advanced version yet, and that's why they want it, want *me*. But I'm free from them; I've got the teleporter, and now I need to run with it. They're after me, and they won't hesitate to use you to get to me; therefore, *we* need to run with it." Alison took

Roz's hands and squeezed them. "That's why I came to get you. That's why we're running." Roz opened her mouth but found it too dry to speak. "Please run with me, Roz."

Roz forced herself to take a deep breath. Her head was spinning. Her aunt's words ran round and round her head. It was something, she decided. It was enough, for now. She nodded. Alison sagged in relief.

"I will tell you everything when we're somewhere safe," Alison promised, squeezing her hands one last time before dropping them.

"Okay," Roz replied. "But I'm going to hold you to that."

The edge of Alison's mouth twitched into a hint of a smile, and she nodded.

"I'm going back to the camp," Roz told her. "Are you coming?"

Alison shook her head and looked down at the teleporter.

"The teleporter still isn't working the way it should. I need to work on it." She looked pointedly away from Roz, but Roz could see a twitch of guilt. "Alone."

23

FRIENDS IN LOW PLACES

OLISE PINCHED HER NOSE as she was awoken by a clatter. Sleeping in the cockpit again... The stress must have been getting to her. Bleary-eyed, she saw Phin – equally delusional and with gravity-defying bedhead – stumble in with his arms out for balance.

"The woman!" he exclaimed. "The name is fake, but we – *you* – have tactical implants, right?"

At the mention, the detective, who still sat behind Olise working away, seemed to brighten up and sit forward.

"So we watch those back, find her face. Find any info we can." He waved his arms around. "Cross-reference it. Find her."

"Yes, *yes*," Harsha said, growing excited. "I have some, too, but I wasn't there in time to see her." He turned to Olise.

"I don't save mine," she said. "It all gets deleted."

The detective's reaction almost made her smile: stress. He buried his face in his hands. *You're in over your head*, she thought and bit the inside of her lip. Like it or not, it was in her interests to keep him around now. If he went back to the law, who knew what he would tell them? Yes, they were all in it together now.

"I'm going to choose not to ask why."

"But you know nothing online is really ever deleted, right?" Phin scoffed. "It needs to be saved so it can be processed, even if only for a second."

"You think you could find it?" Harsha asked.

"There's no *find* about it," he replied. "Olise can request it. With a law enforcer's backup, say if it were necessary for solving a crime, they should give it pretty quickly."

Olise met Harsha's gaze uneasily but nodded. A detective with access to her data? To be able to find her online? To be able to find the Thalers? She shuddered. But if it would help Drake, if it would help them reunite before Sven could catch up with them...

"Let's do it."

***

One data request, one fast food breakfast, and one check of Phin's still-running scan later, they were drawing into Buse-a-Thes. As Olise pulled on a jacket and chose a solitary weapon, the two men followed suit.

"You two are staying here," she told them. She pre-empted Harsha's protest. "I'm visiting an old friend for some advice, and that's not illegal. Doesn't mean they'd take kindly to me bringing *you* along."

After docking the ship, they'd taken the shuttle to the closest city to the Thaler estate. Even then, she was going to leave the pair in the city centre before making her own way out to the Thalers. Certain precautions had to be taken. Harsha seemed to remember himself and relented.

Olise always found it weird, after slumming it in some of the most crowded, most disrepaired space stations, to walk on a planet with fresh air, across sprawling grounds of natural greenery into a red brick mansion. It was even weirder without Drake by her side. She just hoped the Thalers meant what they always said – she was family now.

Nobody stopped her on her way in. In fact, she received a few nods and a remark on how she was looking well. These people, for better or worse, cared about her. Guilt that she'd doubted them squeezed her heart.

"He's through here," one said, opening a door for her. Sure enough, sitting by a window drinking tea out of a cup that was comically tiny compared to his large hands was the broad-shouldered patriarch of the family. He beamed when he saw her.

"Olise! I wasn't expecting to see you back so soon, but it's always lovely to have you." He stood, picking up a teapot from a side table, and poured her a drink. As he moved towards two armchairs by an unlit fireplace, she joined him. "How are things? That's some good intel you and Drake gave us. We appreciate it."

"I'm going to start with the bad news, Remo." She sat in the armchair and took a gulp of tea. "Drake is missing and I need your help finding him."

"Missing how?"

"That's the good news," she said. "Well, the better news. The thing causing the attacks isn't a weapon, it's a teleporter."

Uncle Remo was silent for a long moment, shaking his head before taking a drink.

"From anyone else, I'd think it was a joke." He sighed and met her gaze. His grey eyes were striking. Tough, but not unkind. At least, not to her. "So he's teleported off somewhere?"

"I don't know where," she agreed, "but soon, I can give you pictures of the women he was with. Wherever he is, he's out of contact range or his communicator is broken or..." She didn't finish. Uncle Remo looked away. "I'm going to find him," she said instead.

"Of course you are," he replied, holding out a hand. "Because you'll have our support."

"There's a lot of people after this thing, Remo," she said. "A small army stormed the building behind us. Private military types."

"We'll keep our ears open on all fronts," he assured her. "What's your next move?"

"I dunno." She sighed. "I can't sit and sit and wait for info. I'll stay on the move. We have a plan. A route to find each other and leave notes if we get separated." She shook her head. "But if he were in any of those places, he would have found a way to contact me. Or you. Satra Bal's on that list. It's just on the other side of the system. If he couldn't get me, he would have found a Thaler there." She leant back in her chair and closed her eyes for a moment. "I'm not sure who else to trust. We found a kid on the way. Drake told you that. He's good. Too good. I think he's going to need an intervention like me, and god knows I can't do that."

Uncle Remo listened patiently. What was it about the Thalers that made her so compelled to speak her otherwise guarded mind? "But there's a detective." Uncle Remo straightened up. Olise nodded. "Right? He's looking for the innocent woman who also disappeared and also wants to catch this teleporter bitch. We're using him for information, but I wish we didn't need it. I don't know how things will go down when all of this is over. They're miles away, by the way. I didn't bring them here, just in case. Though I think he's smarter than to try and bring the law down on you."

"I trust your judgement," he said as they both stood. "You and my boy are almost unstoppable." *Only when we're together,* she thought. She opened her mouth to mention Sven, then thought better of it. There was only so much they could ask of the Thalers and they had burned that particular bridge. "If you need anything..." Remo continued.

"I know," she replied. In truth, talking with him made her feel like a weight had been lifted from her shoulders. "Thank you."

***

"So yeah," Phin finished, pacing around the small shuttle. He was erratic, jittery, maybe a little frantic. It made Harsha dizzy to watch. "That's how I met Drake and Olise."

Harsha pinched his nose and fought to suppress a sigh.

"Are you *okay*?" he stressed.

"What? Yeah," Phin said. "I've got three assignments due next week, but I've already done one, and I barely speak to my family so no one knows I'm gone. Told my flatmates I'd gone home."

"So nobody knows what you're going through?"

"If I told anyone, I'd have to go home, and I can't leave in the middle of this."

"Yes," Harsha sighed, "yes, you *can*."

"Yeah, I *could*," Phin allowed. "They're not holding me hostage."

"What are you trying to prove?" Harsha asked gently. "I appreciate that you feel involved now and you've lost the 'ignorance is bliss' bubble, but at the end of the day, you're a young civilian with his whole life ahead of him. This is dangerous. There is no shame in turning away."

"There is though," Phin protested. "This is the first time in my life I've done something useful."

"I'm sure that's not true." Harsha reached out to put a hand on Phin's shoulder, but Phin ducked away. "It's not your job to save the galaxy. It's not your *fault* if another space station gets destroyed."

"I know that," Phin protested, though his voice cracked.

"Do you? It doesn't look that way from where I'm standing."

"Plus, Drake and Olise will protect me."

"They'll certainly try, and so will I." Harsha clenched his fists, growing more desperate than he cared to admit. "But you've got to understand there's three of us, only two at the moment. Think of how many people stormed that building. We don't even know who they are."

"Why do you care so much anyway?"

"Phin, do you know how many tragic deaths of kids like you I've witnessed?"

They were interrupted by the shuttle door sliding open. Olise stepped in. She looked between the two of them as they froze in space. Phin could not stop shaking.

"Are you taking drugs?" she asked. "Tell me honestly or I'll rip out your insides and check."

"No, ma'am. Just coffee," he said. "And some energy drinks."

"Three of them." Harsha kicked the neat stack of cans next to Phin's seat and folded his arms.

"Run some laps, kid," Olise said, tossing him out into the streets. She turned to Harsha. "And you, calm down. I could hear you half a block away. You'll bring the law down on us."

"I am the law."

"Yeah, and do you want to be caught associating with me?"

Harsha did not answer. She turned her back on him, leaning in the doorway as Phin obediently ran.

"He'd make a good little soldier," Harsha said, collapsing into the chair with one final deflated sigh.

Olise replied, so quietly, so softly, "That's what worries me."

24

Living to Regret Another Day

"These are not exactly my optimum operating conditions," Drake growled, making a conscious effort for the seventh time to stop clenching his jaw. With Alison's gun in his back, his injuries still very much present and aching, and the looming sense of dread that came with what he was about to do, he was far from the mindset he needed to be in.

It had been a rough night's rest. If you could call it that. He'd slept in small, cold bursts, waking to keep one eye on Alison. Now, it was time to back up his ass-saving promises with action, but Olise wasn't here to save him if it all went south. When added to the fact Alison's scouting yesterday reported the settlement to be a military outpost, things weren't looking fantastic.

Getting up to the outpost had been the easy part. The long grasses and reeds hid them from view and strong winds covered the sounds of their movements. Most importantly, the last thing the Ab were expecting was three undocumented humans coming out of the grassland. None of that would help them any longer.

They came to a stop at the edge of the grass, where a collection of domes made out of dark metal were clustered together. Through the gaps between buildings, he could see their target, a number of small space vessels. They were wide, flat and angular to cut through the air.

Drake shuddered at the memory of the last time he had seen one of them in action.

He took a deep breath, wincing at the pain that came with it, and flexed his hands to get the blood pumping to offset the cold. He rolled his shoulders and remembered the three Cs.

"Count the number of people." He could hear two people chatting idly about sports. His tactical implant showed another one hidden from view, as well as a few in the small base's buildings. "Conditions." It was night. Darkness was pierced only by a few spotlights and the lights from the building. A low freezing fog was rolling in over the sea of reeds, obscuring vision. The ground was firm and dry. It was as good as it was going to get for them.

"Complications."

"Whenever you're ready," Alison snapped. A sneer crept over Drake's face as he forced down the urge to strangle this woman.

"Complications," he began again, with force. *The damned bitch with a gun,* he said in his head. *Roz too*, as someone inexperienced and in need of protection. Any alarms they couldn't see or hidden sensors. His overlay hadn't picked any up, but he had scars to prove that didn't mean there weren't some lying in wait.

He turned, grabbing hold of Alison's gun and pushing it away from him.

"I," he stressed, "am going forward alone. I will call you once it is safe."

"I don't trust you," Alison said.

"The beauty of this plan, Alison" – he pulled himself up to his full height – "is that you don't have to. Feel free to shout or shoot me and bring the Ab down on us."

"Are you threatening me?" she hissed. Drake smiled. It was not his warm, charming smile. It was the smile of a man who knew things.

"Not yet." She did not back down. Neither did he. "I'll signal when it's safe," he repeated.

Glancing once more in both directions, he emerged from the corner of the building and cautiously stepped towards the next one. The port remained quiet. Ahead, there was a shipment being moved and beyond that, several unattended ships. They were small; they wouldn't get them far, but they didn't need far. All they needed was a quick hop to a space station two planets away, and then they could fence it for something better. He glanced back at the two women, almost swallowed by the fog. Roz looked close to fainting. Alison was now doing checks of her own. He waved them over, and they came reluctantly. Drake bit back a comment, turning instead to the stretch ahead and evaluating the Cs again. They could get to a ship easily enough, but they were going to need a distraction to cover them breaking in.

He dug around in his pockets using touch, only to try to find what he needed.

"Any time today," Alison snipped.

"Alison," Roz said, sounding tired. "Please."

"We have all the time in the world right now," Drake replied. "Assuming you don't fuck it up for us." She glared. He glared back until he felt what he was looking for. "Aha!" He pulled out three smooth spheres. Gun under one arm, he twisted the tips of each until they lit up blue. Alison's eyes lit up in recognition.

"What the hell are you doing?"

"Giving us some room to breathe."

He rolled one down the road at a gentle pace. After a few beats, he threw the next one a little farther, then finally, he threw the last as far as he could.

"Let's move."

He didn't wait for the devices to start hissing out smoke to make the visibility even worse or for the strange lights and sounds they would provide. By the time his second device had done its work, Drake had his multi-purpose tool and began fiddling with the lock on the ship's door.

"Dirty criminal," Alison hissed. "How many times have you done that before?"

What exactly would you do without this? he thought bitterly. *Ask nicely for the keys?* But he kept the words to himself. They were too close now to start arguing. Moments later, they were inside. They could hear but not see the Ab guards investigating the disturbance.

"Stay down," he ordered the women. They could still be seen through the vessel's front glass screen if someone made it out of the smoke. He knelt beneath the main driver's console and removed a panel. Taking out a similar but slightly less legal tool to accompany his multi-purpose tool, he prodded the electronics underneath. Tiny LEDs flashed on and off as he did so. It was delicate work, but the steps were carved into his muscle memory. He had a fine touch and years of experience, something Alison was only too keen to pick up on.

"I told you he couldn't be trusted, Roz," she stated. "He does it so easily. Who knows what else he can do?"

"He didn't lie to us," Roz protested but kept her voice low. "He told us he was a smuggler. He told us he could help us escape. Let him help us."

"Do feel free to step off the ship at any point in time and find your own way off this hell planet," Drake offered. "You could fix that fancy teleporter of yours and zip away anywhere."

He replaced one panel and tapped around on the floor until he found a hollow sound. Prying the floor panel open, he began to work again. She said something more, but Drake didn't hear it. *The faster we're off this hellhole, the faster I'm rid of her and back to Olise,* he told himself, though in the pit of his stomach, he knew he wouldn't leave Roz, or the teleporter, not while it was all still to play for. He took a deep breath and focused on the task at hand. One step at a time.

He straightened up, stretching his back and rolling his shoulders.

"Right," he muttered to himself, examining the console. "Engine thrusters, wings..." He noted where all the controls were. He had the nastiest feeling that once they took off, they'd be racing against the clock.

"Strap yourselves in," he ordered. "This will be bumpy."

Alison made another comment that he couldn't quite make out. The force of the lift-off almost knocked him off his feet. It had been a while since he had flown something like this, and this was hardly the situation for a refresher. The smoke would buy them a minute if they were lucky. No amount of distractions would cover the sound of lift-off, but hopefully, they could make it into a hiding spot before they could see them.

Too many lights were flashing. There was too much to focus on: messages, alerts, the enemy. Too much for one person. In the very pit of his stomach, Drake felt a knot. He knew what he would have to do. The weight of what rested on him came fully into view.

"I'm going to live to regret this," he growled. "And that, bitch," he snapped over his shoulder, "*is* a threat."

First came pure speed. They needed as much of a lead as he could give them, and they would need more than that.

When the radio crackled on with the conversation of the stolen ride's sister ships, his automatic translator became too much to handle, and he turned it off. They would have to do this the old-fashioned way: blind.

When orbital weapons fired, he dodged them. When the ships left the ground to follow after, he kept them moving this way and that, out of their range, too difficult to lock onto. His stomach churned as he lunged the ship from side to side. The force of his sharp turns pressed on his body, making it tough to breathe normally. Spots flashed in front of his eyes until old instincts kicked in, and he began breathing in a short, steady pattern. His hands were slick with sweat as he worked the ship's controls. He wiped them on his trousers one at a time, never taking his eyes off the controls.

When the ship broke orbit, he kept them close to the bright planet's atmosphere, keeping the ride bumpy and their next move unpredictable. It gave their pursuers a speed advantage, but that was not all Drake had up his sleeve. As the Ab drew almost neck and neck with them, he pulled up hard, looped over the top of them and dropped back into the atmosphere. The ride was hell. The air knocked out of his lungs once again and rattled him in a way that made his teeth ache. But through watering eyes, he could see it had the desired effect. It was a risky move, reckless even, deadly to an inexperienced pilot, but Drake had been trained by some of the best pilots in the criminal underworld. After all, the Thalers had made their name in smuggling. Ideally, the authorities would never know they'd been there, but everyone knew well enough that some situations required creativity. *That* was where Drake excelled.

From there, well, he couldn't call it smooth sailing exactly, but he had smuggled bigger ships and more exotic cargo than this out of worse places than Agh-Ab-2. A quick hide in the mountains with all technology off again, another on the moon, then an inadvisable shortcut through a dusty asteroid cloud, and they were looking at the empty stretch of space in front of them and freedom.

"Are we safe?" he heard Roz ask as he sank back in his seat.

"We won't be safe until something's done about the teleporter," Alison replied.

Drake rolled his shoulders and tried to relax his strained muscles. His head hurt and his eyes were tired. There would be time to probe Alison later. Time once they were on a different ship, in a different system. He began plotting their course back to civilisation.

The hairs on the back of his neck stood up. Before Roz had the chance to call out, before he saw Alison's reflection in the front window, his body was on the move, taking her to the ground and twisting her arm so that her gunshot fired into the wall and not its intended target. She looked furious. He pinned her down. He could only laugh. If he didn't laugh, he'd scream.

"I think it's time you answer some fucking questions."

25

Somebody to Help

Once Phin was sufficiently tired out, they made the half-day journey to the space station Satra Bal. The detective didn't protest, but Olise could feel his gaze burning the back of her head. Her jaw ached from hours on edge, watching the station grow closer and closer. She went over the plan she and Drake had agreed on in her head. She'd need to figure out where and when to leave signs that she had been there. It was all made harder by the presence of the detective.

As they docked, she left the starting message in a hoarse voice: docking the ship as "Primo Comet", denoting her first stop. If he arrived here after she'd moved on, he could guess where she was headed.

"I didn't know your ship had a name," Phin said.

"It's not Primo Comet," she replied. "That's a message for Drake. Drake nicknames it everything under the sun. Mainly his 'old lady'."

"What now?" Phin asked. It was an innocent question from him, but Olise could feel the detective awaiting an answer, too.

"I'm going to travel around the station and leave some messages. At the bounty hunter bureau, at a couple bars and places like that. You can come or you can do your own thing."

Unlike Revalin, Satra Bal was not large enough to allow ships inside, so she'd detached the shuttle to take them on the longer journeys across the station.

She looked from Phin to Harsha. Phin shrugged. Harsha nodded.

"I'll join," Harsha said. "And make some of my own stops along the way."

Olise grimaced.

"Alright then."

***

Of course, Drake wasn't on Satra Bal. She'd known that from the beginning. It was too close, too easy to contact someone without a communicator. She'd known it, but she still sat dejected in a coffee shop, brooding over a hot drink. The artificial sunlight of the space station had long ago dimmed from a gloomy late afternoon into a gentle evening. Harsha, it appeared, had had an equal amount of success. Roz wasn't here either. No one was shocked.

They were an odd bunch. It took several weird glances from passersby in the space station for Olise to truly appreciate that. For starters, she, the kid and the detective were dressed for three different events, all hunched over their coffees in different states of dishevelment. But that was the least of their differences.

"When I'm waiting for info from a case, I review what I know," Harsha offered unhelpfully. Olise rolled her eyes. Even Phin gave him a withering glare as if they hadn't already done it several times. "Or take my mind off things." This got a similar response.

"We won't find a bounty job we can all agree on," Olise said.

"One night isn't enough time for a job, surely," Harsha said. "What do you do when you're not working?"

"We relax, but never for long," Olise replied. "There's always something more. That doesn't matter."

"You need to take a break or you'll wear yourself out."

"You sound like Drake," she said. "What am I supposed to do in a case like this? It's not money we'll lose out on. It's not a criminal who will get away. It's my *best friend* who might die and a" – she had enough sense to lower her voice – "a you-know-what in the hands of people we don't know."

They'd have to stay overnight on Satra Bal, and the hours before they could leave seemed to stretch ahead of Olise. She wanted to risk it, to leave now, but the ship was old and bound to break down if they pushed her too hard. This was not the time for a breakdown; she wouldn't be able to cope with the detective.

Now, they played the waiting game, and Olise had never been patient. The thought made her stomach churn. She wished they didn't have to be on a space station at all. If the people behind the attacks targeted Satra Bal next, would there be any warning, any signs? If Phin was right about the teleporter being behind the attacks… She remembered how quickly Drake and the women had disappeared from the warehouse and shuddered. Then again, Revalin *hadn't* been destroyed. There was still far too much they didn't understand for her liking.

"It will do us all good to sleep in proper beds on solid ground," Harsha said. "Phin has homework to do and a mother to call."

"I keep telling you," Phin protested, "she'll be more suspicious if I call her out of the blue than if I don't."

"Do your homework, kid," Olise told him, tossing her empty cup with practised care into the nearest bin. "And if you can sleep without worrying about Roz," she said to Harsha, "then fine, we'll stop somewhere for the night."

She shivered at the thought. The last thing Olise needed was to be alone. The itch for the familiar drug sticks had started small, but now it was crawling all over her body. She kept asking herself what Drake would do, and the answer was always so clear: help people, take care of himself, take care of *her*. But it was painfully apparent that she was not Drake. Drake would know how to manage Phin. He'd know how to negotiate with Harsha. He could make the best of this, pulling in old contacts, making new ones. *He* was the people person, the man with the plan. She was just the muscle.

These were the thoughts that troubled her, the path she trod round and round in circles as they found a cheap motel and split into three rooms. She sat on the edge of a bed full of lumps, looking out at the garish station. She'd come to terms with the fact Harsha would be reporting back to the powers that be. She hoped Phin was returning to some kind of normalcy. So what was she doing?

"What would Drake do?" she muttered again. He believed in her, more than she believed in herself.

Suck it up and reach out to contacts without him? He'd believe she could pull it off, but he wouldn't want her to if it put her at risk, or Phin, and it *would* put her at risk. Stay in this room alone and sleep? Not if it meant returning to her addictions and ruining all her hard work. Go out on the town and drink away her troubles? That was just another of her bad habits that he was trying to break.

So what *would* he do, in a position where everything seemed so stacked against her? It all came back to the fact she was not him. So... what did *she* want to do? She bit her lip. She wanted to do something, wanted to help someone. She wanted to be someone who, when she found Drake again, he would be proud of. Maybe she still could. Surely, there was a job one person could do in a place like this.

Nodding to herself, she pulled on her jacket and opened her door to find Phin outside it, pacing. He jumped when he saw her.

"Everything alright?" she asked.

"Yeah— I— Well— I—" He took a deep breath.

"Have you finished your assignment?"

"Not yet," he admitted. "I was hoping for a break. Hoping you were going out to do something and I could help. I *can* help," he stressed.

She waved him inside and shut the door softly.

"You know," she began uncertainly. "Someone would miss you if you died." He did not respond. "You don't throw yourself around like you're invincible, but you do throw yourself around. You'd have jumped at any job I suggested right now, wouldn't you?"

He hung his head and sat down on the end of her bed heavily.

"That's all Harsha is trying to say," she said. Never in her life had she thought she'd be standing up for a cop. "Probably has kids of his own. Definitely has mistakes of his own."

She sat next to him. "You don't know us, kid, or what we've been through, but trust us. We just want you to live better than we have."

She looked away, at a loss for words at her own speech.

"Sometimes I wonder if you're too perceptive for your own good. You understand how bad things are too well, how big the universe is, how small each of us is." She sighed. "It's a lot of worry to carry alone."

She glanced from Phin to the city, back to Phin. Maybe she didn't need to go hunting in the city for someone to help. She stood and stretched.

"Anyway, you're out of luck," she said. "I was only going for a walk and a snack. But you can come with anyway if you'd like."

Phin looked at her and, for almost the first time since she'd known him, smiled.

***

"I'm sorry, my hands are tied. You have to hand over the case. It's not our jurisdiction any more." Harsha understood the words. He understood why the rules were there, he did, but hearing those words had never been easy. They weren't easy when he was a fresh-faced detective learning the harsh truths of being on the force for the first time. They weren't easy hearing them on the other side of the table, as a father pressing for *something* to be done about his daughter's case. And they certainly weren't easy now, thinking of Roz and everything that had happened.

"Leave it, Harsha," his colleague said. *"Please. This isn't the same as Kala's case. It's bigger than any of us. Stay out of trouble."*

Harsha made no promises. In fact, he barely grunted a goodbye. He tossed his communicator on his bed and flopped down on top of it, flexing his hand restlessly. *Out of our jurisdiction.* It didn't sit well with him. They all lived in the Interstellar Alliance of Homeworlds. Space stations were being *destroyed.* If it wasn't his jurisdiction to follow the case out of the star system, surely it had never properly been his to begin with. Was it only his jurisdiction after his station was destroyed? No, this wasn't a normal case. It wasn't as simple as closing up the files and handing them over to his counterpart. Not after everything he'd learned. *And all the gaps that remain.* He was curious, he was frustrated, but most of all, he was *angry*. Simple as that.

Maybe it was the bounty hunter's influence. Maybe it was the pressure of the case. Maybe it was all just unresolved trauma, but the more that the law refused to help him help people, the more Harsha began to feel like it hindered more than it helped. Olise could do anything.

She may get in trouble for it, but she could be out there on the ground. Drake had been quick enough to jump into the fray to help Roz.

That could have been me, he thought. *If I hadn't wasted time calling it in.*

He rubbed his face and groaned. *The rules are in place for a reason*, he told himself. But why did following the rules mean Roz had to suffer?

It wasn't fair. Any of it. Maybe it never would be. But he couldn't just stop being a detective any more than he could walk away from Roz now... could he? He shook his head at the thought, but a small voice said, "There's a whole galaxy of options out there". Maybe bounty hunter wasn't a fit for him. Maybe mercenary wasn't either. Maybe the whole god-damned universe was going mad and taking him with it. He closed his eyes, letting out one long sigh. But... maybe it was time for a change.

***

STRIKE OUT INTO THE GREAT UNKNOWN.

Phin felt very small standing in front of the large metal wall – the entrance to the space station – where the bold, red text was painted. It was not the first time. It wouldn't be the last, either, but it did feel different. The thought of going back to anything resembling normal now was so foreign. He was okay with that, but the more Harsha and Olise spoke, the more he wasn't sure he should be. Was he overly attached to the people who, in reality, had *kidnapped* him? Was he really this desperate for a purpose? He sighed. Maybe. His phone was still empty of any new messages. But what else could he expect when he so often fell out of contact with others?

"What are you thinking about?" Olise asked, interrupting his downward spiral. She, too, was looking at the lettering.

"Oh, you know," he said. "Life, death, the universe."

She did not push him for more. Maybe she didn't know what to say. She looked over her shoulder, then turned to him.

"What do we do next?" he asked.

"Drake and I made a plan of how to search for each other. A pattern of places to stop, leading outwards."

"So we follow it?"

"Until there's a better option." She chewed her lip absently. "And keep off space stations as much as we can," she added after a moment. She looked around again.

"You keep looking over your shoulder," he observed. "What's worrying you?"

"I don't know Satra Bal very well," she said curtly, avoiding his gaze. Phin followed her gaze as she looked at their surroundings more slowly. "It's crowded."

Phin nodded. He didn't have many space stations to compare it to but crowded certainly seemed to fit the bill. For a long time, Satra Bal had been the centre of the inhabited universe. It had been the first joint settlement and shared home of different species. As more and more species had discovered the interstellar community, more and more had been added to the space station, inside and out. When he looked closely, Phin thought he could see where one layer of development ended and another began. It was remarkable, but he could see why the many crisscrossing pathways and floods of people would make Olise nervous.

"Is it... about Sven, as well?" he asked. She shut her eyes.

"It's always about Sven," she replied softly. She took a deep breath. "I guess, more accurately, it's about Drake. I want him to be safe. I want us both to be safe, preferably. Half our friendship has been me fucking up and Drake trying to protect me, anyway. Sven's no different."

"I can watch your back again, like at the party," he offered, "if you want," he added hastily.

Olise seemed to consider it for a moment, then nodded. She reached around to her back and removed a small pin. It was barely noticeable on her jacket.

"I tend to keep one on me," she explained. "I do a lot of scouting by myself, and I prefer that Drake has something to refer to if I go missing."

She held it out, and he tapped his communicator to it.

"You seem like a good team," he noted. "How did you meet?"

"In prison."

When he choked on air, she only raised an eyebrow.

"We told you we're not good role models."

"For mafia stuff?"

"Drake? Yeah. Me?" She grimaced. "Nothing as noble."

"Drake said you were ex-military," he prompted tentatively. She straightened up and stiffened. "Was it related to the war near Nonke?"

She gave a curt shake of the head.

"Not as recent as that," she replied. "That's the only recent war in the *inner* systems. There are plenty of little wars in the outer systems. Too many to report on in here. The gist is the same as the Maeh belt war. People arguing over who found what first. It gets... ugly quickly." She shut her eyes and seemed to force herself to take a breath. "I don't like to talk about it," she finished.

"But you help people now," he said.

"We help some."

"Are you happy?"

The question seemed to stump her.

"Yeah," she said after a moment. "There's something about Drake... I'm a lesbian, so it's not romantic, but he... completes me in a way no one else ever has."

"He's a strange guy," Phin said without thinking. "Not what I expected from mafia."

Olise smiled.

"You should meet the rest of the family." She looked at him. "I didn't have anyone, but they gave me somewhere to belong. Some days, I don't think I deserve it, but I am trying. You're not alone in this, kid, and you're not the only person who feels the way you do."

Phin's chest tightened. It was all he could do to nod and hold back tears.

"Come on, let's get something to eat."

26

MESSAGE IN A BOTTLE

Roz should have felt something at the sight of her aunt taking aim at Drake, or at him tackling her in response, but the truth was that she had nothing left to give.

As both parties on the floor, furious and rabid, looked up at her, she could only bring herself to sit, put her head in her hands.

"Time for more answers," she stated. "You promised me the rest of the answers when we were safe. We're safe now, so give me answers."

"We're not safe, not while he—" Alison began, but Roz cut her off.

"We weren't safe in the hour we were alone in the warehouse. We weren't safe in the middle of nowhere on that fucking planet. We're not safe now. Will we ever be safe?"

"We will once this is done."

"And how long will that take?" Roz said, looking up. "You're asking too much of me. You've dragged me into this. You're not yourself, Alison. You attack Drake at any opportunity when all he's done is help."

"I need you to bear with me."

"I can't," Roz said. She grew queasy but pressed on. "Not again. I need to know why my life has been turned upside down. Give me something, *anything*."

Alison turned to Drake.

"Get off me."

Drake obeyed with no small amount of reluctance. He kept her weapon, and when he moved away, he moved towards Roz. She felt relieved, then guilty. How could she trust this stranger more than her own flesh and blood? *Easily*, a voice in her whispered. *She left you all alone.*

There wasn't much space they could put between them. The cockpit they were in contained two seats in front – a pilot and a copilot – and a bench that Roz sat on, with buckles, facing the door. At the back was another door. The entire ship was small, so there couldn't be much behind it. At a guess, one set of facilities for a long-distance journey.

"I didn't drag you into this," Alison said finally, dusting herself down. "Not deliberately. The people after the teleporter, after us, are my employer."

"The research company?" Roz asked. Alison grimaced and nodded.

"They *were* a research company. We had various projects for various investors. At first, it was fine. It was normal." Alison set her gaze firmly on the floor. "Two years ago, it was bought over by a private military, Parare Facie. Initially, it didn't seem so bad. They had a lot of money and resources to pump into all the projects, but one in particular. Mine."

"The teleporter," Drake said, arms folded.

"We made some *amazing* strides with their support." Her voice was hoarse and her eyes sparkled with tears. "We thought we were going to change the universe. But..." Roz held her breath. "It quickly became apparent that they weren't ever going to make the teleporter public."

"Isn't that normal?" Drake said dryly. "So they can sell it off to people?"

"Not when you work for a private military. They are *not* going to sell this to anyone who asks. With the teleporter, they have the power to decide the outcomes of conflicts galaxy-wide. It's a weapon of mass destruction in sheep's clothing. It *could* be used to move doctors to patients instantly. It *could* be used to support supply chains and move supplies to those who need them. Some people would do that, but some would use it for assassination and theft, and realistically, selling this on the black market, they'll make more money and they'll supply more of those people."

"Oh, so you're saying you have morals," Drake said.

"I didn't set out to make a tool for assassinations and war. That wasn't what was *advertised*. What are *you* doing here, anyway? Are you getting paid a big bounty for this?"

"No, actually," Drake said, voice filled with ice. "Some of my family were *killed* in the attacks."

Alison winced but didn't say anything. Her mouth curled as if she was tasting something sour.

"So you ran away with it," Roz changed the subject. "The teleporter."

"Not intentionally. When the truth got out of what they were trying to achieve, they had to threaten our families to keep us in line. They've been threatening *you*. A few of us were trying to find a way to escape or to get information about the teleporter out. We never got a chance to execute those plans." Alison put her head in her hands.

"One day, during a test run in the middle of a field, the teleporter blew up – not unlike the destruction of the space stations. I saw three colleagues die before I passed out. When I woke up, I was alone, covered in other people's blood and in a different star system... with the teleporter." She shook her head. "How many others are alive, I still don't know, but I can only hope they were moved elsewhere and not left to pay the consequences. I knew it was my chance to run. They had no idea where I was, and no idea where to start looking, which bought me some time. But I also knew" – she looked up at Roz pleadingly – "that unless I got back in touch with them immediately and returned to them with the teleporter, they'd come after you.

"I made some tweaks to the teleporter and used it to try and get to you, but I got shot all over the galaxy. Finally, I arrived at a station for the Inter-Planet Express and thought that was my best bet to get to you. It got me to Revalin, but it seemed I was always a few steps behind you and the police."

"So the space stations—" Roz stammered. "It wasn't you... was it?"

Alison shook her head, but it brought little comfort to Roz.

"I didn't set foot on those stations," she confirmed. "My employer has everything they need to make a new teleporter," she continued, "but not the knowledge of how to fix what went wrong. While they rebuilt an imperfect one, I was figuring out how to fix mine. It's still not fixed. That's why we ended up here, but at least it doesn't destroy anything."

"Which brings us to the big question," Drake said. "Why did they destroy the space stations they did?"

"You know our codes?" Alison said with a single, haunted laugh.

Roz's stomach dropped.

"Our games?" she whispered.

Alison's face was grim as she nodded.

"You used to leave me messages on the radio. When I was closer."

"But that, that was *years* ago!" Roz felt dizzy, putting her head back in her hands.

Alison's voice cracked.

"When I first started working with them, when things were good, I told them all about you, about *us*. I was so *proud—*" She took a shaky breath. "When I disappeared... They listened to your show and took a gamble that you were leaving me messages again."

"So it *is* my fault these space stations were destroyed."

"No," Drake and Alison replied in unison. *That must be the first thing they've agreed on,* Roz thought distantly.

"I don't think they intended to destroy those stations," Alison added hastily. "Bad for business, if nothing else. They just haven't figured out how to fix it. The damage the teleporter causes seems to happen as it leaves the space. They wouldn't know they'd destroyed the space station until they were already gone. I have the most advanced teleporter in the galaxy."

"Then we need to destroy it," Drake insisted. "And the plans. Before they figure it out."

Alison scoffed.

"You can't turn back technology," she said. "You can't forget a discovery. Your friend figured out it was a teleporter? They won't be the last. The only way any of this ends is by levelling the playing field. If everyone has a teleporter, a working teleporter, and ways to detect them, it'll ease the trouble for a while."

"That's it?" Drake demanded. "That's your grand plan? Give it to anyone who asks? What about the people coming after you? What about Roz?"

Roz perked up. Her head hurt, but she understood enough.

"Yeah," she said. "What about me? They don't seem to be the kind to take this lying down."

"You think they want to risk being identified as the people who caused the attacks?"

"They could kill you both without that," Drake said. "There are a lot of good hitmen out there."

"What's your idea then? With your vast technical understanding and knowledge of the intricacies of the situation."

"They don't want the news made public, we make it public."

"You think that will stop them from trying to kill us?"

"No," Drake admitted. "But I think between my mafia connections and Roz's detective connections, we should be able to protect her until the galactic community does something."

"So that's it then?" Alison said. "Safety in the arms of a dirty criminal and useless law enforcement?"

"Make a better offer, then," Roz said. Alison stared at her. For a moment, she looked hurt.

"Give me time," was all she said. Roz shrugged, sinking back in her chair and shutting her eyes. After a moment, she heard Alison go through the door in the back of the cockpit, slamming it behind her.

27
Personal Satisfaction

Olise awoke feeling like death. She'd slept too deeply, too long, as she always did in a proper bed. Her shower didn't wake her up, though she had to admit a proper shower was hard to beat. She grumbled as she pulled her leather jacket on, feeling uncomfortable. Just... off. At least today, she could do something, rather than sit and feel useless.

She glanced over her messages as she went down to the motel lobby. It was an empty and unpleasant place to be, dressed in dark oranges and browns. Worn sofas sat by windows looking out onto the street and a battered reception desk watched them. A questionable-looking vending machine hummed in a wall that seemed to hum with it. She ordered a shitty coffee from it and waited for Harsha and Phin to appear.

She was trying to figure out how far away Drake must be if he hadn't been in contact yet. His communicator could be broken – it had happened before, and who knew what the teleporter might have done to it – but even if it was, there were ways of sending messages. Mutual contacts, their plan. But those relied on him being in civilisation, which, given the statistics of it, was only a very small part of the universe. Worse still, he could be a prisoner or he could be... dead. She froze for a long moment until a fellow motel resident tapped her on the shoulder, pointed out that her coffee was ready, and asked her to move.

She sulked on a sofa and tried to wash away the bitter taste in her mouth. Surely he wasn't dead. That was not how the great Drake Thaler passed on. Her only small comfort was that Roz, too, was silent. Whoever that woman was, she seemed to want Roz alive too. All Drake needed was a second to adjust and defend himself, even with the blood he'd left behind.

Phin came down, looking as done in as her, followed by Harsha. Two coffees later, they sat in a row, heaving heavy sighs.

"Good night's sleep all round, then," Harsha said.

Both she and Phin only grunted in response.

"As soon as we're out of orbit, we can put the ship on autopilot and relax," Olise replied, standing and stretching. "Let's move."

The space station was crowded. The damn things always seemed to be when Olise was in a bad mood. She shouldered her way through the throng until someone finally pushed back. She stopped, blinking out of her moody haze and looked up. In front of her was a crowd of at least a hundred people packed at the entrance to the port. A departure board was lit up in red.

"The port's closed?" she exclaimed. "What do they mean *closed*? Thousands of ships pass through here every day; they can't *close*."

"Apparently, they can." Harsha tapped her shoulder, showing her a holographic screen with a news article.

"No ships in or out until further notice," she read, heart sinking. "Bullshit." She scanned the article for an explanation. "Due to recent attacks," she scoffed. "Due to recent attacks, they want to keep us all here as sitting targets."

"They're trying," Harsha said through gritted teeth. "To control the situation. Keep your voice down."

"It won't even help," Phin said, voice hollow. "Not against the—"

"Both of you," Harsha said. Grabbing them both by their jackets, he began the long trudge free of the crowds. As they pulled into a quiet side street, he pinched the bridge of his nose.

"Alright, so what's our next move?" he asked, looking between them. "If it's true, and this place is in danger, we need to move. If it's false, we still can't waste time."

"We don't have any reason to believe this station is a target," Phin said. "All previous attacks happened after Roz's broadcasts. Since she stopped, there haven't been any."

Harsha nodded.

"They were after Sabine," he agreed. "They thought Roz was tied in that way. So unless they're here—"

"They're not," Olise interrupted. "Drake would have found a way to get in touch if he was."

"And if they've abandoned him somewhere? Or have a gun to his head? Or killed—"

"I get the point." She gritted her teeth. "But we know for a fact their you-know-what doesn't destroy space stations, so the three of them aren't the risk."

"That doesn't mean the people chasing them won't stop here," Phin said. "They must still be looking."

"So have they fixed their teleporter too or have they decided to lay off the attacks for another reason?"

"We need information and we need off this rust bucket," Olise said, thinking fast. "Harsha, find out what the local law knows. See if you can get us some kind of permission to leave. I'll do the same but with some friends. And Phin." She paused. Was she seriously going to tell him to go do his homework during a potentially deadly lockdown? "Go back to the shuttle. Be our man in the chair. You helped me and Drake at the party. I need you to watch and listen to everything you can as I go." Both men seemed happy with this.

"I thought you couldn't call in favours," Harsha said.

"I don't want to," she replied. "But we're running out of options and... I owe it to Drake to try."

"Be careful," Phin piqued up. She smiled and glanced over her shoulder at him as she set off.

"You too."

In truth, she was more scared now than she had been in quite some time, but she had meant what she said. She owed it to Drake. Whatever trouble may come of it was even more reason to find Drake quietly.

Finding her nearest set of stairs, she began descending into the belly of the beast.

The lower levels of a space station were invariably more crowded, cheaper and generally grim. The maintenance noises were loud, the environmental controls poor because of the sheer number of machines, pipes, and cables, and it was always home to types like her.

Some buildings, like the emergency services or bounty hunter bureau, extended across all floors of the space station. The building she was looking for was not. Bounty hunter bureaus existed to advertise jobs and exchange information. They followed strict rules and kept the whole operation above board. This left a gap in the market for those willing to be more... flexible with the law. These covert information bureaus were unique yet made up a beautifully mismatched set of sisters across the galaxy. She had never been to one of them on Satra Bal, but she would know it when she saw it.

It was more obvious than most today; a long queue of people stood outside what was decorated as a restaurant, agitated. A restaurant was a common cover for information brokers, happy to work under the table:

it was a place people could come and go regularly, a place where they could stay for extended periods of time, all without raising suspicion. Plus, the background noise of music, a kitchen, and other patrons were good at covering sensitive conversations. Clucking her tongue, she joined the queue at the back. It seemed she was not the only person needing a way out of the space station today, though the more sensible among them did not acknowledge it. Bouncers watched the line, and more than one person was thrown out for speaking too loudly about their true business. One even made the poor decision of bringing law enforcement, who questioned each of them in turn to find a crack in the facade.

"They do the best vegan pasta I've eaten off-planet," Olise said, shrugging. "My friend is already inside, too."

The police officer was more than tired, she knew. He was well aware of what this place was, he *had* to be, and even more aware that if he found evidence, which he wouldn't, a legal case would never go through. Still, he did his due diligence and went inside, only to be escorted back outside a short twenty minutes later by the genial manager.

The manager looked along the queue and sighed, though when he spotted Olise, he smiled and paused. She looked behind her and saw no one. She did not recognise the man, but that didn't mean he wasn't aware of her. Should she leave now in an attempt to escape notice? With the people who knew her, there was a fifty/fifty chance of it being good or bad. The man disappeared back inside as Olise's brain kicked into overdrive. She'd known what she was risking when she came down here, and in part, the damage was already done. As a text rolled in from Harsha saying he'd had no luck with the law, it left her with no choice.

Nothing seemed to have come of it as people came and went, many looking even more frustrated than when they entered. Slowly, Olise made her way down to the front. She did not let her guard down, but neither did she stop thinking about who might be inside. She noted her exits and the weapons the bouncers were using and the three Cs. Count: as she reached the window into the dim establishment, she saw at least eight staff. Conditions: the city was crowded, and she'd been noticed. Complications: she was alone, for one. Alone and not the people person of her dynamic duo. A message from Phin popped up on her screen: *I've got your back.*

I really hope so, was all she could think.

When, at last, she entered the building, a restaurant crammed with both tables and people, she was led into a small booth in the corner with a man with his back to them. When she stopped in her tracks, the bouncer picked her up and pushed her down into a seat, then slid in next to her, trapping her inside. Olise went cold and froze. This was it.

"Of all the people to have come here for my help today," Sven said in one long, smooth drawl, "yours, my dear Tenna, must be the sweetest."

Olise didn't say anything. *Couldn't* say anything, even as the mention of her old, fake identity made her flinch. This man, with a wide, toothy grin, made every cell in her body scream.

"Where's your eye candy?" he asked.

"Busy charming the police and politicians," she lied.

"Need a way off this joint so badly?" He leaned closer. "Why?"

"We have more important shit to be doing."

"Mhm?" He nodded along, eyes wide and hand under his chin. "Yes, Gren told me you paid him a visit, and I've seen you walking around with that detective. Maybe we should invite him to join us? You're not the only people who have an interest in the destruction of the space stations." Olise closed her eyes momentarily. Of course Sven, or the mafia family he belonged to, were involved somehow. How much did they know? What lengths would they go to find out more? "So really, is any of that more important than catching up with an old friend?"

"As I recall," she said, "you owe us a favour."

"Nuh, uh-uh." He shook his head without taking his eyes away from hers. "You've spent too long with the Thalers. My *brother* owed *Drake* a favour, and as *I* remember, you killed him."

"A stray bullet."

"Mhm, a stray bullet." He leant back in his seat. "Look, Tenna, I'm not one to hold grudges, you know me." He held his arms out wide. "But I think we both know lines were crossed that day."

"You can't stop us."

"No," he allowed. "But there is no 'us' right now, is there, Tenna?" He smiled once more. "I don't know where your boy is, but I do know he's not here."

"So?" *Go big or go home.* That was what Drake's voice in her head said now. "You won't get much from just me. *If* you can get me."

"Zef," he said, clicking his fingers. Olise saw a flash of dark metal, no, a *gun,* felt its cold barrel shoved into her ribs. She started to turn, started to reach for her own weapon, but before she could react, the bouncer fired. The world tipped. Her vision blurred as she choked and coughed up blood. Before her hand could get to her gun, the bouncer wrenched it out of its holster.

"Not much," Sven allowed. "Except for a little personal satisfaction."

28

MAYBE HE'S FRIENDLY

Roz stirred from her sleep slowly and unfurled stiff limbs from the ball she'd curled up in. A jacket lay over her. Drake's. He was still hunched over a holographic screen and a collection of tools in the way he had been when she had curled up. He was trying to fix his communicator, and behind a locked door, Alison was trying to fix the teleporter. It was almost as though no time had passed at all, but her watch and the shuttle's navigation readings told her that was not the case. It had been ten hours, almost eleven.

She sat up, clutching the jacket around her shoulders and looking out the window at space. It almost seemed like they'd made no progress there too. However, slowly but surely, they were drawing closer. *There's a metaphor for my life in there somewhere,* she thought, rubbing her eyes.

"Hey," she said, voice rough. The gentle noise of tinkering stopped.

"Hey. Are you feeling any better?" Drake asked. "Having some sleep? And some answers."

"I feel *something*," she replied. "That's better than the last few days."

"I'm sorry you got wrapped up in all this," he said.

"Why? There's nothing you could have done to stop it. Or me, apparently." She put her hand to her head. "I'm just glad you're here now."

Either he didn't know how to respond to it or he had nothing to say. She pulled out a bottle of water and some more rations from Alison's abandoned bag. It was supposedly a different meal than she'd eaten on the planet, but the rehydrated food was as spongy and tasteless as the last. At least it satiated her hunger, and a proper, hot meal was yet another thing she could look forward to in the not-too-distant future.

"How are you getting on?" she asked, nodding at his communicator. "Any luck?"

He sighed again, sinking back into his chair.

"No."

He set his tools down and put his feet on the ship's console. "I need a space station to buy something or a space station to send a message."

"I could try," she offered. "To fix your communicator, I mean. I've never worked on one of these, but I used to tinker with simpler devices, like little radios, when I was younger. I was going to try to fix mine when we had the chance."

"Be my guest," he said, passing it to her. "I would appreciate it. But don't worry if you can't. We're seven hours away from the space station, and I'm a big boy. I can survive without it for a little longer."

"Seven hours is nothing after the last few days," she agreed.

"Tell that to your aunt," Drake snorted. Roz glanced over her shoulder at the locked door.

"Do you think she's up to something?" she asked.

Drake shook his head.

"I dunno," he replied, looking up at her. His eyes were a startling grey, but she could not understand his expression. "I don't trust her. Sorry," he added. He rubbed his face, groaning. "I want to be back in civilisation."

There was a long moment of silence. Roz turned Drake's communicator over in her hands and then pulled out her own and compared the two, pondering them.

Drake seemed to brighten up and took his feet off the console. He looked back at her with a grin on his face.

"What kind of radio does the radio DJ listen to?"

Roz, too, smiled. She joined him at the front of the ship.

"Anything local," she replied. "If I'm this far away from home, I may as well see what's different."

"Also translated as: I do not need to hear yet more generic radio. Sounds good to me," he replied. "Do you travel often?"

"In the system around Nonke, before the war," she said. "It was good for work. But when the war kicked off, it wasn't safe to leave the system. When I moved to Revalin, I just... never got settled in."

She gazed off into the middle distance for a moment before snapping back to attention. "What about you?"

"All I do is travel," he said. "And that's the way I like it. I stop by the family home on Buse-a-Thes sometimes, but the truth is, I've always been restless. There's a great big galaxy out there and not enough time to see it. One day, though, the plan is to retire to Porba."

"World of eternal sunsets," she said.

"I just think it's neat," he replied. "So does Olise."

"You're close?"

"She's my best friend, a member of the family now, really."

"Must be nice," she said, lip trembling a little.

"It is."

There was a long moment's silence before the radio crackled to life. They both pulled a face at the first channel that played – the Ab patriotic songs were hardly for recreational listening. The second was a little better. Although their translators couldn't keep up with the speedy and slightly distorted talking of the presenters, the music was good.

"We can do better," Roz said.

Drake hummed in agreement and switched to one filled with canned laughter. Roz stuck her tongue out, but Drake burst out laughing.

"You can get the talk show of the universe all the way out here?" he said. "Man, we can definitely do better than this."

He kept giggling as he switched again. What came on next made her ears perk up – a morse-code-esque signal.

"Crap again," Drake said. "This is why I don't come out into the outer clusters."

"Wait!" she said, stopping him before he could change it. "This is fun too. Decoding Olbasc speak is one of my hobbies."

"You like solving puzzles, huh?" He waved an arm. "Be my guest."

She jumped into the seat nearest to him and, with a wave of her hand, brought up a holographic screen that he could see. There were dials along the bottom, a moving wave following the signal in the top left, and an array of pieces to drag and drop on the far right.

She watched it for a moment before quickly dragging two pieces into place.

"It's a distress signal," she said. "Easy to spot because they want to be found."

She listened for another moment.

"Hijacked?" she said uncertainly, dragging another block into place. It fit. "Hijacked ship. Hostage situation."

She narrowed in on one part of the signal that repeated over and over again and began to adjust the dials.

"Coordinates."

Drake moved to input them into the console's map.

"Eight-ettah-seventy-four," she read off one by one, "by zan-two-zan by seven-two-three-three—"

"Tan?" Drake finished. Roz looked at him, growing cold. "Those are our coordinates," he said. Both of them turned to face the door that Alison had hidden behind. "Has anyone responded?"

Roz's eyes darted from side to side, desperately trying to focus though panic was setting in. Before she could answer, Drake was on his feet, moving towards the door Alison was in and picking the lock.

"Do you mind?" Alison began, leaping to her feet, but before she could do anything, Drake caught her by her coat and pinned her to the wall.

"What the HELL do you think you're doing?" he demanded. "A distress signal in Ab space after we STOLE from them?" Alison did not respond. For the first time, she looked afraid. *Things have really got away from you, haven't they?* Roz thought with a mixture of pity and frustration. "Who did you think was going to answer? Are you trying to get us all killed?"

"Drake!" Roz called, though it was not in protest of his actions. Feeling had drained from her. Never mind the signal, never mind the map. At the front viewscreen, a ship was heading straight towards them, and it was bigger and faster than them. One step closer to normality and now a whole lot further away. *Eva*, she thought, *if I get through this, I deserve to message Eva.*

"Someone's found us."

29

Cold Hands

Olise had not missed the feeling of dying. Yet as she sat, frozen in the moment in front of a grinning Sven, she couldn't help but feel some relief. This had been coming for so long. The consequences of their actions had hung over both her and Drake for years, and now... now it was time to sink or swim.

The first thing she did was click an emergency button on the side of her communicator in her pocket. It sent a brief warning to Drake. She could only hope it would get through to his communicator before anyone could get to him. Sven sent a warning of his own, taking a picture of her stunned state.

She looked around the restaurant for help and found none. Everyone who knew what was good for them was carrying on as if nothing was happening. She swore but knew that a past version of her would have done exactly the same. She searched the table for anything she could use as a weapon, but the flickering candle in the middle was an electronic fake and, she realised with dismay, there was no cutlery or crockery to use. *Fuck.*

A few seconds later, the only thing she could ever thank the military for automatically kicked in: medical implants. The left side of her torso cramped and tightened as they began automatically pumping drugs into her bloodstream in an attempt to stabilise her. Her pain began to subside, though she could still feel the wound throb. She knew the implant would be clotting her blood, but there was still too much blood over her hands. It could not do anything for the puncture in the lung, though, and she wheezed and coughed and rasped.

"One out of two ain't bad," Sven said. "And you'll make the perfect bait for Drake. Assuming you still have your fancy implants to keep you alive."

"You think he'll—" Her whole chest heaved with the action of speaking. Her vision spun. "He won't come."

"There are a lot of things I can say about Drake," he said. "And loyal, to a *fault*, is one. He'll come and he won't have the Family backing him up on this one."

"Bold," she panted. She tasted blood. She could not finish her sentence. Black spots clouded her vision. God, maybe this was where she died. Sven only laughed. *No*, she thought. Today was not her day to die. Not here. Not like this. Not without Drake. She tried to come up with a plan, any plan, but every time she thought she had something, the thought slipped out of her reach. Every cell in her body begged for a fight, but if she had any chance of surviving this, she had to move as little as possible and let her implants do their work until she could get medical attention. She hated putting her trust in those things, in people who weren't Drake, but this time, her faith was not misplaced. She fainted in and out of consciousness, but she jerked awake when the cavalry arrived.

It was Harsha who kicked down the door and started shooting. He didn't miss a single target; Phin must have told him their positions. Olise ducked behind the bouncer, and when he went limp, she knew this was her chance. She shoved him and willed her legs to move, kicked an adrenaline implant into gear. She staggered, still choked for breath.

Her legs gave way, and she hit the floor, but her fighting instincts took over. She grabbed her weapon back from the bouncer and raised it but didn't shoot. The restaurant was in chaos. Other customers fled, forcing her to cower as they passed over her with no regard for her. She couldn't see Harsha or their enemies. She should drag herself into some kind of cover, she knew, but it took everything she had to stay awake.

When the crowds cleared, the remaining threat had gone with them. All that remained in the restaurant with her and Harsha were the dead. Harsha rushed towards her, slung her arm around his shoulder and hauled her up. With what little energy she had left, she searched the faces of the dead for Sven but didn't find him. He was gone. Of course he was. Together, she and Harsha staggered out of a fire escape where Phin was waiting with the shuttle.

"Almost there," he assured her as Harsha dumped her and returned to the restaurant. Sirens were drawing close. "Just stay with us a little longer."

She couldn't catch her breath enough to answer. She caught a glance of herself in the restaurant window. She looked like death, one side of her soaked in blood and more running from her mouth down her chin.

Phin kept talking as they sped away from the restaurant. Olise barely heard him. She fought to stay conscious and lost.

***

The Satra Bal detective heaved a heavy sigh. Harsha would have felt sorry for him if his thoughts were not preoccupied with Olise. He sat in cuffs in a barren metal interrogation room across from some local law enforcement.

"This is some mess," the detective admitted.

"Sorry about that," Harsha managed.

"Your precinct says you're not here on their orders."

"They're correct." There was no point in lying. "There was no time. I'm still working on the case."

"Not by their records." The detective put his head in his hands. "What you've done here won't make a difference. Not when Sven got away, not when half a dozen people could take his place."

"It *did* make a difference because my friend is alive and in a hospital, and she's a vital piece of this puzzle."

"By all accounts," the detective continued, not acknowledging what he'd said. "They started the fight. Because of that, because you're law enforcement and they're criminals, they're not likely to press charges, and you can probably cry self-defence. But Harsha." The detective looked up at him, expression cold and serious. "You're going to lose your job for this."

Harsha nodded. The more time had passed, the more he knew that would be the only outcome. Until he could solve the case, at least.

"What's driving you, man? This clearly isn't just another case. Did you lose someone in the attacks?"

"Not in the attacks, no."

"You need to find a way to let this go. What you're doing now isn't police work."

Harsha bit back a response. *Then maybe police work isn't as good as I thought it was.*

"Are you out of your mind?" was all the detective said. A crazy laugh escaped Harsha's mouth, and he considered, for a brief moment, that he might be. But deep down, he knew he wasn't. He was angry, grieving, losing faith in the system he'd spent so long upholding. He couldn't deny there were limitations of the job, none of them could, but neither could he deny there was a certain rush after doing what he had and *knowing* with certainty he had helped. The badge would never have let him do that. So maybe the badge had to go. Now that *was* a crazy thought, he told himself. But it stuck with him, echoing round his head.

"So am I free to go?"

"For now." The detective uncuffed him. "Telling you not to go anywhere is a bit redundant given the lockdown, but..."

"I know the drill," Harsha said, though he knew he would break it if he had the chance.

It was time to recoup, reassess and pray to every god that everything worked out.

30

Karma Incarnate

"Dolvenni pirates?" Even Alison began to pale as she saw the reading over Drake's shoulder. He wanted to savour it, but there was no time.

"What exactly did you expect in this sector?" he snapped, taking stock of what equipment he had left and grabbing his gun. "Best-case scenario, we were rolling the dice with a random bounty hunter. Worst case, the Ab found us and took their ship back. Depending on how long you've had that beacon going, it could be all three." Alison was silent. Roz was sitting in a chair, looking distant, hands shaking. No matter how much he tried to calm himself, he couldn't. His heart pounded. Fury burned inside him, made worse by the fact it felt completely justified.

"Are you happy now?" he demanded.

She did not reply. The anger drained from him as their ship was rocked by a shot from the large, ungainly pirate vessel. It was an amalgamation of several ships and pieces of no doubt stolen tech. They would catch up with the shuttle no matter what they did. They could blow it to pieces no matter what they did. They would board them and outnumber them no matter what they did. So what remained?

He paced. What would Olise do? He looked around the ship anew. It was strange that the interior was so sparse. Surely, there had to be some equipment stored somewhere. He began tapping on the metal wall panels and floor panels.

"Have you finally gone mad?" Alison asked.

"Given you're alive and aren't gagged, I think I might be," he replied.

"Aren't you going to do something?"

"To fix another one of your problems?" Drake replied. "Unfortunately so." When, at last, he heard a hollow noise, he pressed the panel in, and it unfurled with a hiss. Behind it lay gear to repair the ship, including space suits and tethers.

"Right," he said, clapping his hands together. Both women jumped to attention. "We don't stand a chance against all of them in this little ship."

"Fantastic," Alison said. He ignored her.

"So we're going to board them first."

Alison opened her mouth, but Drake cut her off.

"With a ship like that, they'll have to send out some kind of tunnel to grab us and dock us – and they will do that if we don't put up a fight. Those tunnels usually have multiple exits. We climb outside this ship and walk along the top of it until we find one and slip inside behind the pirates. Then we retract it from their side, leaving at least a few of them stranded here."

"Your plan is to fight?" Alison said again. "Can't we negotiate?"

Drake stared at her, dumbfounded.

"They will *laugh* in our faces, take what they want, and kill us or sell us, anyway. There can't be that many," he continued. "Not on a ship of that size. But more than us."

"And they know their ship," Roz offered. "We don't."

Drake grimaced.

"I know." He paused, looking down at what little he held in his hands, all too aware that he was still injured. "I don't see any other chance," he said. "If we can pull it off, that ship will be faster and be less conspicuous for us to dock at a space station. If we can't, well, we'll be in the same position as if we wait for them to board us now."

"And what about us?" Alison said.

"You can do whatever you like. Be boarded, get yourself killed or captured. Let them pry the teleporter from your cold, dead hands and sell it to the highest bidder." He glared at her but quickly turned to Roz. "I can't make you do anything," he said, "but I do think this is the best way to survive."

"You think they'll kill us on sight?" she asked.

"I've seen it happen. If they don't, we'll wish they did."

"You think you can do this?" she asked. Her eyes were so bright, so quick. He could not lie to her.

"I think if we want any chance of getting out of here with that teleporter, it's our best shot."

Roz nodded.

"Then help me get into a space suit," she said.

Alison, for once, did not disagree and, after a moment, followed suit.

Fifteen minutes later, they were standing in the airlock, tethered together. Around the waist of the space suit were a series of smaller tethers. Drake clipped his gun and multi-purpose tool to them and pulled them taut. He was aware of Roz and Alison watching him. He did not ask if they were ready or if they were sure. The pirate ship was almost upon them. Using a control panel on the wall, he opened the airlock.

The world around him fell silent. The back of the pirate ship glowed a vibrant blue from its engine. Its tunnel stretched across the void towards them. The soundlessness of both was uncanny. All that filled Drake's ears were the sounds of his own harsh breaths. Seeing the pirate ship with his own eyes sent a shiver down his back. It loomed over them, many times bigger than their vessel. *What the hell are you doing?* he asked himself.

He moved cautiously to the edge of the airlock, peering out to find anything to hold on to. He'd only been in the vacuum of space a few times before – only once by choice – and it was no easier this time than any other. Heart pounding, he grabbed a handle protruding from the ship's hull. *Easy does it*, he told himself, cautiously pushing himself out of the airlock and pulling the rest of his body around onto the hull. His stomach churned at the feeling of weightlessness. *I'll never get used to this*, he thought. He swallowed heavily and forced himself to take a deep breath. *I never want to get used to this.*

Drake found the next handhold, then leant to the side, peering into the airlock, and waved for Roz and Alison to follow. Slowly but surely, he led them up the side of the ship onto the roof, using the tethers that bound them together to help Roz and Alison where he could. The ship rocked as the pirate's tunnel connected and locked on. Roz stumbled backwards and tripped, thanks to the lack of gravity upwards. Drake grabbed the tether between them and pulled hard, reeling her back in. From the brief glimpse he got of her through her helmet's visor, she looked pale and sick.

I've done worse, he told himself. He dropped to his hands and knees, keeping one hand firmly gripped onto the ship at all times, and moved towards the edge once more. The tunnel was a small step down. Long railings ran the length of its exterior. He leant down, hooked their shared tether onto it, and then led them forward. *I've done worse and survived.*

But Olise was always there. There was a knot in his stomach and the burn of bile in his throat. *You survived until you met Olise*, he reminded himself, but back then, he'd had the Family's support. *You've learned so much from all of them. It'll be an hour at most*, he reassured himself. *Then it will be over one way or another. Time will march on no matter what you do. It'll all be over in an hour.* He closed his eyes and readied himself.

He watched the suited pirates walk across through small windows in the tunnel. They crept in the opposite direction, Drake feeling around for any sign of an entrance. In the end, he tripped over it, stomach lurching as he did not fall to the ground as his mind expected. It was a hatch, once painted red, now chipped, with large metal handles to pull it open. He pulled himself into a crouch beside it, forcing some deep breaths. Counting to three, he hauled open the hatch and clung on for dear life as air rushed out.

Before his heart stopped pounding, he pulled himself inside. He only took a second to adjust before spotting and throwing himself towards one of the tunnel's control panels. One of the pirates poked their head out of their boarded ship, but they were too late. The bridge between the two ships was retracting before their eyes. Drake pulled Roz and Alison into the corridor after him, then closed the door at the retracting end of the tunnel. The pirates fired. Drake flinched at every gunshot that vibrated against the door, but he knew it would take more than a small gun to pierce it. Closing the hatch they'd climbed through, he pressed another button to bring some air back in. Even once his suit told him it was safe, he dared not take his helmet off yet. *Too bad*, he thought, as sweat rolled down his face.

"That was the hard part," he said aloud, trying to believe it. The space suit hid his shaking hands. His muscles were tense, painfully so. There was no going back now, not with everything on the line.

Rolling his shoulders, he readied his gun, pressed himself into the wall, and opened the inner door to the ship. A quick glance each way told him there was no one on their way... yet.

"Let's move."

Alison, it seemed, was content to follow orders for now. She pulled out a gun of her own – the gun she had shot him with, he remembered with a punch of bitterness – and nodded for him to take the lead. He would have to trust that she wouldn't try to kill him again.

He edged forward into a corridor made up of sheets of metal, some new, some rusted, all patched together. He turned on his tactical implants, letting the visual portion search for any signs of life. No doubt the pirates had seen the bridge disconnect. Someone must have been on their way. He turned a corner, and a shot narrowly missed his shoulder. He cursed, ducking back. Of course they'd been lying in wait. That was the smart thing to do. How many had he seen in that instant? He already couldn't remember. Olise would have known. This was her domain. *Olise isn't here*, he growled at himself. Was he really so helpless without her? No, he was a Thaler, with all that entailed. He could take a few lazy thugs.

He activated another visual implant in his tactical suite, his vision going blank for a brief moment. He would suffer for this later. Migraines and nosebleeds often followed such a quick and dirty implant usage. Still, there was nothing quite like a thermal view to give you the slightest advantage. There were three blobs of heat around the corner: two small balls, heat dulled, potentially by some kind of makeshift barricade, and one tall and unobstructed. The tactical implant estimated three people, and Drake nodded to himself. He turned to the women, holding up three fingers. Alison nodded. Would she cover him? He hoped so.

He leapt out, firing at the standing pirate before jumping up and kicking off a wall to get a second. Alison followed suit, catching the third. She nodded at him, though she did not look pleased about it.

"How many did you say there were?" she asked.

"On a ship like this? Ten to fifteen," he replied. "We left three on the shuttle. Three here. If you give me a moment..." He squeezed his eyes shut as he added yet another implant. His eyes began to water; his nose began to run with what he knew must be blood. The world before him flickered a strange grey-blue, but as he layered a zooming implant on top, he began to make out more heat shapes in the distance. "There's one over there," he said, pointing through a wall. "And two up top, in a control room, I guess."

Roz and Alison both squinted at him as if for the first time.

"How many implants do you have?" Roz asked.

"Oh, you know," he said lightly, though in truth, his head was beginning to throb. "I've accumulated a few over the years."

Another shot sounded, followed by the hissing of air. Drake looked down slowly to see a hole in his arm, straight through his suit. He barely felt the pain layered on top of everything else. He could only sigh.

"I'm getting really tired of this," he said, turning and firing his gun at the source behind him. "He makes ten."

He looked around beneath them and behind them, trying to cover all angles. The base of the ship burned a bright white in the thermal view. *The engines*, Drake guessed with a shudder. *How many could be hiding down there?*

"I can't see much below," he told Roz and Alison. "The engine's interfering with my implants. We'll need to find out ourselves."

"Which direction first?" Roz asked.

"Down," he and Alison replied. "We can't risk him sneaking up from behind," Alison said.

"Yeah, exactly," Drake said. "Ahh," he groaned, turning off the implants. A brief reprieve, no matter how brief, would go a long way. "Let's make this quick."

And quick it was with Alison onside. For now, at least. It was good to have someone to watch his back. It would be better if it was someone he could trust. Still, she covered him when a second man attempted to catch them off guard, even if it was just because Roz was right beside him.

He should have felt cold dread as the three of them made their way to the control room. This could have been Alison's next chance to take him out and send him out of the airlock with the pirates. But, in truth, he was tired. Too many implants in too little time, too little trust in Alison, and too much pushing through his injuries. *I've picked up all of Olise's bad habits too,* he told himself, wordlessly slumping into a seat. His headache grew worse. Lights flashed in front of his eyes. Before the last pirate went cold, he applied a medical patch to his wound and closed his eyes. He slipped into a hazy sleep, unsure if he'd wake up again.

31

A Long Way From Home

It was so strange looking at Olise in a hospital bed, Harsha thought. She looked like an entirely different person. The tattoos were still there, so were the scars, but the way she lay limp, hair stuck to the sides of her face...

When she woke up, and the doctors had assured them she would, he would be glad for more than one reason. His gaze turned to Phin, who was curled up in a hospital chair, face still illuminated by the glow of his communicator. It had been a long night by Olise's bedside. Now, the grey hours of early morning cast a sickly light on Phin's figure.

"All I wanted was to help Drake and Olise," Phin murmured. "But not like this. Don't say it," Phin warned after a moment. Harsha kept his mouth shut. "And don't look at me like that."

"What am I supposed to do? You told me not to say it. Sven's the biggest name you've never heard."

He did not protest, but he did unfurl, leaning forward and clasping his hands.

"She's my friend."

"She's in hot water. Drake, too, by the sounds of it."

"I can help them out of it."

"It could get you killed."

"Mr Sobol, I know you have experience, and I know you mean well, but with all due respect" – his voice cracked as he looked up at him, gaze fierce – "there is one unknown in all this, one surprise element that no one expects or knows how to counter, and it's *me*. Drake and Olise have people after them. You're an officer assigned to Roz's very public case. Olise told me herself that I was never meant to be a part of this, but I *am,* and only you and they know about that." He looked away. "I may not be a soldier, but we've already established none of this is about a weapon. And I know it doesn't *have* to be me who helps. I know I'm not special, but goddamn it, I'm *here,* and that's better than nothing." He sighed. "I can't walk away. I won't."

"Kid—"

"Thing is, I'm not a kid," he snapped. "I know I'm still young, but at the end of the day, I'm legally an adult, and I don't need your permission to stay."

"You're right," Harsha said after a long moment. "You *are* right. I just don't want to send another young body home to their parents. I know what it's like to be on the receiving end of that."

"I'm sorry," Phin said.

"Everyone is," Harsha said. He leant back in his seat. "So long as we're on the same page."

"I don't even think I have a page anymore," Phin said.

"I know how it feels." He stood, looking out of the window at what was otherwise a pleasant day. "Let me get you some food and a drink *without* caffeine in it." He looked at Phin, who looked back to Olise. "I'll bring it up."

Phin nodded.

"Thanks."

He walked down to the hospital cafeteria, passing by floods of concerned faces and weeping families. He swallowed a lump in his throat as he passed by a ward of young people. The cafeteria could only be described as distastefully cheery, in stark contrast to all its occupants. A merry tune played quietly in the background as a serving robot passed him his order. In a way, he understood it. The cafeteria in the police precinct was the same. You had to find some way to separate the work you were doing and the rest of your life. He'd been good at it once upon a time, but that had all changed when he'd lost his daughter. Everything had. Now, he couldn't separate that from anything.

It was almost a relief to return to Olise's side out of the uncanny valley.

He passed a sandwich and a juice box to Phin before tucking into his own.

"What's Roz like?" Phin asked. "I've heard her on the radio. She seems nice."

"She is. Very warm. Very honest." He took a large bite of his sandwich. "I met her under great duress, and let me tell you, that makes her an angel compared to most people I work with. I have more sympathy for the other side after I'd been on it when my daughter was killed, but still... grief breaks people." There was a moment of silence. "I'm not very good at light conversation, am I?"

Phin snorted.

"I'd offer to take over," he said, "but all I can talk about is physics."

"You have anyone special back home? A partner?"

"Nah," he replied. "All the men I've dated in physics and engineering have been..." He waved his hands around. "Let's politely say unusual."

Harsha laughed.

"That bad?"

"I got a scholarship into a really fancy school. Most people there have far more money to throw around than me and they act like it."

"Well, good for you," Harsha said. "For getting into a good school and knowing what you want."

There was a moment of comfortable silence. Perhaps he'd been forcing it too much. Phin was an easygoing person. His face drained of emotion again, though, as he asked, "Do you know anything about the people after Olise? They wouldn't tell me much."

"Sven?" he replied. "He's a big fish. Even Olise seemed afraid. I'm beginning to piece it together. Why even the Thalers can't help them. Sven is dangerous on his own, but he becomes more dangerous when you learn he's cosy with the Macar." When Phin looked clueless, he added, "Another mafia. If the Families don't want a war, and they generally don't, then whatever this conflict is, it's personal."

"Can't be good." Phin took a long sip of his drink. "But they'll be back together soon enough." He said it with confidence, though Harsha could hear his voice waver.

"They better be," he said.

They finished their food in silence. Harsha pulled out a bag of sweets from his pocket. They were old-fashioned Earth sweets, the kind his grandmother had always given him. She was the last of his family to see Earth. Phin took one but pulled a face when he smelled it.

"What is this?"

"Liquorice, from Earth. Well" – he squinted at the bag – "an Earth invention. These were apparently mass-produced in some factory on a distant moon." He chewed on one, feeling his jaw ache. "Are you from Earth? Stupid question," he corrected himself. "When did your family leave Earth?"

"Pretty early," Phin replied, spitting the candy into the empty sandwich wrapper. "My great great great times something grandfather was one of the first settlers in Alpha Centauri."

"Wow, that's a story," Harsha said.

"Yeah, my family lived there for a while, then moved to Dotu-8 when times got tough."

"You ever been to Earth?" Phin shook his head. "Me either. I've always thought that's weird. For millions of years, humans were on Earth, and I've never seen it. For me, it lives on through old sweets."

A long rasp cut through their conversation.

"Who the fuck" – Olise's breath caught in her throat, and her fingers twitched, though her eyes were still closed – "is eating liquorice. Put that" – another gasp – "shit away."

She took her time opening her eyes, the edges of her mouth turned up. Both Harsha and Phin broke into smiles. Harsha tucked the sweets away again.

"Glad to see you back in the land of the living," he said.

"If you can call it that," she wheezed. She moved a shaky hand to her side. "I really thought that was it this time."

"It would have been if Phin hadn't told me what was going on."

She held out a shaking fist to Phin, who bumped it.

"Thanks, kid."

She shut her eyes again, breaths short. "About Sven."

"All quiet so far," Harsha said. He wanted to reassure her, but they both knew it could mean any number of things. She shook her head.

"Not that," she said, then wheezed. "Not just that. He's after information about the destroyed space stations, too. Should have seen that coming." Harsha straightened up. "He saw us together, mentioned you specifically." She raised a weak finger to point at Harsha. "You need to be careful." She locked gazes with Harsha and nodded subtly at Phin. "We *all* need to be careful." Harsha nodded.

"Do you have any idea what Sven's next move might be?" Harsha asked. "We're not exactly in hiding."

Olise grimaced and shook her head.

"We have the same plan as we did yesterday," she told them. "Get off Satra Bal as soon as possible. We'll have a better chance of losing Sven in space." She doubled over and coughed, then flopped limply back onto the bed. "How bad is it?" she asked. "How long until I'm back on my feet again?"

"A day or two and they'll release you, but you're still going to need to rest for a few weeks," Phin said.

"What a time for an injury like this," she moaned. Her eyes sprang open again and were full of their former fire. "I guess I've had worse odds." She paused, rubbing her face with one weak hand. "Harsha," she said. "Thank you. For coming after me. I know it won't be good for you."

Harsha smiled and waved a hand. The formal termination notice from his work hadn't hurt as much as he thought it would. He'd followed his gut throughout his entire career. People said that was what made him a good detective. Why should this be any different?

"Don't mention it." He chuckled. "Helping you out and killing some of those men probably balances out law-wise, anyway."

Olise snorted.

"Even I know that's not how the law works."

Harsha's pocket buzzed. A notification popped up. He was halfway to dismissing it before his brain processed the name:

"Rosalin Dayne."

32

Deep Breath

For a while after they had seized control of the ship, Roz sat staring at her hands. She was aware Alison was watching her, but every time she tried to speak, words escaped her. She turned puzzle pieces over and over in her head, trying to make sense of what her aunt had done, but anger and hurt roiled inside her, muddying everything.

Eventually, her aunt stood, and Roz jumped to her feet.

"Where do you think you're going?" she asked, seething. Alison recoiled.

"To work on the teleporter," Alison responded. Her voice was calm but wavered at the end.

"You don't get to lock yourself in a room again," Roz told her. "Work on it out here where we can see you."

"Roz—"

"*No.*" Roz rose to face her. Her hands shook. "What the *hell* were you thinking?" she snapped. "You don't want to trust anyone, *fine*. But *how*" – her voice cracked – "is rolling the dice with random spacefarers better than one person we kind of know?"

Alison didn't answer, but her face flushed. She looked away.

"Well?" Roz prompted.

"What do you want me to say?" Alison said softly. "What would make you feel better?"

"That you had any kind of plan!" Roz roared. In the moment of silence that followed, Roz panted, and as she exhaled, the anger flooded out of her body, leaving only exhaustion behind. "That you're sorry for any of it," she finished weakly. Alison's eyes were filled with tears.

"We needed," Alison began, croaking, "to get on a ship where no one knew who we were or where we were from. We could have pretended..." She closed her eyes and took a breath. "It doesn't matter now," she resolved. "And as for being sorry." Her voice cracked again, and this time, she began to cry. Roz flinched. "I am more sorry than anyone will ever know. I'm sorry that the distress signal called pirates and not someone else. I'm sorry I was wrong about my employer. I'm sorry that all those people on all of those space stations have died," she spoke quickly and breathlessly between sobs. "I'm sorry when I wake up in the morning, and I'm sorry when I go to sleep at night. In every quiet moment, I am sorry." She gulped, and her expression hardened once more. Roz's stomach knotted watching her aunt's distress, but not enough to stop or comfort her. *I need this,* she thought. *Maybe we both do.*

"I can say it until I lose my voice," Alison continued, "but it won't change anything. It won't *fix* anything. We need to keep moving. I need to keep refining the teleporter. I need to keep you *safe* and then... try to mitigate the remaining damage the teleporter has caused – and *will* cause – the best I can. I need to do *something* to make Parare Facie pay for what they've done." She wiped her face roughly and walked away. At the door, she hesitated.

"I *am* sorry, Roz," she repeated but did not look back.

Roz let her go and sank heavily into her seat. Accompanied by the electrical hum of the ship, a low, constant chatter consumed her brain. Thoughts about Alison and the teleporter, thoughts about Drake, about Eva, all clamoured over each other. She couldn't just sit there, she decided. She needed to do something. To be in control of something. Looking wearily around the pirate ship for inspiration, she shoved her hands in her pockets and felt the cold touch of her broken communicator on her skin. She pulled it out and stared at it. Would she even be able to fix it? She turned it over in her hands. She glanced at the multi-tool clipped to Drake's belt. Surely, it couldn't get more broken. The better question was: did she want to fix it? She couldn't say she'd missed the torrent of social media comments and news articles, but she couldn't hide forever, and she owed it to Harsha to report back. *A series of steps*, she thought. Maybe she owed it to herself.

Roz took a deep breath, grabbed Drake's tool, and cracked her communicator open to see what she could find.

***

Roz almost regretted fixing her communicator. Her email inbox grew larger and larger as the media sought anything from her. But she could ignore them. She had been doing that since day zero. What she couldn't ignore were Eva's messages and the twisting in her stomach when she saw them again.

How are you doing? This is crazy.

Followed, days later, by:

I know I'm probably not the person you want to speak to right now, but they say you're missing and I'm worried. We don't have to talk, but please react or something to let me know you're okay.

It was real. An actual conversation. From *Eva*. Wasn't this what she wanted? She paced in circles, reading the messages from Eva over and over again. There were no hidden meanings here, she told herself. Someone who used to care for her was checking in. Even so, every time she began typing, her mind went blank.

It's insane. She responded eventually, throwing her arms up in the air. What more could she say? Nothing about the teleporter and nothing about where she was, maybe not even the people she was with. She glanced at the crumpled figure of Drake. He looked like death, but he was snoring loudly, at least.

But I have people who are helping me, she sent after a moment.

She set down her communicator and walked away.

The control room was spacious enough to do that on this ship. Three panels and chairs sat up front beneath the forward-facing screen. Another sat in the middle, behind them. Behind that again sat a large table that Roz recognised as a holographic display. Everything was a dull, grubby metal, patched up in places with something in a different colour. Drake had already found the small, worn couches at the back of the room, and Alison had found what appeared to be a small captain's quarters off to the side.

She looked from the window to Drake to the communicator, and then back to the window. Her head spun. The absence of anything to focus on in the void outside only intensified the gulf inside her. *Window. Drake. Communicator.*

Would Drake be okay? He'd already applied some basic medical supplies to his injuries, but neither he nor she was a doctor. While commercial ships often had small medical robots to diagnose problems, she could not see the telltale green markings of one in the pirate's ship. *Don't die,* she begged silently. *I don't know what to do if you die. People will miss you. I'll miss you.* She turned instead to his communicator. He'd spent the last few days saving her life. The least she could do was fix up his communicator so that when he awoke, he could contact his friend.

She picked it up gingerly. It was no different to her own, but it felt like a crime to be holding it without his permission, not that she could access any of his data, anyway. *Don't even think about breaking it*, she told herself with a grimace.

When her own communicator pinged with a notification, she jumped out of her skin then turned stiff.

"Oh my god," she choked. Taking a deep breath, she took one heavy step towards it. What if that was Eva? What if it *wasn't*? There was only one way to find out. She forced herself to take another step. If she could survive the last few days, she could survive reading one message. What was it Harsha had said? That she would live to grimace through whatever came next? She wasn't out of the woods – or rather, enemy space – yet, but in this moment, it was strangely comforting. She picked up the communicator.

"Experience Luxury~ like nowhere else!" A holographic advert burst outwards, showering her hand with sparkles. "While you're in Ab space, stop by—"

"Fuck! Off!" she snapped at the device, shoving it deep into her pocket. She slumped into a chair, putting her head in her hands. *While you're in Ab space...* The words echoed in her head. Cold washed over her. Of course the ads knew where she was. They always did. Maybe it hadn't been such a good idea to fix her communicator after all. If the ads knew, what else, or *who* else might know too? Between the people after her and Drake, she'd seen a whole world of gadgets she'd never thought of before. Maybe someone was lying in wait for her to come back online.

Should she turn it off, just in case? But then surely, any damage was already done? And surely, if she could be tracked by her communicator, someone would have found her long before she'd ever left Revalin.

As her finger hovered over the button, a new notification popped up, and this one *was* from Eva.

That decided it then, didn't it? Biting her lip so hard it went numb, Roz opened the message.

I'm glad to hear it, came the reply. *Are you safe?*

It came with a strange mix of relief and sadness. Yes, Eva had replied and seemed to be worried about her, but she wasn't *with* Eva. She wasn't with Eva because of things *she* had said. And was she safe?

"Am I?" she mumbled. She looked at the door Alison was behind, then back to Drake. He was covered in blood. Weary from all the battles he'd fought. *All the battles he's fought to protect me and find out the truth.*

Safer than I was, she concluded, *but I don't know about safe.*

She looked out the window into the deep, all-encompassing dark. What time was it for Eva, she wondered? Never mind Eva, what time was it for *her*? Time hardly existed when travelling outside of civilisation. The lighting cycles on the ship sometimes dictated it. Other times, it was dictated only by when you slept and ate. Roz was definitely the latter at the moment.

She looked away, despite the fact that Eva was not there.

Listen, she began again. *I want you to know that I'm sorry for everything. I shouldn't have left the way I did.*

She watched Eva's bubble pulse as she was typing for what seemed like a lifetime.

You don't have to worry about that. You have enough on your plate at the moment.

I've had a lot of time to think. Just wanted you to know, Roz replied.

I'm sorry too.

Roz sighed and fell back into a seat. She wanted to cry. Crying seemed to be a permanent reaction of hers these days. What else did she feel? She closed her eyes. There was relief down there, somewhere, trapped under everything else. Relief to have replied, relief that Eva had listened, relief that no matter what came next, she had apologised. That was enough for now.

I'm scared for you, Eva sent. *So keep me updated, okay?*

Thank you.

"A series of small steps," she said under her breath. "I can do this."

She opened her eyes, straightened up, and found Harsha in her communicator's contacts. It was time to call him, to report on all she'd learned, the whole tangled mess. Nodding to herself, she started the call.

33

Take it from the Top

"Hey, you're finally awake."

As Drake's vision came into focus, he managed, "I don't feel it."

Dried blood was crusted on his nose, down his face, and on the front of his shirt. A high-pitched ringing rattled around his head. Roz was kneeling in front of him, holding out a glass of water and a... communicator. He looked up at her in shock.

"I managed to fix it for you," she said with a small smile. "I promise I didn't read any messages. I just— I fixed mine, talked with Harsha and—" He didn't know what to say. Her face turned solemn. "You should call your friend. She and Phin are with Harsha on Satra Bal."

She stood up to leave him, but he caught her by the arm. She flinched.

"Thank you, Roz," he said. "For everything you've done."

"Thank you for the same."

Stretching his stiff limbs, he walked out of the control room and down the hall until he found a small viewing deck. From a drinks cabinet, he poured himself a glass of something unnaturally pink and sat in a low chair, looking at the stars. His hands shook. Why had Roz said it the way she had? There was only one way to find out. The wait as he called Olise was one of the longest of his life. On the side, messages began flooding in. Sven. The name made his blood run cold. *We'll see you soon,* the message read, accompanied by a smiley face and a gruesome picture of Olise. With his own aches and pains and worries, he could have fainted. But Roz had said to call her, not anyone else. When at last she picked up the call, she was unmistakably in a hospital. Alive, but not well.

"I'm glad to see you," he gushed, sagging in his chair.

"Me too," she replied, sounding exhausted. "When you couldn't get in contact, I was so fucking worried."

"The t—" He stopped himself, not sure who could hear on her end. "It knocked out my comms. We were in Ab space, but we're out now. Roz said you were on Satra Bal. You were looking for me?"

Olise nodded.

"Trouble is, the whole fucking place is in lockdown against another attack."

"You're kidding."

Olise shook her head.

"Of all the places to be stuck" – Drake sighed and took a long drink – "it had to be the same station as Sven." He pinched the bridge of his nose. What a time for all this. "How are you?" he asked. He turned down the light of the room, leaving everything in a faint off-white glow, and shut his eyes. When she spoke, her voice was small, smaller than Olise ever was.

"I'm terrified," she said simply. "I know we have it coming. I know it's our own fault." She stopped to catch her breath, clutching her side. "I know we should have seen it, been ready..."

"We're helping people, that's not a weakness."

"You and your bleeding fucking heart," she said with a wheeze. She had a lump in her throat. "It is now. It is when we're apart. It is—" She took a deep breath. "Drake, I finally have something to lose."

His chest ached. He wished he could have been with her.

"I know."

He set his glass down and stood, striding to the window. "But I'm on my way to you. We *will* figure this out. I'll have the family keep their eyes and ears open. They might not be able to get us out of this, but they can still lend a hand. We have their network."

"It will take you weeks to get here if the blockade isn't still going, and I'm bedridden."

"I am currently on a ship with a working... device, and you aren't alone anymore."

"...no," she said. "I suppose not."

"Grab the kid and the detective. Let's make this a group call."

With a grin on his face and a body full of more reckless energy, Drake stormed back into the control room. He rapped on Alison's door and threw a hologram of the call up into the middle of the room over the planning table.

"What is it? What's going on?" Roz said, jumping to her feet. Alison emerged from her isolation, approaching the table tentatively. Phin and Harsha appeared behind Olise.

"We all have problems," Drake began to a distinctly lukewarm response all around. "Luckily, between us, we have quite a diverse skill set. Between us, I reckon we can solve them all."

"Why would we want to do that?" Alison said. "We don't know each other."

"We all came to be involved in this mess for one reason: we want the attacks to stop. Why are they happening? Because dangerous people are trying to get the teleporter, and Alison is trying to hide it from them. Her plan to stop it? Release it to everyone and level the playing field. Harsha, Olise, and I can help with that. Alison and Roz will need protection while things die down. We can help with that too. Phin needs some closure and a chance to go home and speak to a therapist." Phin opened his mouth to protest, but Drake continued. "Harsha, man, feel free to pitch in with what you want. I don't know you."

"I just want to solve the case."

"Cool, again, Olise and I can help with that."

"I'm seeing a theme," Alison said dryly. "What do *you* want?"

"Olise and I can and will help you, but we can't help you if we're dead." He clenched his hands, knuckles turning white, though he kept a signature smile on his bloody face. "There are some people after us. People who almost killed Olise. People already on Satra Bal. People who are also investigating the space station attacks and, when they hear about it, will *kill* to get their hands on the teleporter first."

"So will half the galaxy," Alison said dismissively. "Anyway, we're weeks away from Satra Bal."

"We're not, though, are we?" Drake replied. "Here's what I'm thinking: teleport us in. Olise and I take care of our problem, with backup from anyone willing to help. You and Roz can stay somewhere safe. Then, you teleport all of us out. We expose the teleporter to the galaxy, take down a private military, go out for ice cream, and part ways as unlikely friends."

There was a long moment of silence.

"Alison, you don't look happy." Drake sighed. "What is it this time?"

"I don't trust you people."

"You don't need to."

"And I'm not comfortable being complicit in illegal... whatever you call this," she finished instead.

"There are no laws around teleportation at the moment, as I'm sure you're aware, given your line of work and choice of employer."

"Not by choice."

"Bold of you to assume Olise and I have a choice. We've spent the last seven years running from this. They've already attacked Olise. This is just self-defence."

"And if we get caught in the crossfire?" Alison asked.

"I'm not going to force you to fight with me, Alison. I'm not going to force anyone. You're welcome to drop us off and then hide until it blows over." The weight of all their gazes became too much, and he looked away. "We just need an... *edge*," he said softly.

"If you don't help, he'll be with us for a long time," Roz added. "These people are after him. The police might follow. This could all get messy."

Alison stared at Roz for a long moment then relented, sighing and folding her arms.

"Believe me," Drake said. "The last thing I want is for any of you to die for this. Or me and Olise, preferably."

"I'm all for helping each other," Harsha said. "We've all come this far, and frankly, I think we're all most likely to get out of this alive that way. But I'd like to know what we're dealing with. Olise told me it's Sven, but why?"

"Shortly after Olise and I started working together, we ended up in a bad spot. A crew of mercenaries, Sven's crew, came to our rescue, but their help came at a cost. We couldn't pay – we were broke – so we ended up working for them. I learned he was from a rival mafia, the Macar, and promptly decided to use a fake name. Olise was also under a different name at this point." Drake clucked his tongue. "The first few jobs we did with them were fine: smuggling people and things in and out of places. We were almost friends."

"Apart from the fact you were lying to them," Harsha said. Drake grimaced.

"That is where the problems begin, yes," Drake continued. "A job went wrong. A couple of high-ranking members died, including Sven's brother. They were mad at us for fouling up the job, but it was nothing that couldn't be repaired. Until a few weeks later, they found out I was a Thaler. And," he said with a long sigh, "to cut a long story short: the Thalers were furious with us and didn't want a war with the Macar, the Macar wanted us dead but didn't want a war with the Thalers, but Sven, Sven just wants us dead, no holds barred."

"Is killing Sven going to cause problems with the Macar?" Phin asked.

"Both mafias agreed this was personal because they don't want to fight each other," Drake said. "So, in theory, no, but... we'll see." He fumbled. "It might not be enough to save us from Sven's friends. It might not be." He said it as if repeating it would drill it into his own head. "But it would be enough for now. Enough for us to see this whole teleporter thing through. And more than we thought we'd get." He looked at Olise, who nodded. "And who knows? Sven has a lot of friends, but they might not stick together once he's gone. Everyone might want a piece of what he had. Cue infighting and forgetting about us. For a while."

He looked around the room to a lot of concerned faces. He sighed.

"Like I said, none of you need to be in the line of fire. We just need an edge," he repeated.

"What did you have in mind?"

"If you're up for it, and only if you're up for it, I'm thinking we use you guys to our advantage. Olise and I have always been by ourselves.

Nobody really knows about any of you. This helps keep you safe and gives us a heads-up.

"I think we need to play with what Sven knows and what he *thinks* he knows," Drake continued. "He knows Olise, Harsha, and Phin are on the station. He thinks I have no way of reaching Olise. If he's researched Phin – which I'm sure he will have if he saw you together – he'll think he's harmless. I think we set Olise up as bait," he stated. Olise nodded in approval.

"Sven said he wanted me to lure you in," she said. "If he sees an opportunity to recapture me, or even just kill me, I think he'll take it."

"So we have Olise alone somewhere, maybe looking as if she's going to sneak off the space station? Harsha, I think we need you as far away from her as possible initially to sell the story. If you could tip off the local law enforcement that Sven will be there, that would be helpful. We don't know how many allies Sven has on Satra Bal, but he can probably outnumber us easily, and timely arrival of some law enforcement would probably stop them being able to overwhelm us."

"I can't make any promises," Harsha told them. "I lost my job for the stunt at Sven's restaurant—"

"Something that I'm very grateful for," Drake interjected.

"But I'll try. I just need to... frame it in a way that they can't refuse."

Drake was aware of Phin staring intently at him. He tried not to meet his gaze.

"Phin," Drake began. "We're keeping you as far away from this as possible—"

"I'll be your eyes again," Phin protested. "I'll watch Olise again. I'll use your little drone and watch the streets nearby."

"You can do that from the other side of the space station," Drake stressed. "Alison," he continued, "if you can teleport me in, then I can hide and ambush Sven when he thinks Olise is alone."

"I'm not getting anywhere near this mess," Alison said. "I want to be in and out long before this happens."

Drake shrugged.

"Okay," he agreed.

"The longer you're on the station, the more we lose the element of surprise," Olise stated. "We need a way to hide you from Sven and anyone else who might be watching. From security cameras, from implants."

Drake nodded slowly.

"We need to get you a cloaking implant," Olise finished. Drake winced. A cloaking implant would shield him from view with visual implants, true, but they'd need to get their hands on one first.

"Good luck with that," Harsha snorted. "They're regulated beyond belief."

"More importantly," Drake added, "they're expensive. *Very* expensive."

Olise shrugged, her expression unapologetic.

"I'm just saying it's an option. Probably the easiest option. I'm open to suggestions."

Drake looked from Olise to Harsha.

"Do we have any other options?" he asked the detective.

"You'd need to be out of the range of any visual implants to be properly hidden," Harsha replied.

"Which makes ambushing Sven difficult," Drake finished.

"Or find something to block or mess with the implant's detection."

Olise hummed thoughtfully.

"What about hiding you near something hot? That would hide you from thermal implants. The lower levels of Satra Bal have a lot of the engineering works and lots of factories and warehouses, which are all hot. We'd still need to hide you from direct line of sight, but with the right space..."

"Hide behind some machinery or something," Drake mused. "That sounds reasonable to me. Harsha, any notes?"

The detective considered it for a moment, then shook his head.

"So, when are we going to do it?" Drake asked.

"Tomorrow is the earliest I could be released from the hospital, but it might be the day after," Olise told them. "But I can look into warehouses from here. It probably even adds to the story – trying to run as soon as possible."

"We'll reach the space station Inrov-Ine within an hour or two," Drake said. "I'm going to go shopping, see what I can restock, see if there's anything that might be useful. Alison." He turned to the woman. Her arms were folded, but her face was wrinkled with thought, not disdain. "I know you're working on the teleporter. Will it be able to do what we need it to do?"

Alison looked up at him, and he was suddenly struck by the familial resemblance between her and Roz.

"I'm close," she said with a nod. "I need to do some practice runs, but I think I've fixed the problems that landed us on Agh-Ab-2 and left us stuck there."

Drake closed his eyes for a long moment, then opened them again to find all eyes on him.

"I think this is coming together," he told them. "Thank you. Let's..." He searched for some inspiring words and faltered. "We can do this," he said instead. *I hope.* "Let's get ready."

34

Promises

Roz stared out of the ship's window, watching the bulky form of the space station Inrov-Ine draw closer. It had been hard while travelling in the depths of space to remember that this was Drake's goal. It was hard to feel like it was a win after the conversation with the whole crew. So she stared out the window, trying to steady herself with deep breaths. Drake said he was breathing easier now they were out of Ab space and into something more familiar. Roz wished she could say the same. There was still so much to do.

She glanced over her shoulder as Alison entered and closed the door softly behind her. With a small, metallic clink, she placed two coin-sized disks on the counter between them.

"What are they?" Roz asked.

"Trackers," Alison answered simply. "One for me and one for you."

Roz looked from Alison to the small devices and back again.

"Just as a precaution," Alison added. "I'm going to try teleporting a few times. I want to check the accuracy of where it takes me and that the same malfunction that landed us on Agh-Ab-2 doesn't happen again." She sighed. "If I'm right, and my changes have worked, I'll be back soon. If I'm wrong, if I end up somewhere random, if I get stuck there, I want you to know." She slid one of the devices back across the table and into her pocket. "And I want to know where you are so I can get back."

She pushed the second disk closer to Roz, who stared at it for a long moment.

"Promise you'll come back?" Roz asked, a lump rising in her throat. Alison nodded hastily.

"I promise," she replied.

"Okay." Roz took the second disk. "Be careful."

"I will."

***

Stars in his eyes and hope in his heart, Drake dashed from shop to shop on the space station. It was crazy to think that in less than a day, the plan had changed from getting a new ship to gathering weapons and gadgets like a child in a toy shop. It didn't quite drown out the growing anxiety, but it helped. An equipped bounty hunter was a prepared bounty hunter. With Harsha and Phin volunteering to give the element of surprise, things were looking a little less grim.

Still, as he returned to the ship they were soon to abandon, he couldn't help but feel a sense of finality. Maybe this would be the end, with no Porba in sight. He steadied himself. He entered a quiet room that looked like it had once been a kitchen and spread out his purchases, slowly and methodically checking each and putting them in their place.

"You keep getting into trouble for other people, huh?"

Roz's voice behind him made him jump. He relaxed, forcing a tired smile as he turned.

"Only the ones worth saving."

There was a moment of awkwardness. Roz half shuffled into the room but clearly did not want to make him feel like she was prying. She opened and shut her mouth to speak a few times but looked as if she was struggling for words. He did not rush her.

"I'd like to help," she said finally. "Not combat, obviously. But you, uh, you mentioned that Phin is going to be your eyes from afar, right?"

"Yeah, that's the plan," he said, setting down the object he was holding softly and turning to face her. Her lip wobbled.

"I can be your ears," she offered.

His gut told him no, just as it had with Phin. Part of him regretted asking them for help. They were, after all, civilians who had been dragged into this. But they'd seen enough to know it wouldn't be pretty, and the other part of him knew it improved his own chances of survival. He could see in Roz's eyes the same fierce determination. It was the fire of someone who had been on the sidelines too long and wouldn't be passive again.

"I know what I'm getting into," Roz began, a little frantic, taking his silence as rejection.

"I know," he replied, stopping her in her tracks. "That would be helpful, thank you. You two should talk and figure out what the other can do."

He picked up the object again and resumed packing.

"I... spoke to Eva," she said. "Got a lot off my chest. No matter how this ends, with the teleporter, with the people after us, with her, I feel okay."

"Good," he said with a smile. "I'm glad."

"How can you be so calm?" she asked. He could feel her eyes on him. Shivers ran down the back of his spine at the thought. "I've been preparing myself for the worst, preparing Eva for the worst, and I'm not even in the line of fire."

"I'm not," he admitted. "I'm just... ready."

"You think you'll win?"

"I think this is the best shot we've got. I..." He took a breath, nodding to himself. "A lot of good people did their best to get us this far. You fixing my communicator, Harsha and Phin saving Olise. Countless more. Now it's up to us." He slid two parts of a gadget together with a satisfying click and then took them apart again in one smooth motion. "If we don't make it, can you do me a favour?"

"Yeah."

"Make sure Phin gets home. And the pair of you, don't blame yourselves. Olise and I always knew the risks and the consequences." He stood up straight and rolled his shoulders. It felt like there was a great weight pressing down on him. His jaw was locked, his heart sombre. Bounty hunting was hardly a safe profession, but had he ever stared down death like this before?

"You're going to get through this," Roz said. "We all are. Then we're going to a fancy tea place to trade stories, remember?"

He glanced over his shoulder, a smile briefly passing across his lips. He held up a fist. She bumped it.

"Fancy tea it is. Let's go deal with your aunt."

***

For what felt like the hundredth time, Olise stopped to catch her breath. She improved by leaps and bounds each day, but they didn't have any more time to wait for her to recover. Everyone was painfully aware of that. She was grateful for the help. Nobody treated her as weak. They all knew what she was capable of.

She and Harsha sat in a silence of focus and understanding. In either of their professions, everyone had a way to steel and prepare their nerves. Roz had apparently made it onto the station in one piece. It was hard for Olise to believe it was true that, in mere moments, she had travelled so far. She had gone straight to where Phin was hiding. Perfect timing, in Olise's opinion. Phin's nerves had begun to fray. Alison had escorted Roz personally, Drake had told her with an eye roll. He had told her all about that woman and what she'd tried to do. Olise grimaced at the thought that it was just the two of them alone, waiting for their moment to bring Drake in. She longed to see him again and for this whole mess to be over, but if their plan was going to work, Drake had to appear at the last minute. They could not give Sven the chance to learn he was nearby.

The plan was simple. Don't change what wasn't broken. Their age-old formula of surprise and misdirection. For the first time, the roles of her and Drake would be reversed. She was the bait, the front face, the one doing the talking. He was the surprise, the gun in the shadows.

"Do you think it will be enough?" Harsha asked, not looking up from his weapon maintenance.

"It's the best shot we've got," she replied. "You know, in another life, Drake could have been a magician. Surprise, misdirection, clever tricks... Those are all his ball game."

"And you?"

"I don't know. Seeing through all that, perhaps. Planning, thinking, on my feet. I never wanted to be a soldier, but I'd be lying if I said it didn't come easily to me." She paused. "I hope we can fill each other's shoes well enough."

"Drake's right about one thing: they can't possibly see this coming. They run this space station? Then they meant it when they said they were certain he's not here – because he isn't. He'll be here before they can understand what's happening."

"Thalers always love being fashionably late," Olise said, laughing as much as her lungs would allow. "In fact, I'll put money on it that he says that to them."

"One for theatrics as well, then."

"What's life without a little fun?" she replied, swaggering her shoulders in an impression of her best friend.

"You seem good for each other."

"We are. He definitely saved me, but I like to think I've helped him too. He wasn't so fresh and cheery when I met him. He's my best friend, my family."

"All the more reason to see this through, then."

"What about you?" she asked. "Who's waiting for you on the other side?"

"Ah," he sighed. "Some friends, some co-workers, you know. I was married, but after my daughter... my wife, my ex-wife, didn't like the detective I became. I agree with her." He looked up, and when he smiled, Olise couldn't help but smile back. "But if it's any consolation, I think you've changed me, too. And Phin and Roz."

"Yeah, well," she said. "Galaxy-threatening destruction has a way of changing our perspective."

"Do you think it'll last? When we go our separate ways?"

"I think we all have a bigger impact than we realise. That's what Drake would say, anyway."

"He seems like that kind of person. You can't save the galaxy, but you can save one person."

"Maybe we *can* save the galaxy," Olise countered.

"Yeah, but that's a one-off," he said. "I hope."

***

"Uh, hello?" Roz stepped inside the unlocked motel room cautiously, Alison at her back. The curtains were drawn, and the room was gloomy, but she could see the edge of a bed and a couch around a corner. A blue glow on both betrayed someone's presence. Walking farther in, Roz found someone who looked so normal that her heart ached for him straight off the bat. She'd seen Phin once before in their group meeting, but half-hidden behind Olise and Harsha, it had not properly conveyed how young or how tired he was. *You really were dragged into this like me, huh?* she thought. He jumped to attention, dismissing the collection of holographic screens around him.

"Hiya," he said meekly.

"Hey," she replied.

Behind her, Alison investigated the rest of the room, opening the cupboard and checking the bathroom. Phin's eyes followed her anxiously.

"Your face matches your voice," he blurted. "Sorry," he added hastily, looking away.

Roz shrugged it off.

"I've got used to people saying that kind of stuff."

Finally, Alison returned to Roz's side and nodded.

"I'll leave you to it," Alison said. "Lock this door when I'm gone. And any trouble, call me straight away."

Roz nodded.

"I promise," Roz told her. "Stay safe."

Roz followed her aunt to the door and locked it behind her. When she turned back to Phin, some of his tension seemed to leave him.

"So... you listen in to radio and stuff?" he asked. "Like for Drake?"

"Yeah. And you watch security cameras and stuff, right?"

He nodded.

"I'm just happy to be helpful." He brought up his screens again but looked distant. "This whole thing is crazy. For you, more than me."

"That's certainly one way of putting it," Roz replied. "I'm sorry you got dragged into it all. Sorry that Alison... threw you under the bus."

Phin sucked in a breath. Roz winced.

"Yeah." There was a moment of silence. "Feels like we're at the end now, though, doesn't it?" he said, glancing at her.

It hurt to draw a breath, but she forced herself to do it and nod.

"Be back on the radio in no time," she replied. Her jaw clenched. She drew up holographic screens of her own listening and decoding tools. Her stomach flipped. She was just a hobbyist. Was she prepared for this? What even was this?

"W-will you play a song for me?" Phin asked, interrupting her thoughts. "If you go back on the air."

Roz did a double-take.

"'Cause things will go back to normal," he said. "I don't think Drake will have it any other way."

"Yeah, I guess so." There was still a canyon between her and it. A great distance that she couldn't begin to cross.

"So, will you? Play something for me."

A series of small steps, she thought. *Play a song for Phin.*

"Sure. What?"

"Opaque by Parcl."

"I..." Roz broke out into a grin. "I take that offer back." She shook her head, holding back a giggle at the absurdity of it all. Waiting for a mafia fight discussing some of the worst music in existence. "*Why?*" she asked. Phin snickered too.

"Because I started listening to it ironically, and now I think it's actually funny."

Roz shook her head again. She felt giddy. When was the last time she'd smiled like this? When was the last time she'd *laughed*? A warmth spread through her chest, and it almost filled the gaping hole anxiety had left there. Almost.

"Fine," she relented. "*Fine*. If we get out of this and I get back on air, I'll... I'll play Opaque for you."

Phin giggled mischievously. Roz allowed herself a brief moment more of that dream, then took a long, steadying breath. Her gaze fell back on her screens.

"What's our plan? Where do we start?"

35

The Last Laugh

Olise walked through the street, clutching her side and taking deep, regular breaths. She glanced this way and that, looking for any signs of trouble, and found them. There was at least one person following her and another staring a little too intensely from their seat outside a coffee shop. She did not react. It was good. She didn't need to watch her own back with Harsha, Phin, and Roz on the case, but she needed to sell the story: she was alone, desperate, and in a bad physical state. That much, she did not have to play up.

She'd rented a warehouse near the docks, on a bottom level that smugglers came in and out from. She made some fake payments and orders to said warehouse, everything carefully pointing to her trying to flee.

She hobbled into the warehouse, immediately hit with a sickening wall of heat. That was good, too, but she huffed and tugged her jacket open. She flicked on the lights to reveal the warehouse's sparse contents. A few large metal containers were stacked to different heights along one side of the building. Rickety-looking stairs climbed up one wall to a mezzanine level that went around all sides of the building. The back wall was dominated by thick pipes that dipped underneath the floor, the source of the intense heat. They were part of the space station's vast engineering system. That was what made the warehouse undesirable to most, but perfect for her. She sent the green light to Drake.

Now came the hard part, the waiting. She took one unsteady breath, then another, leaving her visual implants on and keeping her gun in her hand. She walked a lap of the space, taking it in. *Count*, she thought to herself, beginning the three Cs once more. They didn't know how many people Sven would bring with him, and they wouldn't know until they were almost at the warehouse. There were three entrances to the warehouse, the front door and a door on each side. She blocked one side door by pushing a container in front of it and blocked the other by bending a stray piece of scrap metal to wrap around both handles. Neither action would slow Sven's people for long, but it was worth trying to control the flow of people.

Conditions. The warehouse was big enough for a fight but lacked good cover. Maybe if she moved some of the containers... She stared at them for a long moment and then shook the thought from her head. She didn't want to give their plan away. She kept walking. Near the pipes had been the deciding feature of the warehouse: a hatch in the floor with a ladder to a basement level. The pipes were a good start – if Drake stayed close to them, no thermal implant would be able to spot him – but he still had to stay out of Sven's line of sight. Hiding under the hatch would ensure he was close to her *and* hidden. She looked upwards. She'd need to defend the stairs up to the mezzanine if she wanted to avoid being surrounded. Where was she best positioned? Maybe sitting on the stairs was the answer. She *was* injured. Maybe it was worth playing that up more. She sighed. This storytelling and scene dressing was really more of Drake's thing.

Complications. Fewer than two days ago. Phin and Roz's monitoring helped keep them in the loop. Though they didn't know if Harsha's reinforcements would come, or how many they would bring, the possibility of backup was more than she and Drake had ever had before.

She put her hands in her pockets, returned to the stairs, and sat down. *It will be enough,* she told herself. *It has to be.* She let herself fall into a calm, meditative state as she waited for Drake. *This is my thing,* she reminded herself. Drake was good at stories and charm. Planning and fighting were her domain.

It was hard to describe the presence of the teleporter. The one thing she was certain of was that there *was* a presence. It was far less aggressive than her first encounter with it. Her hair stood up on end and her ears popped. As she heard a familiar voice and saw a familiar grin, relief flooded through her. He rolled his shoulders, blinked as though his eyes were adjusting, and rushed towards her.

"Not a fan of that," he said. He embraced her carefully. "How are you?"

"As ready as I'll ever be," she replied. "This ends today. One way or the other."

Drake nodded. Olise looked past him, to where Alison stood, already adjusting the controls of the teleporter once more. Drake followed her gaze.

"I'm leaving now," Alison said shortly.

"Thank you, Alison," Drake said and sounded genuine. "We really do appreciate this."

Olise nodded.

Alison did not smile, but her harsh expression softened, and she nodded. With a push of a button, she disappeared once more.

"Where do you want me?" he asked.

"The basement hatch is back here," Olise told him, leading him over.

They're on their way. The message made them both straighten up. Drake opened the hatch and stared into the darkness below.

"Time to make myself scarce. But I have your back," he added.

"And I have yours."

They shared one last meaningful look before Drake dropped the short distance down and closed the hatch behind him. Olise returned to the stairs. She tried to return to her meditative state, but she couldn't ignore the messages flashing across her communicator. Phin told them what appeared to be going on. Roz told them, from listening to communicators, what was actually going on. Harsha had managed to convince some law enforcement officers to check out the warehouse. Everyone was on their side. Everything balanced out. Drake had always claimed to be a believer in the natural order. That people in need should be helped, and no one should die before their time. Was this their time? The way his jaw had been set told her that even he wasn't sure. If they lived to see the other side, Olise could almost believe what Drake had been saying all these years was right.

Sven walked in through the front door with two men. They had their weapons drawn, and the Roz and Phin house of information assured them there were more at each exit. It almost seemed like Sven was here to talk.

"The bigger they are, the harder they fall," he said. "Isn't that right, Tenna?"

She suppressed a grin. He was here to gloat. Perfect.

"Yes, that's what it looks like to me," she replied evenly.

He looked around and then back at her expectantly.

"What are you waiting for?" she asked him, leaning back against the stairs.

"I'm waiting for whatever it is you're planning," he replied simply. His grin lessened into the slightest hint of a smile. "You're not this basic, Tenna. We both know that."

"There's nothing here for you, Sven," she said with one long sigh. "Nothing here but me."

"Maybe that's enough." He stepped towards her, and she straightened up sharply, feeling her injured side throb. She levelled her gun at him, and he stopped. "I think you know something about the destroyed space stations," he continued. "*I* want to know that something."

"Or what?" she scoffed. "Like I said, there's nothing here for you. Drake's the only thing you could ever hold over my head, and you know it."

"I'm still waiting, Tenna," he said, frustration creeping in. "What's the plan here? What could you possibly stand to—"

Three gunshots fired off in close succession. On the ground floor of the warehouse, everybody froze. Olise's wound throbbed and ached, but her heart beat harder and faster. Sweat rolled down the back of her neck. The noise had come from below them. Sven's knuckles went white around the grip on his gun. He smiled and relaxed. With a wave of one hand, he sent one of his men to investigate the hatch. With the other, he pointed his gun at her anew.

"You know all these warehouses are connected, right?" He waved his gun hand around in circles. "Some of these warehouses are so small, so dingy. If you buy two next to each other, you can open the walls to create a bigger space. It's so convenient; I own half the street."

I have visual, Harsha messaged. Sven took another step towards Olise, and she leapt to her feet.

"Drop your gun, and I'll make it quick," Sven stated.

Olise took a deep breath, trying to fight her racing heart, trying to focus. Her gut said shoot. Her heart said it might spell the end for both her and Drake.

"Drop yours, and I'll make it quicker," she replied through gritted teeth.

"Always so damn cocky," Sven tutted, shaking his head. "You've spent too much time around Drake, but surely, *this* is your limit."

"My limit?" Olise laughed. "Bold of you to assume I have a limit."

"Give it up," he roared. "I want to see you beg for what you did to me."

"Look, Sven," Olise said. "I know there's some bad blood between us. I know we messed up. I know *I* messed up. But I'm here for a noble cause. Some Thalers were killed in the attacks. I bet some of your Family were, too."

"And you're the only one who can stop it?" he mocked.

"Something like that, yeah."

"I don't believe you," he sneered. "I'm going to kill you, then I'm going to squeeze everything I can out of your communicator, your implants. I'll go after everyone you've worked with and learn everything you've learned and then I'll kill them, too."

Should she shoot? Was Drake alive? Would not shooting save him if he was? Cold certainty settled over her. She pulled the trigger.

Several things happened at once. A strange sense of calm came over Olise as her body moved without thinking. *It'll be what it'll be,* she thought, giving in to her combat instincts. Her gunshot hit Sven's shoulder, and he stumbled back. He pulled his trigger too, but his shot went wide. The gunman by Sven's side also fired at her, but Olise was already on the move. White-hot pain radiated across the left side of her face as it grazed her and punctured her ear. Her vision blurred and her ears rang, but her limbs kept moving on their own.

Behind her, the hatch banged open, and more gunshots filled the air. Olise twisted, putting her back to the warehouse wall, keeping Sven, his gunmen, and the whole warehouse in view. The gunman at the back of the room had toppled over backwards into a rapidly spreading pool of blood. Olise held her breath. She saw a flash of pink and blonde hair, and that was enough. She turned her attention back to Sven, whose eyes were locked on the hatch.

A shot rang out from the back, striking the gunman by Sven, and Olise followed it up with another. As the gunman collapsed to the ground, Drake popped up and forced a smile. Sven shook his head.

"On me!" he roared. At once, the front doors to the warehouse burst open, and Olise heard something hit the side doors. The sound of gunshots echoed from outside, but nothing crossed the threshold. No people, no weapons, no shots. From what little Olise could see, it seemed like something else had taken the reinforcement's attention. *The cavalry is here*, she thought with what little relief she could muster. Harsha and the law enforcement had arrived. Drake jumped out of the hatch and began to run towards Olise and Sven. The sleeves and front of his jacket were soaked in blood. *It can't be his,* Olise told herself over and over. *He wouldn't still be standing if it was.* Sven whirled around to Olise, taking aim. "*How—*" he began.

Olise didn't give him the chance, *couldn't* give him the chance, to finish his sentence.

"We do know something you don't know," Olise replied, shooting him one final, fatal time. By the time Drake reached her side, Sven was dead. He looked her up and down, then turned to Sven.

"It's done," he said weakly. "He's done." He gave a stiff nod. Olise grabbed his arm.

"We need to get out of here," she told him. "Away from Sven's people and away from the law enforcement."

She looked around desperately for an opening. Drake nodded but looked dizzy and distracted. "Are you okay?" Olise asked. He nodded again and shut his eyes briefly. When he opened them again, he looked focused.

"It's been a long slog to get here," was his only response. "We can talk later. Let's get out of here."

Olise weighed up their options.

"Take that bloody jacket off and put your gun away," she ordered, shoving her own gun in her jacket pocket. "We go out the front. Hopefully, law enforcement is causing enough of a distraction that we can slip past. We only need to make it a couple blocks before there's enough of a crowd to hide in." She pulled her hair over her throbbing, bleeding ear and tried to wipe the blood from her face. Drake carefully rolled up his jacket to hide most of the blood and propped it under his arm. He looked at her cut face and grimaced.

"Keep your head down, and I'll do that talking," he told her.

Despite everything, Olise smiled.

"Good," she replied. "I'm done pretending to be you."

36

BIGGER FISH TO FRY

ONLY HARSHA HUNG AROUND to see the law enforcement win control. He answered their questions and gave them all the information he knew they needed to know. This did not comfort them. He was an outsider, no longer a detective, and even he could admit this didn't look great for him. But with a gang on their doorstep and the promise of no more interference from him, maybe they would wave it away one last time.

"Harsha, man," the detective said as he arrived, looking haggard. "You need to stop doing this."

"Don't worry, this is my last time."

"I'm going to ignore how ominous that sounds and take it at face value." He looked at the collection of thugs, half in body bags, half being dragged out in handcuffs. "And the perpetrators are just mysteriously gone."

Harsha shrugged.

"I'm not a cop," he replied.

"Yeah, which is why I don't know how you managed this." He shook his head. "I'm almost tempted to thank you."

"Think of the credit that comes after the paperwork," Harsha offered.

"Something will fill this gap," the detective replied. Harsha recognised the anguish. "It'll all balance out."

He sighed but turned back to Harsha and shook his hand. "Now if you'd be so kind as to get on the first ship out of my jurisdiction..."

"With pleasure."

***

Roz did not look up when Harsha returned to their meeting point in the cheap motel the trio had been staying in. That was another worry checked off her list, but not the biggest. Not yet.

"Well, the local law wants nothing more to do with me, but what remains of Sven's group around here will be locked away for a while."

"Welcome to the club," Drake said, "and thank you."

"Of all the things I've done for a case," Harsha said. "Putting them away was one of the easiest."

"Fantastic," Alison said dryly, returning from her hunched position separate from the rest of the group. "Let's get out of here."

"Finally, something I can agree with," Drake said. "How do we point it at my ship?" After a moment of cooperation that was uncomfortable for them both, they took their places around the teleporter. Harsha and Phin eyed it warily.

"It'll be fine," Roz assured them. "Most of the kinks are worked out." Both of them raised an eyebrow at "most" but said nothing. Alison gave them no warning. A wave of fuzziness ran over them, and the world blurred. A short moment later, they were on the bounty hunter's ship, ready to fly anywhere. Harsha, Phin and Olise gathered at the nearest window.

"Just like that," Harsha murmured.

"Guess I have been taking it for granted," Drake said, following them. Roz forced herself to take a moment to look outside, but in truth, thinking about it made her sick. This piece of technology and everything it currently stood for had torn her life apart and left her lost and alone. No, she realised as Harsha put a hand on her shoulder, and Drake pulled her out of her daze, not alone.

"Yes," Alison said. "It's a fantastic marvel of technology. Can we marvel once we're on our way? I'll feel better if we're moving."

"You're quite agreeable today, Alison," Drake said, beginning to shepherd them. "Are you beginning to like me?"

"I'm *beginning* to see the light at the end of the tunnel," she replied through gritted teeth. Drake laughed. Perhaps he could, too. No matter how hard Roz tried, she could not. For so long now, the dreams of a normal life, of Eva, had kept her going. But now... the further along they got, the longer the tunnel became. Once they released the teleporter, then what? If the private military were going to keep pursuing Alison, then they would pursue her too. If Drake and Olise's story proved anything, it was that different names, different locations, always moving... They would only protect you for so long, no matter who your friends and family were.

All sound faded away like there was a bubble between her and these strange people she now called friends. A million tiny hands pulled her apart. Where did this end? How much of her would be left when it did?

They started flying. Roz didn't know where. It took until they called a group meeting to discuss the future of the teleporter that she began to thaw, and even then, it was not the medicine she was looking for. Drake opened his mouth to speak, but Alison cut him off.

"First," she said. As all eyes fell on her, she grimaced and looked down at the floor. "I wanted to…" She whipped her head up as if someone had yanked it and looked Drake in the eye. "I'm sorry your family were killed in the teleporter disasters." She turned to Phin. "I'm sorry you got wrapped up in this because of me." Then to Olise and Harsha. "You chose to be here, but I'm sorry all the same." Finally, her gaze turned to Roz. "Sorry isn't enough for what's happened to you, but…" She reached out and took Roz's hand. Roz barely felt it. "I'm sorry." Each of them nodded in response. There was a heavy moment's silence, but slowly, their gazes returned to the teleporter sitting on the table between them.

"Are we definitely doing this?" Drake said. "Because once we do it, we can't undo it. Once it's out there, it's out there, for better or for worse. For both of you." He looked from Roz to Alison. "You said they threatened Roz to keep you in line; that's why they've been after her. If we release it, they're not going to take it lying down."

"I know. I know." She grimaced again. "But what happens if we don't?" Her tone was grave and her knuckles were clenched and shaking. She looked ashy. "There's no war because Parare Facie uses the teleporter to get anywhere they want, take out all their enemies, take whatever they want, all while the galaxy flounders to catch up. The teleporter *must* be made public."

There was a solemn silence.

"Would they definitely be able to trace it back to you?" Harsha asked, arms folded and eyes closed, apparently in deep thought.

"They know I escaped with a version of the teleporter," Alison replied. "Then we ran from them in the warehouse on Revalin. I look pretty guilty of *something,* and they don't do things by halves. Why take the risk?"

Roz shrank underneath the gaze of Drake and Harsha. Drake's eyes seemed to beg her to protest, but she could not. How could she, when her accidental involvement in this had already cost so many lives?

"What," Drake began nervously. "What's tying you two to all this? We can get rid of records. We could bribe people. Threaten people." He sighed. "I just... I'm not sure I'm comfortable if this sacrifices Roz in the process."

"Me either," Alison admitted. "I've been thinking about that." Roz's head shot up. "You say your family can offer her protection, and I – I believe you," she said after a moment. "The problem is me. Under no circumstances can they know that she's not involved because that makes her a prettier target than before, as leverage." Alison reached out and took her hand, the first sign of comfort since their reunion. "I think we have to put on a play," she said finally. "We need to have footage of me supposedly dying and of someone taking the teleporter from me. *Then* we release the information."

"We'll struggle to fake a death certificate for more than a couple of days," Harsha said.

"He's right," Olise said. "Even if you went completely off the grid, changed your name, your appearance... People have done more than we could ever think of and still been caught."

"We have time to work something out," Alison said. "From what we've seen, their teleporter is still far from perfect." She looked around the table. "You've proven to be a resourceful bunch. Will you help me?"

"Yes."

Roz could have faded away. So much trouble. So many people. For her. She could barely squeak a thank you.

Olise turned to Phin.

"You set up a..." She waved a hand around as if trying to find the words. "A *thing* to try to find the teleporter after Roz and Drake disappeared from Revalin."

Phin nodded, but as Alison's focus shifted to him, he shrank.

"Did it work?" Alison asked.

"Uh, no, not really," Phin managed. "I'm not sure if you were too far away, or if I was too slow to start it, like does it need to be on all the time, or if I was even looking for the right thing."

"Will you show me?" she pressed. "After this conversation."

Phin nodded hastily.

"My teleporter doesn't release as much energy as the earlier versions," Alison continued. "But there will still be a 'fingerprint' of sorts. If we can release something to find teleporters, it can only help control the situation."

"Hey," Drake protested, "it's Phin's idea. You can't just release it without his permission."

Alison waved a hand dismissively.

"He can keep the credit," she said. "But if it works, it needs to be public."

"She's right," Phin agreed. "And if it'll help, I want it to be public. That's why I came with you and Olise: to help."

"If you're sure," Drake said. "While you're doing that, I'll see who might be able to help us hide or protect Roz and Alison."

"I'll find out what tracking systems are being used by the law and any others I can find and see if there's a loophole we can exploit," added Harsha.

"I'll watch our backs," Olise said.

"I just... I don't know what I would do without you all," Roz managed. Drake, as usual, gave a bold grin.

"Luckily, you don't have to. You've helped a lot of people, Roz. It's time somebody returned the favour."

37

The Best Lies are Partly True

Roz should have been asleep. Everyone except Drake seemed to be. She was exhausted. She'd been all over the galaxy in the span of a few days. Instead, she lay in a makeshift bed in the bounty hunter's storage space, listening with her eyes closed as the quiet music Drake was listening to in the cockpit drifted down to them. She winced at the sound of boots on metal but did not open her eyes. She had a good guess of who it was, and she did not have the energy for a conversation.

"Are we heading towards that moon base?" Alison asked. Her words were quiet, but all noise seemed to carry through the bounty hunter's ship.

"Yeah, we need fuel," Drake replied.

"Can we stop there for a bit?"

"Sure," he said. "Can I ask why?"

"I just... I..." Alison stuttered. "I owe Roz a lot of things. More than I can give her now, but the least I can give is some alone time and a talk."

"Alright," he replied. "I understand. And I understand that you never meant for things to affect her. I know how that feels." There was a pause. "You're the only family she has left, right?" She heard him sigh. "Tell me you're not going to leave her alone."

"She's not alone," Alison replied. Roz's breath caught in her throat. "And she's always been fine without me. I'll do whatever I need to keep her safe and give her a proper life. I owe it to her and to my sister."

"I don't like the sound of that," Drake said. Alison snorted softly.

"Yes, well," she said. "You and I have done nothing but butt heads. But we both want what's best for her."

"My family and I will protect her," he assured her. "They would protect anyone I asked, but Roz, who's kind and innocent? No question."

"Good," Alison said. "Good. Thank you." There was a long moment of silence. "Now do me a favour and pay attention and dock. Don't kill us all now."

"Yes, ma'am."

Alison walked away, boots thudding on metal. Roz focused on her breathing, counting the seconds as Drake communicated with someone on the moon. The ship shook slightly as they docked, and the sound of heavy boots returned. Roz flinched when Alison touched her, giving the appearance of startling awake. Her eyes were heavy, and she was exhausted. It was not a difficult part to sell.

"Come on," Alison said gently. "You and I are going for a coffee."

Roz got up wordlessly and followed. It was a crisp, clear morning on the moon and it did something to pull Roz from her coma-esque state. Alison did not say anything as they walked or as they bought coffee. It was only when they sat under a tree in an artificial park, looking up at the stars, that she finally said softly, "This isn't the ending I wanted." She put a hand to her forehead, frowning. "For either of us. The teleporter... I guess I got caught up in the wonder of it all. I should have run at the first sign of the military. I should have tried to escape."

"Someone else would have made it instead of you," Roz offered. Her hands shook so much she could barely drink.

"And someone else's family would have been threatened," Alison agreed. "But it wouldn't have been *you*. Your mother..." She took a shaky breath.

"Mum wouldn't blame you if she were here," Roz said. Alison's eyes began to sparkle with tears. "And the reality of it is that she *isn't* here. She's not the one who had to make those decisions."

"I appreciate the thought, Roz," she whispered. "But if she could see us now, I doubt she'd have anything nice to say. If I could change things—" She choked.

"I know," Roz clutched her hand. "I know."

They sat in silence for a while.

"I love you, Roz."

"I love you, too."

"Play a song for me when you're back on the air?"

"Stop talking like this is a goodbye," Roz snapped.

"Even if it would keep you safe?"

"Even if—"

"I've got to go, Roz." She shook her head, at a loss of what to say. She opened her hands and stared at her palms. "I'm sorry. Forgive me."

"When? *Where*?"

"I'll make sure you're safe."

"That's..." A lump rose in Roz's throat. "That's not really an answer. Or an excuse. Or an explanation."

"I know."

"You're like a tornado," Roz continued. Her eyes welled up.

"I know."

There was a moment of silence. Roz sniffed and wiped her eyes.

"Will I see you again?" she asked.

"I hope so," Alison replied, but she looked pointedly away.

"Is this it then?" Roz indicated her coffee cup. "One last cup for the road?"

"I just wanted some time," Alison said. "One last, selfish moment."

They stood, walking slowly back to the ship, both trying to hold back tears. When they reached the docking bay, Alison stopped. She opened her mouth to speak, but Roz cut her off.

"Don't say you're sorry again," she said. "I know. I know, and I'm sorry too."

She shrugged, lump in her throat. She looked Alison in the eyes. *She looks her age*, Roz thought. Her guard was down. Her armour, her confidence. All gone.

"What more is there to say?"

"Promise me you'll take care," Alison said, holding out her hands. Roz took them.

"You too."

Alison squeezed her hands, then let her go.

"And get some sleep," Alison said. "You look worse than I feel."

***

Drake forced a smile when Roz and Alison returned, happy to pretend he hadn't overheard the last of their discussion. As Roz made an apology and went to bed, Alison made a coffee and stood by the window at the rear of the ship, watching the landscape of the moon outside.

As their day came to an end, Olise and Harsha rose. Space travel was like that; unless you had a moon, planet, or station to go by, time hardly felt real. Tempting as the smell of their coffee and breakfast was,

Drake stood and stretched, ready to hand over control to Olise. When he turned, he found Alison waiting for him.

"There's something else I need to do," she said. Somewhere on this trip, he noted, her commanding presence had died. She wrung her hands. She looked a *mess*, not that he was going to be the one to tell her. He shrugged.

"We can wait a while longer."

Alison nodded, lips pursed.

"Anything else you want to divulge?" he offered. She shook her head.

"Okay, well" – he opened the door for her – "good luck and take care, I guess."

She hummed in response, jumping the short distance down to the moon's surface and setting off without so much as a glance back.

"Okay," he murmured to himself. When he shut the door behind her, he found Olise and Harsha both looking at him expectantly.

"Do you want me to follow her?" Olise asked.

Drake thought about it for a moment, then shook his head.

"Don't get me wrong, I know she's tried to kill me a few times now, but she's left Roz and the teleporter, and they're the only things she cares about. I don't think we're in danger."

"And if she's the one in danger?" Harsha said.

"She doesn't want us helping," Drake replied.

"True enough," Harsha said with a sigh, turning back to the holographic screen he'd set up in front of himself. Olise did not seem convinced. She looked around the interior of the ship.

"If she brings her trouble back with her, I'll be ready."

"Alright, well, can you do it from the cockpit?" Drake ran a hand through his hair, feeling exhaustion weigh down on him. "I'm going to report to Remo, then get some rest."

Olise nodded, patting his back as he passed.

When his cabin door slid shut behind him, he sighed, kicked off his shoes, and flopped onto his messily made bunk. He allowed himself a minute to close his eyes, then groaned and turned on a light before he could fall asleep.

With a lazy wave of his hand, he brought up a screen and called Remo. His uncle took long enough to answer that he mustered the energy to sit up. He frowned at his own appearance, but there was little that could be done without a good night's sleep. Soon enough, Remo answered, albeit in a dressing gown, coffee in hand.

"I hope I didn't wake you, Uncle," he said. "I forgot to check the time."

"It's 8am, my boy, and I'm hoping you're going to start my day with some good news."

"Uhhhhhh," Drake said. "Yes and no. Olise told you about the teleporter?"

"So it's real? Really real?"

"Oh yes," Drake said, shutting his eyes. "And about as much of a complication as you can imagine."

"You don't seem yourself, Drake," Remo said, brow furrowing. "What's going on?"

"Well, Uncle, I've been shot about four or five times in as many days." He winced as he changed position. "And the situation is about to blow wide open. Long story short, we're going to expose the teleporter. Listen," he cut his uncle off with a wave. "I promise, as soon as it's over, we'll come straight to you and explain everything. You'll know it when you see it, trust me," he added. "In the meantime, I need a favour."

"Anything."

"You know the DJ? Roz Dayne?" Remo nodded. "She's innocent. But she's in a lot of danger. I need to borrow some guys on Revalin, maybe Nonke. Just to keep an eye on her."

Remo paused. It was an excruciating moment. Then he nodded.

"Alright, Drake. You've more than earned that much." His gaze turned serious. "But I want a good explanation for all of this later, alright?"

"Yes, sir," Drake said. "Now, if you'll excuse me, I'm going to steal some sleep before this all kicks off again."

Moments after the call ended, before he even dismissed the screen, Drake flopped back again and fell asleep.

***

Drake awoke to the sounds of Olise and Harsha bickering in hushed tones.

"Out of my way," Olise said. "I'll do it."

The door to his room slid open and bright light poured in. He squinted into it to find them both at his door and Phin hovering, looking pale, behind them.

"What happened?" he asked, adrenaline rushing through his stiff limbs. He sat up, though his head spun.

"Alison's dead," Olise said flatly.

"Dead how? Dead where?" Drake exclaimed.

"Dead in the shady part of the city. Dead by an assassin hit hired by the name Sabine Coren."

"Security footage and police believe she was killed as part of a robbery. The killer took something from her body," Harsha continued.

"I'm going to tell Roz. I've done conversations like this before. I just wish I didn't have to. We wanted to give you a heads-up."

"The teleporter's still here, isn't it?" Drake said. "What the hired killer took wasn't it?"

"How'd you know?" Harsha said.

"The play," he replied, flopping back onto the bed. "Alison said she was going to put on a fucking play. She's teed the whole thing up for us."

38

Mind the Gap

It's such a simple button, Drake thought, staring at Roz's blown-up holographic screen. Alison had left her the trigger, of course. The teleporter's blueprints, energy readings linking it to the destruction of the space stations, and half a dozen files Alison had taken from her employer sat ready to be published on the galactic internet and sent directly to scientists, media companies, and law enforcement. One click, or one slip of the hand, and that was it. The teleporter was released to the galaxy. Drake, Olise, and Harsha all stared at it as Phin watched them with wide eyes. Roz watched her own hands as she clasped them tightly.

"We have to do it," Roz said, breaking the silence. All eyes fell on her. "It can't all be for nothing."

There was a general round of nods but still, nobody moved.

"I'll do it," she offered in the following silence.

"Are you sure?" Drake asked.

"We have to follow through with Alison's plan. We can't let those people run freely with the teleporter. The longer we wait, the more suspicious this becomes."

Another round of nods. Roz raised her hand and held it for a moment. When no one objected, she pressed the button.

"Done," she said simply. "Now let's see what fresh hell it brings."

They drifted around the room in solemn silence, waiting for something to happen. It took around ten minutes before the galaxy at large began to realise what had just popped up all over the galactic Net.

"It's been noticed," Phin reported, eyes glued to his communicator. There was another round of nods.

They watched downloads of their release increase, information posts go up, and news stories begin to break left, right, and centre. It did not feel like a victory.

"What now?" Phin asked. No one was quite sure of the answer. Celebrating didn't feel right, but neither did parting ways, not yet. Folding his arms, Drake closed his eyes.

"Coffee?" he offered. Over the past few days, it had been the thing to fill the space. He looked out of one of the ship's windows at the moon base, where they were still docked. "It might be good to get some fresh air."

There was a long moment of silence.

"I kind..." Phin said. "Kind of want to go home."

Harsha grunted and nodded in agreement. Drake nodded.

"We'll take all of you home," he said. "By ship," he added. "I'm not sure I want to touch the teleporter. And if you need anything in the future, just get in touch. We'll be roaming."

"And it'll be no trouble," Olise said, staring at Phin.

There was another moment of silence. Drake was the first to move. Dusting himself off, he said, "Anyone need anything before we set off?" There was no reply. "Good. Then let's go."

Phin's home was closest, though "close" was a relative term. It took almost three days of dozing and Drake trying to lighten the mood with songs for them to reach their first stop – the moon Enna. It was beautiful, the surface marbled different shades of green.

"It's lush down there," Olise said, staring at it, mouth open.

"Come visit sometime," Phin said. She smiled.

"You won't be able to get rid of us," she said, clasping his hand. "Keep in touch. Keep in *school*. Keep out of trouble."

"But if you need anything," Drake said, shaking his hand. "To talk about all this. If you ever think you're in danger. If you ever need a little bit of work."

Phin smiled.

"I know where to find it."

"Hey, we can probably give him a reference, right?" Drake looked to Olise. "He did work for us for a bit."

"How should I know?" She pulled a face and shrugged. "I'm not sure anyone cares about our opinion."

"Well, kid, you've been great. We'll check back soon, alright?"

"Alright." He gave an awkward wave to Harsha. "It was, uh, nice to meet you, sir," he said. "Weird circumstances, but still."

"Nice to meet you too, Phin," he replied. "And the same offer stands for me." He pulled out a business card. "You can ignore the detective part, but it's still the easiest way to reach me."

"Those are *nice*," Drake said. "Should we have business cards?" he asked Olise.

"With our friends? Best not."

Phin turned to Roz who did sit up and try to smile at him.

"Same for me," she said softly. "You know where I am."

"Ditto. Don't forget to play that song for me when you're back on the air!"

Roz smiled.

"Anything you'd like," she replied. "Even Pacl."

"I'm going to take you up on that."

They watched him go, and, although he put on a cheerful front, Drake only felt his heart sink.

"We'll be back!" he called after him. "That's a threat!"

Phin waved and laughed and it wasn't until he disappeared into the distance that they departed. He took a breath, then spun sharply, forcing a smile back on his face. He looked to Harsha.

"Where can we drop you off?"

"Revalin," he replied. "But I don't think I'll be there for long."

"Oh? Do tell."

"Well, I don't think the law will take me back, and, in all honesty, I'm not sure I want to go back."

"You thinking private detective?" Olise said, leaning towards him.

"That," he agreed. "Or bounty hunter. Maybe a mix."

"I think a mix would suit you," Olise agreed.

"It seems I'm a little less bound to the rules than I thought. I just want to protect people."

"You do. You did," Roz said.

"What about you, Roz?" Drake asked. "Are we dropping you off there too?"

"I could do with picking up some stuff, if you don't mind," she began. Her lip wobbled and she looked away. "But there's nothing left for me now."

"So Nonke?" Drake said.

"Yeah." She blinked away tears. "Yeah, I have to try, anyway."

"You're going back to Eva?" Harsha said.

Roz shrugged heavily and awkwardly, exhaustion casting shadows across her face.

"We've been talking throughout all of this," she said. Tears fell from her eyes, but she hurriedly wiped them away. "I haven't told her I'm coming back yet," she added quickly. "But I will. On the journey back, I'll message her. I don't expect anything, I can't expect anything, but I hope she'll meet me. Just to talk, in person." She took a breath. "But mostly, I want to reconnect with my friends. I want to apologise. And Nonke was my home, *is* my home. After everything that's happened, I want to sit in the gardens after a night shift with a hot chocolate and watch the sunrise."

"Sounds like a plan," Drake said gently.

"Yeah," she agreed. "I just... all I've wanted is to go home, and now I get that chance, I..." She sobbed and curled up into a ball. "It's finally over." She looked up at Drake. "It is, isn't it?"

"Yeah, it's over. The Family has agreed to keep tabs on you and on Parare Facie. We'll make it clear that if they try anything with you, they'll be trying it with *us*, and I'm willing to bet with the cat out of the bag and Alison..." He faltered. "I'm willing to bet it's more trouble than it's worth for them."

"And you can call me, too," Harsha said. "You still have my card?" Roz shook her head.

"It broke when we teleported to Agh-Ab-2."

He pulled a new one from his pocket and offered it to her.

"T-thank you."

They slept and ate before dropping off Harsha, but the departure was just as weird. It was always going to end this way; he'd said it himself, but Drake still felt so... detached from it all.

He must have been sitting in a deep gloom because it was Olise who turned the tables on them and said, "This isn't just an end; it's the beginning of something new."

He nodded and saw Roz nod too.

"A new line of work for us. A second chance for Roz."

"It'll all work out," Drake allowed.

"How much have you told your Family?" Roz asked.

"I gave them the basics with the teleporter info, told them about you, but have I explained anything?" He sighed. "Not yet. There's an awful lot to explain."

"Tell me about it." It was her turn to sigh. "I've got so many business emails asking me to sell my story, but I don't even know where I would begin. I probably need to speak to the police first. Explain…" She waved a hand vaguely. "I don't know. I don't know how much I should say, about Alison, about the teleporter."

"Sounds like your prospects of getting back on air are good, then."

"They're calling it the story of the century," she agreed. "Maybe not as a DJ. Not right away, anyway. But Harsha's investigation proved I had no knowledge of what was going on and people liked my work before all this, so yeah, we'll see."

"Will you go back to your old job?"

"We'll see how everything goes." She choked on a laugh. "Maybe this will just be a proper ending to my life on Revalin, not a fresh start. I don't plan to jump straight into work, anyway. I need some time."

"Sounds like your calendar is pretty free to schedule a catch-up. When I come back, I'm expecting some fancy recommendations."

They both smiled.

"You can come too, Olise," Roz offered after a moment. Olise smiled.

"Thanks, but I'll cause trouble somewhere else."

"What are you guys going to do?"

"I think we'll find ourselves with a lot of teleporter-related work," Drake replied. "People escaping jail. People going missing. People starting fights."

"Let's take a break first," Olise said. "I have a feeling there will be trouble for a long time after this. But Alison was right," she added. "Better for everyone to be on the same page."

"And Phin's teleporter finder evens it out even more." He put his hands in his pockets. "Hope he makes some money off of it. Or at least the recognition gives him a good future."

There was a moment of silence.

"Do you really think we'll go back to normal lives after this?" Roz asked, fidgeting.

"I think it depends on what you call normal," Drake said. "Things change, and we move forward. Were things normal after you changed your whole life leaving Nonke?"

"I'm not sure you're helping," Olise said.

"You told me we were all just ships passing in the night, right?" Roz said. Drake nodded. "So we met, and now we continue on our way."

***

It wasn't the first time that Roz had sat staring at a message from Eva that read something to the effect of "This is crazy", and yet she still couldn't think of a better response than "Yeah, it is." Eva, and what felt like half the galaxy, had messaged her a few hours after the release of the teleporter.

Was it really a teleporter? Eva said, asking the questions on everyone's minds. *What does it mean for everything?*

Let's leave the second question to the smart people, Roz told her. *But yeah, I've been teleported twice now.*

What did it feel like?

It makes your skin prickle and your ears pop. It's very strange.

She lingered in the back of Drake and Olise's ship, watching through a small porthole as the soft, all-consuming darkness pricked with stars flowed slowly by. Before answering Eva's first message, she had thought long and hard about how much to say. It wasn't just a case of how much she trusted Eva; it was whether certain information put Eva at risk.

My part in this is done now, Roz said finally, redirecting the conversation. *Law enforcement has said I'm free to go back to my normal life. Well, normal, apart from the 4000+ emails and messages I've ignored.*

Her communicator was still overflowing with people trying to speak to her. She wondered if it would ever stop. She'd thought that once the teleporter had been released, she wouldn't be interesting to the media anymore. The opposite had been true. For better or worse, her name was inextricably linked with the new invention and the destruction it had caused.

What's your plan now? Eva asked.

I really don't know, Roz replied honestly. *I wasn't fired, just suspended, so I still have a job and a home in Revalin. Well, an apartment in Revalin. It's never really felt like home.* Her hands were slick with sweat. *I'm coming back to Nonke for a bit,* she typed with shaking hands. Her face burned. *Can we meet up and talk?* She forced herself to take a breath as her heart pounded. She squeezed her eyes shut, waiting to feel the telltale buzz of a message from her communicator. Seconds stretched into ages. Roz let the gentle background noise of the ship consume her. She fought the urge to check her communicator. Would Eva respond? *How* would she respond? Had she already moved on from Roz?

When the reply came through, Roz jumped out of her skin, sending her communicator flying across the floor. She scrambled to pick it up, hastily tapping the screen to reveal the message.

I'd like that, was all it said.

Warmth settled in Roz's chest. She returned to watching the stars outside the window. Tension flowed out of her body, and for once, she thought it might last.

***

Drake traipsed into the family manor a very tired, slightly defeated man.

"You really got invested in this one, huh?" Olise said, punching his arm. He managed a weak smile.

"Says you, Ms Mentor," he teased. "Harsha told me what you did for Phin. You did good, Lis. Did what I probably couldn't."

"Let's not go that far," she said. "I was just... paying it forward. Guess all your talk got to me."

"Yeah, well, you got to me too," he said. "You should have seen me on that pirate ship. You'd be proud."

"The important thing is we all made it out in one piece." She clutched her side instinctively as they climbed the stairs. "Mostly," she wheezed.

They walked into Uncle Remo's office. He stood up, arms wide. He smiled, but his brow was furrowed.

"I hope you can put some sense into all this, Drake." He hugged them both, shaking his head. "Wonderful to see you both, wonderful to see you up and about, Olise, but" – he pressed a hand to his brow – "what in the ever-loving fuck is going on?"

"We can answer almost everything," Drake assured him. "But first, pour us some whisky. We're going to be here a while."

"Dear lord," the Thaler patriarch said, but he did make his way to the drinks cabinet.

"Do you want the long version or the short version?" Olise asked.

"All of it," he replied with a wave of his hand. "I want to hear everything."

"Right, so..."

The sun sank beyond the horizon, and the clouds blew in and it began to rain. They barely stopped to eat and by the time they were finished, his uncle had made several pages of notes and turned away four other appointments. When they finished, Remo leant back in his chair. There was a long moment of silence as he poured them each another drink. He shook his head.

"I'm too old for this." He turned to look out the window.

"Tell me about it," Olise muttered.

"You did well, kids. You've done right by us," he said, looking back over his shoulder. "We won't ever forget that."

"Do you want to tell the families of the Thalers who were killed or will I?" Drake shifted uneasily. "This whole thing has been a mess from start to finish. Misunderstandings and mistakes every step of the way. I'm not sure how much comfort it will bring them."

"It's an end. A conclusion," Uncle Remo told them. "It'll be better than never knowing what killed their family. I'll tell them," he said after a moment. "You" – he turned to point at Drake – "look a mess. Go rest, for god's sake. Olise was almost killed a few days ago and she looks ten times better than you. Why so glum?"

"I dunno," Drake said with one big sigh. "It's... not how I thought this would end." He shook his head. "I just need to rest."

"Then stay as long as you need," Uncle Remo said. "We'll look after you."

"We've got other plans, but thank you," Olise said. Drake's head shot up.

"Do we?"

"Yeah, man, trust me."

He smiled.

"You know I do."

***

"I thought it might be a good time to visit Porba," she explained several hours later, "But then, I thought you would say our work wasn't done so…"

She hadn't let him see the navigation panel or whatever she'd stopped off to buy. She smiled as she finally allowed him to see where they were. A moon, with beer and pizza waiting for them. But not just any rocky but breathable moon. One of the first places they'd been together when they'd done exactly this.

"Lis…" He struggled for words.

"Help me get the deck chairs out," she ordered, but he could not move. "Drake, you're everybody else's rock, and look what it's done to you. We figured out the mystery. We helped Phin and Roz and Harsha." She gave him a can and held out her own. He clinked it against hers, still stunned. "We're free of Sven! I know it feels like a lot – because it has been. I know you don't know what our next move is and you're too tired to laugh it off."

She pointed up at a distant red dot in the sky. "Remember what you told me last time? About your natural order, about a life better than one I had ever dreamed of? About the spaceships passing in the night?

You said '*One day, I'm going to retire to Porba knowing I did some good and met a whole bunch of people along the way*'." She grinned at him and he grinned back.

"This isn't an end, it's also a beginning."

39

PLAY A SONG FOR ME

FOUR MONTHS LATER

PHIN STARED AT THE stairs in front of him, knees shaking.

"This is ridiculous," he told himself. "After everything you've been through, you can do this." He nodded to himself, and as the Dean of his university called his name, he climbed the stairs to the stage to receive his degree. His face burned as he walked, but he forced a smile. He saw his mum smiling and waving from the crowd, dabbing tears with a handkerchief. It wasn't until he was walking off again that he saw that she was not the only one who had come to see him. At the back of the allocated seating on the large grassy plain by the lake were Drake and Olise, suited and booted and grinning like fools. They gave him a wave, and he grinned.

He could barely sit still through the rest of the ceremony, desperate to catch them and speak to them for the first time in weeks. They kept in touch, but they were often in and out of a sensible signal range. He couldn't believe they'd come. They'd asked for the date and address, but even so... he hadn't expected them. As his mum gushed about him to an acquaintance she'd spotted in the crowd, he found them and told them so.

"Nah, kid, of course we came," Olise told him.

"We've officially taken our first holiday in years," Drake added. "I set up an out-of-office reply and everything."

"Oh my god," Phin sniggered. "Well, I'm glad you're here. It's nice to see you."

"It's nice to see you, too. You look well. Are your family here to see you?"

"My mum," he said. "She's very excited."

"So she should be!" He raised an eyebrow. "Just mum? No Mr Sayer in the picture?"

"He's around," Phin warned. "He just can't make it today. Couldn't get leave from the war."

"Hey, it's not me you need to worry about." Drake laughed. "Olise is the one with a thing for older ladies. That being said" – Drake straightened his collar – "Mums love me."

Phin looked to Olise, who shrugged while grinning. And it was true. As his mum ended a conversation with her friend's cousin's sister-in-law and returned to them, Drake's natural charisma shone.

"Phin," he said brightly, "you never told me you had a sister."

His mum laughed and let him kiss her hand, feigning embarrassment though, in reality, only Phin was embarrassed.

"Phin," she said. "Who are your friends?"

"These are Drake and Olise," he replied nervously. "They're— I worked for them for a while," he said. "Just a couple of weeks."

"Yeah, he was our intern on an independent research project," Drake said, smiling. "He really brought a fresh pair of eyes to the situation."

His mum straightened up, ruffling her fur coat like a mother hen, blushing.

"Honey, you never told me that!" she replied, smiling and hitting his arm lightly.

"Ah well, it was short-lived, unfortunately," Drake replied. "The funding ran out. You know how these things are, but we'd love to have him back again in the future if he'd like."

As Drake walked arm in arm with his mother towards the lake, Phin could not help but marvel at what an easy liar and charmer he was.

"Did he prep that speech about the research project?" he asked Olise.

"All the best lies have some truth in them," she replied. She punched him gently on the arm. "We're proud of you, kid. And if you're ever looking for work, you're always welcome with us. But also, if you want to keep out of trouble and just meet for pizza and beer every so often, that's fine with us too."

"Thanks," he replied, choking up a little. "That means a lot." He cleared his throat. "So, uh, what have you guys been up to?"

"Oh, you know, jobs here, jobs there," she replied. "We're staying out of trouble... mostly. A lot of jobs around teleporters. Your thing that detects them? Still works like a charm."

"I'm glad to hear it." Phin quirked a smile. "You'll never guess who offered me a job," he told her.

"Alright, I'll bite. Who?"

"Parare Facie," Phin said. Olise snorted and folded her arms. For days after the release of the teleporter, the galaxy had been filled with chaos and theories and talk of the teleporter. When the dust had settled, all eyes had turned to the private military for answers. They were too big to pin the blame on any one person, or even a group of people, but they would not escape unscathed. They were at the centre of an interstellar inquiry, being picked apart for all the galaxy to see. They'd offered an apology, a statement that the destruction of the space stations had been a regrettable series of accidents from unforeseen side effects of the teleporter. It might reduce the crime, but the inquiry was already raking them across the coals for using an unfinished, undocumented teleporter in the inner systems. "I turned them down, of course," he finished.

"Have you got something else lined up?" Olise asked. "Don't let me stress you out. I'm not trying to make you come with us."

"I've been offered a position to develop my teleporter finding technology for an actual company, for proper money."

"I don't blame them! Surprised it's taken anyone this long to a) try to make money off this whole disaster and b) hire you to be the one to do it." She smiled. It was distant, Phin thought, but it was warm and genuine. "You know where to find beta testers, anyway."

"But I... I might still take you up on your offer one day."

"I'll look forward to it. Come on," she said, pulling him along. "Let's catch up. We've got some celebrating to do."

***

Harsha had come to appreciate that there was a certain kind of meditation to long space journeys. He was a slow learner or, more accurately, a stubborn one, but in this moment, he finally understood what Roz, Drake, and Olise had tried to tell him.

He sat by a small, circular window on his interstellar transport, hands clasped and legs stretched out as far as the rows of seats would allow him. The steady hum of the transport wrapped around him like a heavy blanket. Gentle chatter from the other passengers lay neatly on top of the sound as the universe passed by slowly outside.

He couldn't help but smile. There was a long road ahead of him, it was true, but for the first time in years, he felt a warmth and an energy at the prospect. It had taken him an embarrassing amount of time to recognise the feeling as excitement. But he was. Excited. Hopeful. Alive.

It was time to forge a new path for himself, to explore new horizons. He put in one earphone and closed his eyes, waiting for a familiar radio broadcast to start.

***

Roz rose as the sun set. She untangled herself from her bedsheets and trudged to her kitchen to find Eva with a meal waiting for her. Radio chatter drifted through the air. Their apartment was small but full of love. Eva's paintings dried in a corner and her latest work in progress was set up on an easel by the window. The walls were covered in art and antique records. Books were scattered across a coffee table, surrounded on all sides by different coloured couches and cushions. In one glance, it sang more of home than Revalin ever had.

"Big day today," she said, kissing Eva's forehead.

"What's today?" Eva asked, wrapping her arms around Roz's waist.

"Phin's graduating," she replied. "A couple of galaxies away on a much nicer day than today." Their windows were splattered with raindrops and fogged up by the cold – Roz's favourite weather. The lights of the city flickered and blurred together in a warm glow. It made everything feel so much less lonely. Though, Roz considered, as she tucked into her food, she rarely felt alone these days, least of all because she was reunited with Eva and their friends.

There was something so much less intimidating when she knew there were people like Drake and Olise causing chaos, Phin feeling like she did, and Harsha keeping them safe. It wouldn't be long before she saw them again, separately, their ships not quite coming into port at the same time. But this was all she could ask for and she was content with it. It wasn't Radio Broadstrokes; it wasn't her dream, but her dream had changed to a future with a girl with big blue eyes and paint over her arms and a motley crew led by a man with pink frosted tips.

She smiled and, in that moment, was complete. She got up and dressed, ready to face the day, or night as it tended to be, ahead of her. With one last kiss from Eva, she set out.

"Time to humiliate Phin on live radio."

She returned to her studio and turned on Ambo to find a picture of Phin, Drake, Olise and Harsha and a picture of her, her mother, and Aunt Alison waiting for her.

Her gaze lingered on Alison for a long moment, then dropped to her hands. It was a strange mix of gratefulness, guilt, and grief that wrapped itself around the space in her heart reserved for her aunt. The more time went on, the more she realised that Alison had done the best she could to help Roz but there would always be a small part of her, the child in her, that was angry that her family had left her alone again. Life would go on, she knew. She could be upset at their ending and play songs for her aunt at the same time, and that was what she was doing. It wasn't one of their games, wasn't anything especially secret, just a quiet signal alongside the radio broadcast spelling out "I love you".

Plus, Roz wasn't fully alone. Not any more. She looked from her photos to her workstation and had never been so ready.

"Good evening, weary travellers. This is Nonke Radio 1, and this is Roz, here for you through the quiet night." Roz's fingers danced across the controls in her own special kind of magic. Here, with Ambo, and Eva waiting for her, she was home. "Before we play our next song, I have a little message here congratulating Phin Sayer on graduating with the highest honours in Physics and Adaptive Technology at Freestrand University. We're all very proud of you, and we hope you're celebrating tonight. Next on the list for you, get a better taste in music. Tonight, however, here's something special just for you: Opaque by Parcl."

She bit her lip through a smile as she turned up the song and danced in her seat to what was, frankly, the most ridiculous song she'd ever heard.

And as she weaved her stories and made the music work, she thought of Phin and Harsha and Drake and Olise, each out there on their own journeys, their very own ships in the vast night, and the universe didn't feel so big.

Acknowledgements

People who have known me for a long time will remember that I used to be adamant I would never publish a book. Well, I was wrong, and it's been a very long, but very rewarding journey to get here. I couldn't have done it without the support of the following people.

Firstly, thank you to my developmental editor Rachel for helping me bring out a version of the novel that's better than I ever imagined. Thank you also to my copy editor, Amanda, and proofreader, Oskar, for their support in polishing it all up.

Thank you to my readers, Miles, Merlyn, Jess, Briar, and Kayla for their feedback and encouragement.

Thank you to Miles (again), Daffodil, and the ladies of Frog Queue Elles for being my hype squad, and to Aavi for being my constant sprint partner through so many drafts.

Finally, and most importantly, thank you to all my friends, family, and colleagues who, when I said I wanted to publish, responded universally with excitement and support. It has meant the world to me.

About the Author

K. P. Kilbride is a permanently windswept Scottish science fiction author writing stories about strangers coming together to save the galaxy and themselves. Inspired by the likes of Terry Pratchett, her works are set in a far-future take on the Milky Way galaxy in which humanity has reached the stars, encountered aliens, and settled into a comedically mundane coexistence.

Outside of writing novels, Kilbride enjoys many creative hobbies, such as pottery, playing and running TTRPGs, worldbuilding, baking, and painting.

For updates and more information, go to https://www.kpkilbrideauthor.com/

www.ingramcontent.com/pod-product-compliance
Ingram Content Group UK Ltd.
Pitfield, Milton Keynes, MK11 3LW, UK
UKHW041943200725
461008UK00002B/75